T0144363

The Anti-Pamela

The Anti-Pamela

Or, Feign'd Innocence Detected

Eliza Haywood

MINT EDITIONS

The Anti-Pamela: Or, Feign'd Innocence Detected was first published in 1741.

This edition published by Mint Editions 2021.

ISBN 9781513291567 | E-ISBN 9781513294414

Published by Mint Editions®

 MINT
EDITIONS
MintEditionBooks.com

Publishing Director: Jennifer Newens
Design & Production: Rachel Lopez Metzger
Project Manager: Micaela Clark
Typesetting: Westchester Publishing Services

Display'd and Punish'd

Syrena was a Girl, who even in her Cradle gave the promise of being one of the compleatest Beauties of the Age: As her Years encreas'd, and her Features grew more settled, her Loveliness encreased in Proportion; but what was most to be admired in her was, that the Innocence which is inseparable from Infancy, and which is so charming, even in the plainest Children, never forsook her Countenance; but continued to dwell in every little Turn and Gesture long after she came to Maturity, and had been guilty of Things, which one would think should have given her the boldest and most audacious Air.

Her Mother, though in very mean Circumcumstances, when she was born, flatter'd herself with great Things, from the growing Beauties of her sweet Babe; and tho' she had other Children, this alone engross'd her whole Attention: I say her Mother, for her Father, at least him, whom the Law would have obliged to own her, died soon after she came into the World; and was incapable of receiving any share either in the Profits or Disgrace of our little *Syrena's* future Conduct.

Being therefore left entirely to the Care of a Parent, who had been a Woman of Intrigue in her Youth, was far from repenting what she had done; and one of the most subtil Mistresses in the Art of Decoying that ever was; the Girl was not out of her Bib and Apron, before she instructed her in Lessons, which she had the wicked Satisfaction to find, her Pupil knew not only how to observe, but also to improve.

She had not reach'd her thirteenth Year, before she excell'd the most experienc'd Actresses on the Stage, in a lively assuming all the different Passions that find Entrance in a Female Mind. Her young Heart affected with imaginary Accidents (such as her Mother, from time to time, suggested to her might possibly happen) gave her whole Frame, Agitations adapted to the Occasion, her Colour would come and go, her Eyes sparkle, grow Languid, or overflow with Tears, her Bosom heave, her Limbs tremble; she would fall into Faintings, or appear transported, and as it were out of herself; and all this so natural, that had the whole College of Phycians been present, they could not have imagin'd it otherwise than real.

Thus was she train'd up to deceive and betray all those whom her Beauty should allure; but she had not so soon as she wish'd an

Opportunity of discovering how well she should behave, when what had yet only been Ideal, should come to be real Matter of Fact; for being very little of her Age, the Men took no farther Notice of her, than to say she was an exceeding pretty Miss—a very fine Girl—that she'd soon be a delicate Creature, and such like Compliments, that were nothing to the Purpose at present.

About this Time several of her Mother's Relations, as she had some that lived well, and in good Repute; knowing the Indigence of their Condition, and that they were obliged frequently to have recourse to them, for even the common Necessaries of Life; began to ask what was intended to be done with *Syrena*, for the other Children were all taken away by the Friends of one side or the other; to which finding no determinate Answer, they advised the Mother, to put her to a Milliner or Mantua-maker, tho' the latter they seem'd to think most proper; not only because there required no Stock to set up, with, when her Apprenticeship should be expired but because also they thought that in that Business, having to deal only with Persons of her own Sex, she would be exempt from those Temptations, her Youth and Beauty might expose her to in the Millinary Way. One of these Gentlewomen was so good, as to promise she would give Fifteen or Twenty Pounds with her to a Mistress she should approve. The Mother durst not refuse so kind an Offer, and assured her generous Kinswoman she would enquire about it; but as this was not the manner in which she desired to dispose of *Syrena*, she still found excuses to evade the Matter, and pretended she could not hear of any fit Place.

As there seem'd no room to suspect the Truth of what she said, or that a Parent would not be glad her Child should be in a way of getting a handsome Living; this truly honest and worthy Friend, took upon herself the trouble of looking out for a Mistress, and in a short time was inform'd of one who had very great Business, and was a Woman of a sober and unblemish'd Character. The Mother of *Syrena* had no Objections to make, the Terms between them was soon agreed upon, and the Girl was to go one Month upon Trial; after which the Indenture was to be made, and the Money paid by the good Gentlewoman, who had taken all this Pains, out of a conscientious regard for the Preservation of a young Creature, who she thought deserv'd it; and who might otherwise be drawn into those Snares, too often laid for Youth and Innocence; especially where there is an Indigence of Circumstances, and which a much better Education than could be expected the poor *Syrena* had been blest with, is not always a sufficient Guard again.

Syrena, who had always been sooth'd with the hopes of living grand, either by Marriage, or a Settlement from some Man of Condition, could not endure the Apprehension of sitting all Day to run Seams; nor was her Mother better pleased at this putting her Girl out of Fortune's way, as she call'd it; but as she resolv'd it should not be for any Continuance, she was the more easy, and made the other so too. Care was to be taken however not to disoblige their Benefactress, and they both affected the highest Gratitude to her, and Satisfaction in what, indeed, was most irksome to them.

Here one cannot forbear reflecting, how shocking it is, when those who should point out the Paths of Virtue, give a wrong Bent to the young and unform'd Mind, and turn the pliant Disposition to Desires unworthy of it; but more especially so in Parents, who seem ordain'd by Heaven and Nature, to instil the first Principles for the future Happiness of those to whom they have given Being; and tho' we cannot suppose there are many, who like the Mother of *Syrena*, breed their Children up with no other Intent than to make them the Slaves of Vice, yet if we look into the World, and consider the number of unfortunate Women (as they justly call themselves) I believe we shall find the Miseries these poor Creatures undergo, and frequently involve others in, less owing to their own Inclinations, than to the too great Indulgence and false Tenderness of their Parents; who flattering themselves that by breeding them like Gentlewomen, and setting them forth to the utmost of their Abilities, and often beyond, they shall be able to make their Fortune by Marriage; give them Ideas no way to their Advantage. What Compassion is due to a Mother, who having no Portion to give her Daughter, shall fill her Head with Notions of Quality; give Half a Crown for the cutting her Hair, when perhaps half the Money must serve the whole Family for a Dinner; make her wear Gloves, Night and Day, and scarce suffer her to wash a Tea-Cup for fear of spoiling her Hands; when such one, I say, shall cry out Daughter is undone, and exclaim against the cruel Man that has robb'd her of her Child; who can avoid accusing her as the first Seducer of the Girl's Virtue, by flattering that Pride and Vanity in her Nature, which without some extraordinary Providence, indeed, must render her an easy Prey to the first Temptation that offer'd itself. But as this is an Observation, that must occur to every thinking Person, I ought to beg my Reader's Pardon for the Digression, and return.

The Day prefix'd for the Departure of *Syrena*, the good-natur'd Kinswoman came and took her up in a Hackney-Coach with her Mother, who it was thought proper should go with her, and a Trunk with a few Cloaths in it; which the other looking over, told her, it should be better fill'd if she was a good Girl, and behaved herself well. I hope Madam, answer'd the young Dissembler, I shall never do anything to forfeit the Favour of so kind, so generous a Relation; and if I could be capable of any Pride, it would be to carry myself so, that the Mistress I am going to, should give you such a Character of me, as would convince you I am not unworthy of your Favours. This Speech, accompanied with a thousand modest Graces, so charm'd the Person it was address'd to, that she took her in her Arms, and said, I have not the least doubt about me, that you will deserve much more Encouragement than is in my power to give; but, added she, you may be assur'd I will do all I can. Many such like Expressions of Kindness on the one side, and Gratitude on the other, pass'd between them till they got to the end of their little Journey, where they were very handsomely receiv'd and entertained by *Syrena's* intended Mistress; and our young Hypocrite so well acted her Part, affecting to be highly pleas'd with the Place and Person she was to be with, and testifying no farther Regret at parting from her Mother, than just so much as served to shew her Duty and Affection, that she was look'd upon as a Prodigy of Sweetness and Prudence.

Thus was she enter'd on a new Stage of Life; but in what Manner she was used, and her Behaviour in it, can be no way so well represented, as by her own Letters to her Mother; the first of which was wrote three Days after their Separation.

Thursday Afternoon

Dear Mamma,

Tho' my Mistress has promised I shall go to see you next *Sunday*, if the Weather proves fair, I could not forbear writing to let you know how I go on. I assure you all here are very kind to me in their way. I lie with my Mistress's Sister, and breakfast and dine with them; for they say they see something in me that deserves better Treatment than any they have had before; but all this don't make me easy. I could not live as they do for the World; and I believe I shall find it a hard Matter to stay my Month out, they are such an old-fashion'd sanctify'd Family.—

Ah, Mamma, what a difference between this and home! we rise every Morning at Eight o'clock, have but one Hour allowed for Breakfast, and then to Work—the same for Dinner, and then to Work again—no Tea in the Afternoon, unless Company comes—and then at Night, my Master who has a Place in the Stamp-Office, comes home about Nine; he and my Mistress and her Sister sit down to eat a bit; after that, I and the Maid, and an old Woman that has been a Nurse in the Family, are called into Prayers, and so to Bed—This they call a sober regular Life—my Stars! defend me from such formal Ways—I am quite sick of them already. I pretend, however, to be mighty well pleas'd, and do everything they bid me with a great deal of Chearfulness, but it goes so against the Grain, that I know I can't do so long. Therefore, dear Mamma, remember your Promise, and contrive some Way to get me as soon as you can out of this Bondage, who am,

Your dutiful Daughter,
SYRENA TRICKSY

P.S. They don't know of my Writing, so I have no Compliments to send you.

MONDAY Morning

Dear Mamma,

I Fretted myself almost sick that I could not come to you Yesterday; but you saw it rain'd incessantly—indeed I long to see you; and the more, because an Adventure has happened to me, which I don't know but may come to something, if I manage right—I'll tell you exactly how it was, and then you will be the better able to advise me.—You must know, Mrs. *Martin*, my Mistress's Sister, and I, lie in a dark Closet, within the Dining-Room; so I go there as soon as I am up, to comb my Head and put on my Cap in the great Glass; but I am always in such a Hurry to get my things on before my Master and Mistress comes down, that I never minded who observed me.—I was observed however, and all my Motions watch'd, from the first Day I came it seems, as you shall hear—Last *Friday* some Silk being wanting for our Business, and the Maid sent out another Way, my Mistress bade me step for it: I ask'd if she had any particular Place where she bought.—Yes, said she, but that's too far off: for I generally buy a large Quantity together of a wholesale Dealer in the City, so you may go to the Haberdashers at the Corner of the Street, and get a Quarter of an Ounce for the present, but be sure you match the Colour; with these Words she gave me a bit of the Damask, and I said no more, but went on my Errand—The Shop was very full of People when I came in, and among them a fine Gentleman with a lac'd Hat and Cockade, looking over some white Stockings—so I was oblig'd to wait till most of them were dispatch'd;—all the time I could see the Gentleman had his Eye upon me, and when all were gone besides ourselves and the Gentlewoman behind the Counter; How do you do, my pretty Neighbour, said he? Very well thank you, Sir, answered I, blushing and curtsying, as you bid me when any Stranger spoke to me, but I han't the Honour to know you—for that Matter, cry'd he, the Honour would be wholly on my side, if you had found anything in me to take Notice of; but I assure you I lodge just over against you—I was at my Window when you came out of a Hackney-Coach, accompanied by two grave Gentlewomen, who I suppose were your Relations; I saw too much of you then, not to wish to see more; and I can tell you the Pleasure of looking on you, while you are setting those pretty Locks of yours in Order, has made me an early Riser. As he spoke these Words, he took hold of my Hair as it hung down on my Neck, on which I frowned, and snatched away my Head—I did not know that I had any Over-lookers, said I, but since I have, shall be more careful for the future; then I turned to the Woman of the Shop, and desired she would make haste to weigh me the Silk, for I could not stay. Nay, my sweet Miss, said he, you must not be angry,—I mean no Harm to you,—I have only a small Favour to beg of you, which you must not refuse me. All the Favours I can grant, answered I, must be small indeed. What I have to ask is such said he, it is no more than to chuse a Pair of Stockings; I am obliged to make a Present of a Pair to a young Relation in the Country, and would have your Fancy;—Pray let us see some of your best Womens Silk Stockings, added he, to the Woman; yes Sir, cry'd she, and immediately turn'd to reach a Parcel down. I have no Judgment, upon my Word, Sir, answered I, a little peevishly—so pray Madam let me have the Silk. No, no, I bar that, cry'd he, first come, first serv'd, you know Miss is the Rule; and as I was here before you, I insist on having my Stockings before you have your Silk. I said nothing, but pretended to be mighty uneasy, tho' in my Heart I was well enough pleas'd.—Well! the Stockings were brought, and he would have me chuse; so I pick'd out a pair of white with Pink

Clocks, for there was none with Silver. He made me a Compliment on the Genteelness of my Fancy; and having paid for them, and two pair of fine Thread for himself, now, Miss, said he, you must accept of what you have made Choice of, and put them into my Hand with a Squeeze, that made my Fingers ake for an Hour after;—I was very much surprised I confess, not expecting any such thing, but I threw them down on the Counter, and told him, I never took any Presents from Gentlemen: He attempted to force them upon me again and again, but I would not take them all he could do; and there was a great Scuffle between us. At last finding I was resolute, he put them with the others into his Pocket, and went out of the Shop very much out of Humour. After he was gone, the Woman of the Shop began to banter me, and told me, I had made a Conquest; but I seemed to think nothing of it, and went away as soon as I had got my Silk. I prevented my Mistress from asking why I staid so long, by telling her, the Shop was so full of Customers, that I could not get served, at which she seemed not at all surprised. When I began to consider on what had pass'd; I thought I had been a little too rough in the latter part of my Behaviour; for tho' I did not repent my having refused the Stockings (tho' indeed they were very pretty) yet I did, that I had not done it with more Complaisance.—I verily believed he loved me; but then, as it was a Passion of so late a Date, it might want a little Hope to give it Strength; and tho' it was necessary I should seem coy, yet it should have been such a Coyness, as might give him room to fancy I might at last be won; and so have drawn him in by Degrees, till it was not in his power to go back. These Reflections kept me awake all Night, and when Morning came, I dress'd me at the usual Place; but that I might not seem too forward, I put the Window-Shutters a-jar, so that I could see him through the Crack, without his distinguishing me.—I was glad to find he was at his Post, because it look'd as if he had not given over all Thoughts of me;—I wanted to shew myself to him too, but could not tell how to do it, without making him think I did it on Purpose.—At last I bethought me of our Cutting-Room, which is over the Dining-Room;—I ran up there, and finding the Window open, stood sometime; but he not expecting me so high, never lifted up his Eyes; so I took a Bottle with some Mint growing in it, and threw it into the Street; the Clash made him look up; he seem'd pleas'd to find there what he had so long been looking for in another Place, and kiss'd his Hand with a great deal of Gallantry and Tenderness; I seem'd confus'd, but made a Bow, and soon after retir'd.—I saw him no more that Day, but Yesterday and this Morning we have exchanged Glances several times thro' the Glass.—Dear Mamma, I am impatient to know if I have behaved hitherto as I should, and how I shall proceed for the future; for I am certain by all his Ways he loves me, and that something may be made of him, for he must be rich; he goes as fine as any Lord, and has a Man that waits upon him: So pray write your Mind with all Speed, and send it by old *Sarah*; but don't let her give it me before any of the Family, for fear they should expect me to shew it them; but she may come as with a Compliment from you to them, and to know how I do:—So dear Mamma, no more at present, but that I am

Your most dutiful Daughter,
SYRENA TRICKSY

MONDAY Afternoon

Dear Mamma,

As I was coming from putting my Letter to you, into the Post-house; who should I see in the middle of our Street, but my Lover, (for I think I may venture to call him so now) talking to another fine Gentleman—I found he saw me, and it presently came into my Head to make tryal of his Love; so instead of going home, I turn'd down a little Court, I don't know the Name of it, but it goes into Covent-Garden, and walk'd slow. I had not gone many paces before I heard somebody come very fast behind me, I did not doubt but it was my Gentleman; and so indeed it proved; for having overtaken me, so my little cruel Dear, said he, taking hold of my Shoulder, have I caught you abroad once more.—I pretended a great Fright and Confusion, and desired him to take his Hand away; not without you'll tell me where you are going, and permit me to accompany you said he. Lord, Sir, cry'd I, trembling, I am only going to—to—where my Dear, again demanded He? Only to Covent-Garden, answered I, for a little Fruit. Well, said he, and where's the mighty Business if I go and buy a little Fruit too—I beg'd he would not—told him we should be taken notice of—and said all I could, but he swore he would go with me, and go with me he did.—When we came among the Stalls he would needs fill my Pockets with the best the Market afforded; I would have paid for them, but he would not let me, and I thought it would be carrying the thing too far, to make a bustle in that publick Place; so I thank'd him, and was going to take my

ELIZA HAYWOOD

leave—No, said he, since Opportunities of speaking to you are so scarce, I am resolv'd you shan't quit me now, till you have heard what I have to say; and with these Words took hold of my Hand, and attempted to pull me into the Tavern, at the End of the Piazza.—I was frighted now in good earnest; and snatching my Hand away with more Strength than could be expected from me; what do you mean, Sir, said I, what do you take me for? For everything that's charming, answered he—By Heaven! I would rather die than offer anything should give you cause of Offence; therefore, dear Angel, oblige me so far, as to go in for one Quarter of an Hour only. Not for a Minute, cried I, I would not set my Foot in a nasty Tavern for the World. Fie, fie, said he, I shall suspect you for a little Prude if you talk at this rate, and look'd I thought as if he took me to be silly. I don't care what you suspect me for, answered I, and turn'd away as if I was going home; but he came after me, and beg'd that since I would not go into a Tavern, I would take a little walk with him in the Church-Yard, just to let him tell me something. This I was not averse to in my Mind, for I long'd to hear what he had to say, and so after some seeming Reluctance I comply'd.—Dear Mamma, 'tis impossible for me to repeat the fine Things he said to me, and much more to express the Tenderness with which he spoke them. He swore that his Intentions were perfectly honourable, that his Heart told him the first Moment he saw my Face, that I was the Person that must make him happy or miserable forever—that he could not live without me, and that if he had Millions he would lay them at my Feet; and sigh'd at every word as if his Heart were breaking—I reply'd very little to all this, and seemed to think him not in earnest; but then he swore a Thousand Oaths, and offer'd to give me any proof I ask'd, tho' 'twere his Life.— Indeed Mamma, I never read more moving Things in a Play, but I did not seem to believe him for all that, and was for hurrying away; but he would not let me go till I had promised to meet him on *Wednesday* at the same Place—So pray let me have your Advice before then, whither I shall keep my word or not, and how I shall behave, for I am quite at a loss—Let old *Sarah* come by all Means—I am,

Dear Mamma,
Your most Dutiful Daughter,
Syrena Tricksy

The Answer to these two Letters came to her on *Wednesday* Morning by old *Sarah*, as she had desired, and contained as follows.

WEDNESDAY Morning

Dear Child,

I Received your Letters, and am very much surprized to find you have gone so far in a Love Intrigue, in so short a Time: I perceive nothing, however, to condemn in your Behaviour hitherto—your Refusal of the Stockings, your giving him an Opportunity to speak to you a second Time, and the Confusion you affected were all perfectly right; but I am a little angry that you so readily believe what he says, and seem assured of his Affection—I doubt not, but he likes you, but my Girl there is a wide Difference between Love and Liking; the chief aim of the one is to make the beloved Object happy: That of the other, only to gratify itself.—Now your Business is by an artful Management to bring this Liking up to Love, and then it will be in your power to do with him as you please.—But after all, I am afraid he is not worth taking much pains about—if he be only an Officer, as I quess by his Cockade, 'tis not in his Power to make you any Settlement as a Mistress—and as a Wife; when Children come, what is a Commission!—Or what a Pension to the Widow, left perhaps in an advanced Age, when 'tis out of one's power to mend one's Fortune anyway.—No, Child! 'Tis your Business to make Hay while the Sun shines—for when Youth and Beauty are no more—Farewel Hope—I could wish notwithstanding you knew his Name, and what Family he is of. He may be born to an Estate, and if so, his Passion must be cultivated.—It won't therefore be improper to give him the meeting tonight, but continue your Shyness; yet so as to give him some little Encouragement too, that you may the easier get out of him what he is; for there is no advising you how to proceed till we know that.—Be sure you write me a full Account of what passes between you, on *Thursday* Morning; and if you come on *Sunday*, shall then give you Instructions suitable to the Occasion.—I hope you do not stand in need of any Caution against indulging a secret Inclination for him; for if it once comes to that you are ruin'd!—No Woman ever made her Fortune by the Man she had a sincere Value for.—Depend upon it in a little time you will see finer Gentlemen than he, be he as fine as he will—let your own Interest be your only Aim—think of nothing, but how to be fine yourself; and by keeping in that Mind you will be happy, and also make so,

Your Affectionate Mother,
ANN TRICKSY

ELIZA HAYWOOD

P.S. I charge you not to be prevail'd upon to go into any House with him—I don't like his asking you to go into the Tavern.

Syrena was rejoiced to find by this, that her Mother approved of her keeping the Assignation, and had before prepared an Excuse to her Mistress for going out—Her Lover had detain'd her so long on *Monday*, that she was oblig'd to say when she came home, that in stepping out to buy a few Apples, she had met with a Relation who was very glad to see her, and to hear she was so well put out; and added, that she had bid her come to see her on *Wednesday* in the Afternoon, for she had something to make her a Present of. Well, said Mrs. *Martin*, to whom all this was spoke; I'll prevail on my Sister to give you leave, for 'tis pity you should lose anything for not going for it. The good Gentlewoman performed her Promise, little suspecting the Truth, and *Syrena* put a handsome Paris Cap in her Pocket, which at her Return, she pretended had been given her by her Cousin; but in what Manner she had in reality been engaged, she gave her Mother a faithful Account of, the next Morning, in these Words.

Thursday Morning

Dear Mamma,

Having your Permission I went at the appointed time, which was Four o'clock, to the Church-Yard.—My Gentleman was there before me, and his Eyes sparkled with Joy as soon as he saw me coming: He ran to meet me; my dear Angel said he, the Place we are in will not permit me to throw myself at your Feet, as I ought to do, to thank you for this Favour; but be assured, my Heart is more your Slave than ever by this Goodness. Sir, I have been taught, answer'd I, that to be guilty of a breach of Promise, is the worst thing almost that a Person can be guilty of, so have always been careful to avoid that Fault with everybody. But may I not hope, returned he, that you make some Distinction between me and others, and that I owe this Blessing to something more than meerly a Punctilio of Honour.—I wish, Sir, said I, that I have not given you too much Cause to think so; for as the Promise I made you was upon a sort of Compulsion, I might have dispensed with it. 'This I spoke, Mamma, in a more tender Air than ever I had done before; in Hopes by seeming open and unguarded to him, he might in reality be so to me; and indeed it answer'd my Expectation, for on my representing the Hazard I run in my Reputation, for meeting by Appointment with a Gentleman, who was a perfect Stranger to me, he readily told me his Name was *Vardine*, that he was of French Extraction, and his Parents among those who quitted their Estates and Country for the Sake of Religion; and that they being dead, a Person of Quality, but who he did not mention, had been so good to procure him a Commission in the Army: He concluded this Narrative of himself with telling me, he expected to be preferr'd, for at present he was only a Lieutenant; and that if I could once be brought to love him, he would make me a happy Woman.—I thought of you then, Mamma, and how lucky it was for me, that I had not set my Heart upon him.—I took no Notice however of the Baulk it was to me, but seem'd very civil and obliging.—He press'd me again to go and take a Glass of Wine with him, but I absolutely refused that; however, being afraid somebody might happen to come through the Church-yard that might know me, we cross'd, at my Request, the Garden, and struck down Southampton-street, and so into the Savoy, where we walk'd about an Hour: he all the time entertaining me with Praises of my Beauty, and the Impression it had made on him. Indeed I staid with him more to accustom myself to hear fine things said to me, and to practice an agreeable manner of receiving them, than anything else—for as you say, Mamma, he is neither fit to make either Husband or Gallant to one in my Circumstances; so I am resolv'd to think no more on him.—I am a little vex'd tho' now, that I did not take the Stockings, for as there is nothing to be done with him, 'twould have been clear Gains; but I did not know then, his fine Cloaths deceiv'd me; and methinks I am sorry he has not an Estate, for he has Wit at Will, and I am sure loves me to Distraction; and so you would say, if you heard him as I have done—but that's nothing to the Purpose—let him love on—I shall trouble my Head no more about him, but wait with Patience 'till something offers more to my Advantage.—He wou'd fain have exacted another Promise to meet him again; but I told him it was not in my power, if even I had an Inclination, I was much so confined; and if ever he had an Opportunity of speaking to me again, it must be Chance that gave it him.—He complain'd bitterly of my Cruelty; but I was not to be persuaded, and left him as much mortified as the Account he had given me of himself had made me.—I shall see you on *Sunday*, and if anything should happen before, then, shall not fail to let you know it—till then I am,

Dear Mamma,
Your Dutiful,
but Disappointed Daughter,
Syrena Tricksy

Hitherto *Syrena* had disguised nothing either of her Behaviour or Sentiments from her Mother; but a very little Time made her alter her Conduct in that Point, and practice on her some of those Lessons of Deceit, she had so well instructed her in. *Friday* in the Afternoon, as she was sitting at Work, old *Sarah* came in: She was surpris'd to see her, and ask'd hastily if her Mamma was well. Yes, Miss, said *Sarah*, very well; but hearing me say, I was coming this way, she desired me to call and give you her Blessing, with these three Yards and a half of Dimitty; she says, if your Mistress will be so good to cut it out, and give you leave to run it up at a leisure Time, it will serve you in a Morning to comb your Head and wash in, and save your other Cloaths; as she deliver'd this Message, she gave her the Bundle, and at the same time slipt a Letter into her Hand unperceiv'd by anybody. The Mistress who was present, said Mrs. *Tricksy* was a very good Mother; and she might be sure, the Girl should find time to make her Gown very soon. *Sarah* then told her, they hoped to see her on *Sunday*, which the other promised, and the old Emissary went away.

Syrena could not imagine the reason of her Mother's writing again, when she expected to see her so soon, and as she thought had no farther Advice to give her, concerning the Lieutenant; being full of Impatience to see what it contain'd, she soon made a pretence for going out of the Room, and read these Lines.

Friday Noon

Dear Child,

Tho' I hope to see you on *Sunday*, I could not refrain giving you some Remonstrance, which every Hour's Delay of, may render less effectual.—I have not slept all Night for thinking on some Passages in your Letter. Ah, *Syrena!—Syrena!* I am afraid you like this poor idle Fellow, more than it may be you are yet sensible of yourself—why else are you sorry he has not an Estate?—If he has not an Estate others have, that, perhaps, may find you as agreeable as he has done.—You have a very great Opinion too of his Wit, and of his Love; suppose you are not mistaken, he is only the more dangerous, and you ought the less to trust yourself with him.—I charge you, therefore, to shun him henceforward—be as industrious to avoid all Opportunities of seeing him, as 'tis probable he will be in seeking them.—You already believe all the fine Things (as you call them) that he says to you; and knowing by Experience, how susceptible the Heart is at your Years, I tremble least all the Counsel I have given you, should not be sufficient to guard you from the Temptation.—Don't think Child, that I want to lay you under any unreasonable Restraints.—No, if we were rich and above Censure, I should be far from putting any curb to Nature; but as all our Hopes depend on your making your Fortune, either by Marriage or a Settlement equal to it, you must be extremely cautious of your Character till that Point is gain'd, and when once it is, you may freely indulge your Inclinations with this, or any other Man.—You see, I do not like most Parents, want to deprive you of the Pleasures of Life; I would only have you first attain, that which alone can give them a true Relish; for Love in Rags *Syrena*, is a most despicable Thing. Therefore, I once more lay my Commands upon you, to speak no more to this paltry *Vardine*; and to endeavour with all your Might, to conquer whatever Sentiments you may be possest of in his Favour, which is all that can restore Peace of Mind to her, who is at present,

Your most discontented Mother,
Ann Tricksy

P.S. Come as early as you can on *Sunday*.

Syrena was not very well pleas'd at the Contents of this Letter: She thought there was no Occasion for this Caution; and that she had said enough to convince her Mother, that she had no regard for anything in Competition with her Interest.—Why then, said she, must I be debarr'd from speaking to a Man that loves me? A little Conversation with him sometimes would certainly instruct me better how to behave to the Sex, than a thousand Lessons—besides, I might get some small Presents from him—but she will needs have it that I am in love, forsooth.— Not I, indeed, I did not care if he was hang'd for that Matter; but there is something pleasingly amusing, in being address'd by a Man that admires one, and can talk well—in the insipid Life I lead here, 'tis necessary I should have some Diversion to keep up my Spirits.—She owns my Conduct has been perfectly right hitherto—why then should it not be so still?—why must I run away whenever I see him, as if I were afraid he would devour me? Indeed, I shan't make myself such a Fool—if Fortune or his own Endeavours throw him in my way, I shall hear what he has to say, and it may be manage, so as to get something of him—poor as she thinks him.

Thus did Vanity, Self-Conceit and Avarice, tempt her to despise the Admonitions of her crafty Mother, and make her resolve to act henceforward of herself.

When *Sunday* Morning came, as she stood drawing on her Gloves at the Window, she saw him at his ready drest; she presently imagin'd he was ready so early, for no other Reason than to watch her going abroad; but she had not indulg'd herself with this Idea above three Minutes, before it was entirely dash'd: He took up his Hat and Cane and went out of Doors, without so much as looking up.—Ha! cryed she in a Pet, is it so—you are strangely alter'd methinks.—Mamma, need not have been so fearful. The Coldness of my Behaviour last time, has certainly made him resolve to give over all Thoughts of me.

So instead of thinking she had been too kind, she was beginning to repent of not having been kind enough; and in the room of avoiding her Man, was fearful of nothing so much, as not being pursued by him,— in this Ill-Humour she went out of her Mistress's House; but was no sooner in the Street than she perceived the Person who had occasion'd it, at the Corner of that Court, where he had once before overtaken her.—Her Heart bounded with Joy at the Sight of him, not doubting if he stood there for any other Purpose, than to observe which way she went. She deceived not herself in this; he soon came up with her, and accosted her with more Gallantry than ever. She pretended to be greatly alarm'd at seeing him—entreated he would leave her, and told him she had suffered enough already by the little Acquaintance she had with him.—somebody, said she, saw us together in the Church-yard, and told my *Mamma*, who is so angry, that she vows she won't own me as her Child, if ever I speak to you again. Your Mamma, answered he, is ignorant of the Respect I have for you—besides all old People have odd Notions in their Heads—But, my Charmer, continued he, this might have been avoided if you had complied with my Request, and gone into a Tavern. O! that might have been worse, cried she. Much better for us both, said he; at least if I am not the Object of your Aversion; for you would have been convinced of the Sincerity of my Passion, and I should have been happy in your being so; but I'll warrant, added he, the same scrupulous Modesty that made you refuse me then, will not suffer you now to accept of a Coach where you are going. Not for the World, replied she hastily, I am going to my *Mamma*, who expects me; and if she should send anybody to meet me (as 'tis likely she may, for she is violently suspicious since she heard that Story) I should be undone; so pray, Sir, don't go any farther with me. He seem'd to believe what she said; but swore that whatever was the Consequence he would not quit her, till she promised to meet him in the Afternoon. O dear! cried she, then we may be seen again. No, said he, I'll be in the Birdcage-Walk in St. James's Park, about Four o'clock, and if you'll come we'll strike up into the Fields behind Buckingham-house, where we may be private enough. Well, said she, I like this better than going into a Tavern, and if I can get away from Mamma, I will do thus much to oblige you. He call'd this but a half Assurance, nor would leave her till she protested in the most solemn manner, that she would be at the Place he mentioned. Had he known her Mind, he might have spared himself the trouble of exacting a Vow from her, for the fear of losing the first Lover she ever had, render'd her in so complying a Humour, that she was ready to grant almost anything to secure him.

The Reception she had from Mother, was such as she expected from her Letter; but by telling part of the Truth, she so cunningly conceal'd the rest, that artful as the Person she had to deal with, was, there remain'd not the least Suspicion in her Breast. The foolish Fellow watch'd me out, said she, but I gave him such Looks, as I believe put half what he intended to say to me, out of his Head; but yet he would come with me, and talk his Stuff, so I told him we had been seen together in the Church-yard, and you had been made acquainted with it, and were very angry; and for my own Part I did not like to be followed about, and did not know what he meant by it; but whatever Designs he had upon me, he should find himself disappointed; that I could neither like him nor love him, nor desired to be lov'd by him, and a great deal more to the same Purpose. And at last he said; he had been a Fool to trouble himself about me, that I was a proud, pert Minx, and so went strutting away highly affronted. I dare say, Mamma, I am quite rid of him now, and I hope you will be so of all your Fears for me. Mrs. *Tricksy* was perfectly well satisfied with this Account, and after a little ridicule on the Folly of Women, who suffer themselves to be seduced by fine Speeches only, they fell into other Conversation, such as the Affairs of the Family *Syrena* was in, and the Methods that were to be taken for her coming away at the Month's End; till the young Gipsy remembring her Assignation, said what a sad Thing it is to be confined, Mamma, now I have not seen you for almost for a Fortnight, and must not stay with you but a small Part of the Day. How so Child, cried the Mother? why said the other, my Mistress dines abroad on an Engagement made long ago, and poor Mrs. *Martin* is almost dead with the Headache, so she begg'd I would come home soon, for 'tis our Maid's *Sunday* to go out, and she should be alone. I thought you had an old Nurse in the House, said Mrs. *Tricksy*; yes, answered *Syrena*, but she has been these two Days with her Grandson who has the Small-Pox. Well then, returned the Mother, I would not have you do anything to disoblige Mrs. *Martin*, or any of them, because they may give you a bad Word to your Cousin—you shall go as soon as Dinner is over.— When the time grew near, *Syrena* played loth to depart to the Life, and seemed ready to whimper, but her Mother forced her away; and she departed laughing in her Sleeve, and applauding her own Ingenuity in outwitting so penetrating a Judgment.

Vardine was in the Park before the Hour prefix'd, and *Syrena* scarce exceeded it; the Afternoon being gloomy, there was but little Company, especially on that side, so they chose to entertain each other there, rather than walk farther; but this was no sooner agreed upon, than there fell so violent a Shower, that had it continued, the Trees under which they stood for Shelter, would not have defended them from being wet.

Happily however for them, and all that were abroad, the Sky cleared up, yet not enough to give any Prospect of a fair Evening, so he could not desire her to stay, without shewing he had little Regard of her Health; they walked pretty fast till they came to Spring-Garden, when it began to rain again: He called a Coach, but there was none in hearing, and they were oblig'd to stand up in a Tavern Entry, tho' when she ran in, she knew it not for such; and when she did, would have quitted it, tho' all the Doors beside being shut, she saw no other Refuge from the Storm. Nothing could have happened more lucky for *Vardine*'s Designs: He had now a very plausible Pretence for persuading her to go into a Room.—It would be a piece of strange Affectation, said he, to chuse to stand in a Place where we are exposed to the View of everybody; (and you see how many People pass) rather than go with a Man who loves you, and whose every Action you may command. With such like

Arguments she was at last prevail'd upon, and he order'd some Wine to be made hot with Spice and Sugar. After they had drank a Glass or two, now, said he, where is the mighty Business of going into a Tavern—is it not better sitting here than strolling the Streets, as if no House would receive us?—'Twould be more comfortable indeed, answered she, if it were not for the Scandal; there is no Scandal in it, cry'd he; beside, who need know it, unless we tell it ourselves, for the Drawers here are as secret as Confessors. That may be, said she, in a sort of Childish Tone; but methinks I am ashamed to know I am here myself. That's for want of knowing the World, my Dear, replied he; in such Weather as this the veriest Puritan would have made no Scruple. Did not *Dido*, tho' a great Queen, run into a Cave with a wandring Soldier to avoid a Storm. Great Folks may do anything, said she, but pray what is that Story? I'll tell you anon, my Dear, answered he, but first pray ease me of this Luggage;—I have had your Stockings in my Pocket all Day, and now I desire you'll take charge on them yourself;—with these Words he laid them on the Table before her:—My Stockings, said she, indeed they are none of mine;—and I won't have them;—but you shall, and you must, reply'd he; you chose them, and they are bought and paid for;—but may be you think they won't fit;—I should know that, because they may be changed;—I can tell in a Moment, by grasping your pretty Leg:—Here he made an offer of doing as he said, but she resisted with all her Strength, crying out at the same time—hold! hold! I will have them—they will fit; and glad enough she was to take them, tho' in reality a little frightend at the manner in which he forced them upon her. He found she trembled, and would not alarm her Modesty too much at once, so drawing back his Hand, don't be under any Apprehensions my sweet Innocence, said he; upon my Soul I mean no hurt to you, and did this only to oblige you to accept my little Present.—Well, I'll believe you this time, answer'd she, but pray don't offer such Freedoms anymore, for if you do, I'll never speak to you again. He then made her drink another Glass of Wine in token of Forgiveness; and that being followed by several others, her young Brain unaccustomed to such an Encrease of Heat, began to grow confused, and she lost all Memory of the Place, or Danger she was in: He ply'd her all the time with Protestations of Love, and sometimes by way of Parenthesis gave her a Kiss, which he had the Satisfaction to find she less and less resisted.

How ought, therefore, the Fair-Sex to beware of indulging even the very Temptation of a Vice, which I am sorry to say is at present too prevalent among them. I need not say I mean that of Drinking, which indeed opens the way to all others; the Example before us of a Girl train'd up in Precepts directly opposite, to giving Way to any tender Inclinations, and taught that the only thing she had to avoid, was the bestowing any Favours but where Interest directed; now, by the meer Force of Liquor, betray'd to yield to the Impulse of Nature, and resign that Jewel, on which all her Hopes of living great in the World depended, to a Person from whom she could have no Expectations, and for whom what she felt could not justly be called Love; this, I say, may be a Warning to all of what Principles and Station whatever; since there are Dangers arising from this pernicious Custom, as well in the Closet as in the Street, tho' perhaps of a different Nature.

The young Officer perceiving the Ground he gain'd, did not fail pursuing the Attack, and bombarded her so fast with Speeches out of Plays, tender Pressures, Kisses, and the more intoxicating Juice of the Grape, that at length the Town was wholly his;—the momentary Rapture over, the Power of Reflection return'd to this unhappy ruin'd Girl;—she reproach'd him and herself;—she wept;—she exclaim'd;— but it was now too late. He said a good many fond things to her, but he made a Jest of her Complaints; why, my Dear, cry'd he, you desir'd to know the Story of *Dido* and *Æneas*, and I have more than *told* it to you, for I have *acted* it to the Life. O wicked! wicked Man! cry'd she, and sobb'd most bitterly:—He then endeavour'd all he could to set her Mind at ease: He made a thousand Vows of everlasting Constancy, and that when his Affairs were once settled, he would make her his Wife; at last she grew a little more composed; and it being now dark, began to think what Excuse she should make at home for being out so late; her ready Invention soon supplied her with one, and a Coach being call'd, he set her down at the end of the Street, after having made her promise to meet him again the first Opportunity, which she was to let him know by a Sign from the Window.

The good People at home were very much frighted at her staying so late, for it was near Nine, and as much rejoiced to see her safe returned: She told them, that being just coming away, the Rain obliged her to stay; and that afterwards a Person who happened to dine that Day with a Lodger in the same House, offer'd to set her down if she would stay her Time; so Madam said she, I accepted her Favour, as it was a bad Evening; and hope you would not be offended; not in the least, answered her Mistress, I am very glad it happened so.

As *Syrena* had a Share of Understanding uncommon for her Years, she could not recollect what had pass'd between her and *Vardine*, without a great deal of Uneasiness; but her Vivacity and Strength of Spirits soon threw it off; she consider'd that as it was past recall, to hurt her Eyes and Complexion, by crying and fretting, would encrease not diminish her Misfortune; and therefore resolved to be entirely secret in the Matter, and get as much as she could from him, in recompence for what he had robb'd her of. How she should contrive any future Meetings with him, was now the chief Employment of her Thoughts; but tho' she rack'd Invention to the utmost Pitch, she could not hit on anything that had not some Danger of Discovery. She saw her Lover the next Morning at his Window as usual, but had no Sign to make but a melancholy shaking her Head, accompanied with a Look that told him, it was not owing to her Inclinations, that they had not a nearer Intercourse. The next Day it was the same, and probably would have continued so till *Sunday*, had not Fortune befriended her Endeavours.

A Gown being in hand, *Syrena* was ordered to go to the Lady's House for Silver Lace to trim it;—what would she not have given to have known this in the Morning,—but it was now too late.— *Vardine* was abroad, and she knew not where to send to him;—it came into her Head however as she was in the Street, not to go, but to walk about a little, and return home, pretending the Lady had not bought the Trimming, and had bid her come for it the next Day at three in the Afternoon: This was feasible enough, and passed current with People that had not the least Suspicion of her Conduct.

Possession had not so far abated the Fervour of her Gallant's Affections, but that he attended the Window as before—and she had the Opportunity of making him know he might see her in the Afternoon; which was done by pointing to the Street, and holding up three Fingers, in signification that Three o'clock was the time. He express'd his Satisfaction by a thousand tender Gestures; but she was oblig'd to leave him in the midst of them, fancying she heard somebody coming up Stairs. She had indeed more than ordinary Reason now for being cautious, not only because Guilt naturally makes People so, but also, because his standing so much at the Window had been taken Notice of: The Maid told her one Day as she was washing her Hands in the Kitchen, that she was sure she had got a Sweetheart since she came;—a Sweetheart, said *Syrena*! what do you mean, *Margaret*? I mean as I say, answer'd *Margaret*;—the Gentleman that lodges over the Way is as surely in love with you, as I am alive.—I never go to the Door or into the Parlour in a Morning, but I see him staring at our Windows, as if he'd lose his Eyes; and it must be for you, for there's no other young Body in the House;—why not yourself, said *Syrena*, you are not old;—no, no, I am not so vain, cry'd *Margaret*; but if I were, he takes care to undeceive me; for the Minute he sees me he pops his Head in. *Syrena* laugh'd, and the Maid being call'd, there pass'd no more between them; but this serv'd her as a good Warning to be circumspect; for she very well knew that if her Conversation with him were once but so much as suspected, it would break the Neck of her Designs every way.

When it grew near three *Syrena* reminded her Mistress, that it was the time for her to go; and received the Praise her supposed Dilligence seem'd to deserve.—*Vardine* was at the usual Corner, and having a Coach in waiting at the end of the Street, they both stept into it, and drove immediately to the same Tavern they had been in before.

The pains she took for this Interview may very well be taken for the Effect of Love, as indeed it was; but not of the Man, tho' something belonging to him. She had seen a very genteel Snuff-Box in his Hand of Pinchbeck's Mettal, which she mistook for Gold: This Box had run in her head ever since *Sunday*; and she languished with Impatience for an Opportunity, which she hoped would make her Mistress of it.

She was not deceiv'd in the Complaisance of her Lover, tho' she was in the Value of the thing she had set her Heart upon; for by praising and looking earnestly on it, she so artfully insinuated she had a mind to it, that he soon made her a Present of it. They past about an Hour together, in the manner Persons usually do, who see each other on the Terms they did; and parted with a Promise of meeting at the same Place at four o'clock, as she came from her Mother's next *Sunday*. After which she went on the Business she was sent, and was dispatch'd time enough not to make her Mistress think she loiter'd; tho', to excuse her stay, she pretended she had waited a good while before the Lady could be spoke with.

She had now nothing to think on, but what she should wheedle him out of next: He had no Ring on his Finger, no lac'd Ruffles, or anything fit for her to ask.—She therefore contriv'd a Stratagem to get a small Sum of Money from him (for she did not imagine he could spare a large one) and executed it in this manner.

When she came to the Tavern, where he was ready to receive her, she put on so wild confused a Countenance, as made him, when about to take her in his Arms, start back and ask if she were not well—Yes, said she, I am well enough in Health—but the saddest Accident—O that I had been sick, or dead, or anything, so that I had not come out this Day!—Then she threw her self into a Chair, and burst into Tears. He prest her very endearingly to tell him the Occasion; but all the Answer she gave him was, O! I must never look my *Mamma* in the Face again—O! I am undone—I durst not go home—I cannot tell what to say, that will pacify my Mistress—Sure I am the most unfortunate Creature in the World.—What, my Dear, said he, nothing concerning me, I hope, is discovered? No, reply'd she sobbing, but I'll tell you the whole Business. You must know, continued she, that my *Mamma*, borrow'd five Guineas of my Mistress, upon a very great Exigence: She gave her a Note for it, and a time was prefix'd for the Payment;—it became due Yesterday, and my *Mamma* having the Money ready, desired the Note might be sent by me, as I was to come this Day.—O! unhappy Day that it is to me, I'm sure.—Here she feigned as if she could not speak again; but then seeming to recover a little—In short, said she, I carry'd the Note—My Mamma gave the Money to me, and I put it into my Purse, where I had a few Pieces of Silver of my own;—but they are all gone together—Either some Rogue has picked my Pocket, or I have pull'd out the Purse with my Handkerchief.—An ugly Accident indeed, my Dear, reply'd he gravely, but might have happen'd to anybody—You must ev'n tell the Truth—O! cry'd she, 'tis a sign you don't know their Tempers; they would tear me in Pieces—My Mistress would think it a Trick between Mamma and me, because I carry'd the Note; and Mamma beside would be obliged to pay—O! what shall I do? I'll never go home again, unless I have the Money—She run on in this manner for a good while, without his offering to interrupt her; which she had cunning enough to look on as no good Omen of Success; and finding she must speak more plain—O! if you loved me half so well as I do you, said she, you would not see me fret so—you'd give me or lend me such a Trifle. I protest, Child, reply'd he, I have not so much about me—Well, said she, you may leave me at the Corner of our Street while you fetch it—That I would willingly do, return'd he, but if you must know, I am not at present Master of so much.—But you can borrow it, cry'd she; nor can I borrow it any where that I know of, answer'd he; I never ask'd such a Favour of anybody but our Agent, and he happens to be out of Town—so you had better own the Truth.—I dare not, said she, and you only perswade me to run the risque of it, because you don't care to part with your Money.—Upon my Soul, answered he, I have it not—See here, continued he, pulling out his Purse, and throwing two Guineas on the Table; this is my whole Stock, besides a little Silver in my Pockets—But you have a gold Watch, returned she, and anybody—the very People of this House, I'll warrant you, would lend you five Pounds upon it till your Agent comes to Town—Excuse me, my Dear, reply'd he somewhat haughtily, I never pawn,—nor can I part with my Watch on any Consideration—we in the Army are oblig'd to observe time—Well, cry'd she, sobbing again, I see that I am miserable—you have ruin'd me, and now neither love nor pity me. That's unkind, said he, I would serve you if it were in my power, but this you ask is not—if these two Pieces, added he, would make your Mistress easy—Give them to me, interrupted she, I'll tell her, Mamma receiv'd but half what she expected, and could send no more than two, but she should have the other three some Day this Week—but then you must be sure to get them for me. He would fain have perswaded her to have told the Accident—He said he could not be assured of receiving Money so soon, and would be loth to disappoint her—In fine, they had many Arguments, he to keep, and she to get the two Guineas:—At length he found himself forced in a manner to recede, and she pocketed the two Pieces—Well, said she, I'll tell my Mistress, that I forgot to bring back the Note—but, my dear, dear *Vardine*, don't fail to procure me the other three by *Tuesday* —I can't promise it so soon as then, reply'd he, you must say *Thursday* or *Friday* —Ay, let it be *Friday* —Since she found she could do no better, she urg'd it no farther, and began to grow more chearful—but the young Officer could not so readily dissipate his Gloom: He was not quite satisfy'd with the Story she told him, and began to fear his little Mistress would become too expensive to him. He conceal'd his Sentiments, however, as well as he was able, and when the Close of Day reminded them of parting, ordered a Coach, and set her down at the same Place where he had taken her up.—As she took her leave, remember *Friday*, and the three Guineas, said she, I shall look for you at the Corner of the Court, about Ten in the Morning, and if you fail, will never speak to you again—And if I do, Child, answer'd he, I'll never venture to look thee in the Face again.

Now did *Syrena* Glory in the Power of her Beauty and Invention, she thought it impossible for Mankind to refuse her anything; and tho' it was with Difficulty she had gain'd her Point with *Vardine*, she imputed it only to the Scantiness of his Fortune; and did not doubt but to find Articles to get greater Sums of him, tho' he even sold his Commission to raise them for her: But her Triumph lasted not long.— *Friday* Morning happening to come into the Dining-Room, before the Maid had quite finished putting it in order—O Miss! cry'd she, you have lost your Admirer—I did not know I ever had any, answer'd *Syrena*; but what do you mean, *Margaret*?—Why, said she, the Gentleman that I told you of over the way, that used to stare up so.—*Syrena's* Heart flutter'd at these Words, and in the present Confusion, she cry'd hastily, well what of him? He has left our Neighbourhood, reply'd *Margaret*; as I was washing our Steps about an Hour ago, I saw a Hackney Coach at the Door with a Portmanteau and other Luggage before it, and presently in stept the Beau, and cry'd, Drive away Coachman. Pish! said *Syrena*, thou art always troubling one with some Stuff or other— What was the Fellow to us, I wonder. She said no more, nor, indeed, was she able, nor to stay any longer in the Room, without discovering her Disorder. She ran up Stairs, tho' she knew not why, she doubted not the Truth of what the Maid had said—She saw the Window open, but no Lover appear—She sat down, pondering on this Adventure, at last recollected herself—Well, said she, a thousand Accidents may have obliged him to quit his Lodging, but that does not follow, that he must therefore quit me.—He will certainly be at the Place he promised at the appointed time—I will at least make myself easy till then.

Soon as she heard the Clock strike ten she ran out, pretending she had broke her Lace, and must go to buy another; but no *Vardine* could she see.—She stay'd a few Minutes walking about the Court, flattering herself still with the Hope that he would come; but instead of him, a sort of ill-look'd Fellow came up to her, and ask'd if her Name was not *Syrena Tricksy*, and on her saying it was, gave her a Letter, which she hastily opening, found in it these few, and little pleasing Lines.

Dear Girl,

Our Regiment is ordered to the *West*, and thence, I believe, to *Ireland*: I was too lately apprized of it to take my leave of you—make yourself as easy as you can—when I come back I shall with pleasure renew my Acquaintance with you,

Yours, &c.
J. Vardine

P.S. I am sorry I could not comply with your Request.

Rage did not so far bereave her of her Senses, but that she ask'd the Fellow a great many Questions, but he either could not or would not answer anything to the purpose; and all she could get from him was, that the Letter was given him by a Gentleman at a Coffee-House, who ordered him to wait in that Court till she came, and deliver it to her.

It must be confessed, this Action of *Vardine*'s was cruel and ungrateful—what must have become of the undone and forsaken *Syrena*, had she been possest of that Softness and Tenderness which some are; but as she was capable of loving in reality nothing but herself, and carried on a Correspondence with him merely on a mercenary View, she was not much to be pitied. The Mortification of her Pride and Avarice, however, gave her Agonies which she before had no notion of; and made her the more easily counterfeit an Indisposition, which was the Pretence agreed on between her and her Mother, for her going Home at the Month's end—and it is certain, she grew so thin and pale, that the Mistress herself imagined that sitting so close to her Work had prejudiced her Health. She had the Good-nature to offer her the Advice of a Physician, but could not help agreeing with everybody who were consulted about it, that it was most proper she should be with her Mother, as best acquainted with her Constitution. In fine, home she was brought, nor could that Kinswoman who had recommended her, take it amiss, when she saw how ill she looked—a violent Pain in her Head and Stomach was the Complaint; and it seemed reasonable to believe, that stooping forward to her Work, had occasioned it. There was again some talk of putting her to a Milliner, which was indeed what Mrs. *Tricksy* aimed at; but the Reasons before alledged against that Business, being now repeated, stopped her Mouth; and nothing seemed now so proper for her, as to wait upon a Lady. All the Relations in general approved of this, and promised to enquire among their Acquaintance for a Place for her.

In the mean time *Syrena* was so far from recovering her former Colour and Vivacity, that she look'd worse and worse; and had sometimes such sick Fits, that her Mother began to be afraid she had counterfeited a Disorder so well, as to bring it upon her in good earnest: But her Penetration did not permit her to continue long in the dark as to the Cause. She soon discover'd, that a too near Conversation with a Man had made the Alteration; and not doubting but it was *Vardine*, accused her in such plain and positive Terms, that the Girl had not Courage to deny it. She search'd her Trunk, and found the Stockings, Snuff-

Box, and two Guineas, with the Letter, which not only let her into the whole Mystery of her undoing, but her being forsaken also. It would be tiresome to repeat the Exclamations she made, or the Reproaches poor *Syrena* was oblig'd to bear; 'tis sufficient to say, that the first Fury of her Resentment over Reason resumed its Place, and as what was past could not be recall'd, all that could be done, was to endeavour to alleviate the Misfortune as much as possible: To that end, she prepared a strong Potion, which the Girl very willing drank, and being so timely given, had the desired Effect, and caused an Abortion, to the great Joy of both Mother and Daughter. After all was over, and *Syrena* pretty well recovered, Mrs. *Tricksy* could not forbear renewing her upbraidings; but the other confessing herself to blame, and professing her future Conduct should retrieve all, at length mollify'd her Passion; and the more so, because tho' she had suffered herself to be beguiled by that young Officer, yet her Management of him afterwards shewed the Instructions given her had not been thrown away; and that she had both a Genius and Inclination to make the most of her Men, and now an Opportunity offered to prove her Abilities that way.

She was recommended to the Service of an old Lady, who wanted one chiefly to attend her in her Chamber, and read to her till she fell asleep. Such an Employment would have afforded little Hope of advancing *Syrena* in the manner she had desired, had it not been for the Family the old Gentlewoman was in; which consisted of her Daughter, who was married to a Baronet, and their Son, a fine young Gentleman of about twenty-two. This last Article rendered the Place extremely acceptable, and our young Deceiver being introduced to the Ladies, her feigned Innocence immediately gained their Favour; and she was received into the House, with the promise of being used very kindly. The second Day after her coming, she wrote to her Mother as full an Account of the Family, as she was able to give in so short a Time.

FRIDAY

Dear Mamma,

How happy would some young Women think themselves to be in my Place, I have so little to do, and am so much respected by the inferior Servants, that I can scarce think I am a Servant myself—it is not required of me to rise till nine or ten o'clock, and then I go into my Lady's Room, enquire after her Health, and give her her Chocolate, which is ready made and brought up by the upper House-maid: After this, I am my own Mistress till about one, when she rises, and I help her on with her Clothes, and see her no more till about eleven, which is the time she generally goes to Bed. I sit down and read to her till she falls asleep, and this compleats the Work of the Day—Her Daughter's Woman has ten times more fatigue than I, tho' her Ladyship is reckoned very good too; but I heard by the by that she is horribly jealous of Sir *Thomas*; and that makes her a little cross sometimes to those about her; so I am glad I have nothing to do with her: I lie with Mrs. *Mary* her Chamber maid, who is a mighty good-natur'd Creature, and likes me prodigiously; it was she gave me the hint about Sir *Thomas*, and bid me avoid him as much as I could; for says she, if he should take any notice of you, my Lady would never rest till you were out of the House; and her Mother is so fond of her, that she would part from anybody rather than give her a Minute's uneasiness—and I can tell you he loves a Girl in a corner—so I find, Mamma, I must take care of my Behaviour—As for the young Gentleman, I never saw him till this Morning as I was coming up Stairs—I assure you he is not at all handsome—you need not fear I shall lose my Heart.—He did not speak a Word, but stared at me when I stopped to let him pass, and I made him a Curtesy—so how things will happen I can't tell; but if anything material occurs, you may be sure of being immediately acquainted with it, by

Dear Mamma,
Your most Obedient Daughter,
SYRENA TRICKSY

P.S. Just as I had finish'd the above, my Lady's Bell rung; so not having time to seal it then, I have the opportunity to tell you, that as I was crossing the passage, I saw the young Gentleman again, coming out of his Father's Closet; I made him another Curtesy, and blush'd, and I thought he look'd a little red too, but did not speak a Word—I hope soon to have more to acquaint you with.

MONDAY

Dear Mamma,

I Long'd to see you Yesterday, but did not think it would look well to ask to go out the very first *Sunday* I came. So I write to inform you, what has happen'd since my last. On *Saturday* Morning, as I was in a Room joining to my Lady's Chamber, tacking a Pair of three-double Ruffles on her Sleeves (for she goes as fine and as gay as her Daughter, tho' she is so very old) Mr. *L*—— came thro' to pay his Duty to his Grandmother, as it seems he does every Morning, tho' I never happen'd to be in the way before. He took no notice of me as he went, but when he came back, So my pretty Lass, said he, you wait upon my Grandmother, I think? Yes, Sir, replied I, rising and curtesying, I am so happy. I hope you'll have cause to think yourself so, returned he, she is a very good Mistress, and you look as if you would deserve her Favours. This was all that past, and he went directly down stairs.—Now whether he had any Meaning in what he said I can't tell, but I could not help thinking it a lucky Omen, that the first thing he said to me should be, that he hoped I should have Cause to think myself happy.—I should think myself happy indeed, if I could get a Husband with such an Estate as he will have—O, what Splendor does my Lady *L*—— live in!—How everybody worships her—tho' I must not set my Heart too much upon it, for fear of a Disappointment—but I have something more to tell you still, Mamma—Yesterday in the Afternoon my Lady, and Sir *Thomas* and his Lady, and Mr. *L*—— went all out a visiting— So it being an idle time Mrs. *Brown* Lady *L*——'s Woman, and the Chambermaid and I were got all together over a Pot of Coffee in the Back-Parlour; and tho' I believe none of us are silly enough to give any Credit to what one may fancy is to be seen in throwing the Grounds, yet to amuse ourselves we toss'd the Cups, as they call it, and were telling one another our Fortunes—when, to our great Surprize, in comes Mr. *L*——: we were so busy, that we never heard him, till he was just upon us—it seems some of the Under-Maids happen'd to be standing at the Door, and he came in without knocking—He found what we were at, and fell a laughing most prodigiously; but the Confusion we were all in is not to be express'd—Nay, nay, said he, I won't disturb you; and since I have caught you, am resolved to make one among you—Come, which of you is the Artist?—I believe, Sir, replied Mrs. *Brown*, who had the most Courage, our Skill is pretty equal; tho' I think *Mary* is rather the best at Invention—Then *Mary* shall be my Conjurer, said he; and with these Words turn'd down a Cup. Poor Mrs. *Mary* was sadly asham'd, and begg'd his Honour would excuse her; but he would needs carry on the Jest, and forced her to take the Cup—Well then, said she, here is a great House, and a fine Lady at the Gate, that seems to expect a Visit from your Honour; and a great deal more such Stuff she run on with. He laugh'd again, and said, as you observed Mrs. *Brown* I find *Mary* is a great Visionary; but she has not happen'd to hit upon my Humour—I don't regard fine Ladies; Beauty and Innocence have more Charms for me than Grandeur—He look'd full at me as he spoke these last Words:—then, I thank you for my Fortune, however, *Mary*, continued he; and I think I ought to pay for it. With this he gave us everyone a Kiss, beginning with Mrs. *Brown*, and ending with me. But indeed, Mamma, I am very much mistaken, if there was not a great deal of difference between his manner of saluting them and me; he seem'd, I thought, only to touch their Lips, but press'd mine so hard that he made them smart. After this, Well, said he, I won't stay to be a Restraint upon you—pray pursue your Diversion, and so went up stairs.

This Accident is very trifling, but everything must have a Beginning; and therefore I thought fit to let you know it, as you shall most faithfully all that happens to, my dear Mamma,

Your most Dutiful Daughter,
Syrena Tricksy

WEDNESDAY

Dear Mamma,

I am not half so easy as when I wrote to you last—I am afraid, I have made a Conquest in the wrong Place.—I find what Mrs. *Mary* told me is true.—Sir *Thomas* can't be content with his own Lady, tho' she is allow'd to be one of the finest Women in the Kingdom, and is not old now; for they say, she was a perfect Girl when Mr. *L*—— was born: Well, if I were a Woman of Fortune, I'd marry none of them.—But I'll tell you, Mamma; Lady *L*—— went with some Company to the Play on *Monday*; after she was gone, Sir *Thomas* came up into my Lady's Room, and staid about an Hour, and drank Wine and eat some Jelly with her, which I serv'd, as it being in her Chamber; when he took his leave I was order'd to light him down; I did so, and when we came to the Door of his Study, he took hold of my Hand and pull'd me in: I was so confounded, not expecting any such Thing from him, who had never before seem'd to look at me, that I had not power to make any Resistance.—Pretty Mrs. *Syrena*, said he, I would not have given you this Trouble; but for an Opportunity to tell you how much I am charmed with your Person and Behaviour—in speaking this he clapped the Door, but did not lock it. I beg your Honour would not talk so to me, answered I, endeavouring to get from him; but he held me fast, and in spite of all I could do, forced a hundred Kisses from me.—The more I struggled, the closer he press'd me to him; and I don't know how far the old Goat might have proceeded, if I had not protested, I would cry out and alarm the House: he then desisted; but still held me with one Hand, and with the other took five Guineas out of his Pocket, and would have put them down my Bosom; say nothing to anybody, cried he, and I'll be a Friend to you: Sir, said I, resolutely, I desire no Friendship, but what I shall endeavour to merit by my Honesty; and as I am Madam S——'s Servant, shall take no Presents from any of her Relations, without acquainting her with it. You are young, cried he, and don't know the World yet; nor do I desire to be inform'd of it by such Means, replied I; and giving a sudden Spring got loose, and ran up Stairs. I thought that I had thrown all the Pieces down, that he attempted to put into my Bosom; but when I came to unlace me, I found one Guinea had slipt in unknown to me.—Indeed, I was a little tempted to keep it, as believing he would not miss it, in the hurry of Spirits he seemed to have been; but then again I thought that if he did, it would look like an Encouragement: So it came into my Head to make a merit to the Ladies of restoring it, and at the time shew him, that any future Attempts he should think to make upon me would be in vain. When I went into my Lady's Chamber in the Morning; Madam, said I, after I had read you to sleep last Night, I saw this Guinea lying on the Carpet, so I took it up, fearing it might be lost, when the Carpet was taken up to be shook, I suppose you happen'd to drop it. No, answer'd she, I never carry Money loose in my Pocket.—I believe, my Son in pulling out some Papers, might let it fall. I beg then, Madam, said I, you will be so good to return it to him. No, replied she, you shall do it yourself. When we go to Dinner, I'll send for you into the Parlour: She did so, and having told Sir *Thomas*, what I had said concerning the Guinea; I went to him, and made him a low Curtesy, offering it to him. No, Mrs. *Syrena*, said he, pray keep it yourself, as a Reward for your Honesty. I humbly thank'd his Honour, and went away; but as I went out of the Room, I heard Lady *L*—— say, Sir *Thomas*, I am glad you have given it to her; and the Butler told me afterwards, that they all were full of my Praises. Sir *Thomas* himself, I find is not disobliged at this Action, for as I went through the Dining-Room this Morning, to ask how Lady *L*—— had slept, she being a little ill with the Headache last Night, he was sitting at the Window, and as soon as he saw me, he rose, and in a low Voice, said, I see you have a Discretion above your Years.—I will offer nothing that shall alarm you; but I must have a Moment's Discourse with you soon. I was vex'd he was there, and only answer'd, I beg your Honour will not think on't, and so left him. As to Mr. *L*——, I have not seen him since *Sunday*, but at Table when I carried in the Guinea, and once in my Lady's Chamber; so I can form no Judgment, how far I am in his good Graces, any farther than my last made mention of.—It is very unlucky that his Father likes me; but I shall shun him as much as I can, without being taken Notice on by the Family.—I am afraid I shan't be able to see you next *Sunday* neither, for my Lady talks of taking Physick; but I am not certain yet, and shall write to you again before then, for I have time enough, if I have but an agreeable Subject. I am,

Dear Mamma,
Your most dutiful Daughter,
SYRENA TRICKSY

THURSDAY Evening

Dear Mamma,

Strange Adventures have happen'd since yesterday Morning; but don't be alarm'd for the Consequence of them, in all Probability will turn out highly to Advantage, one Way or another. But I will not keep you in Suspence. As soon as Dinner was over, the Coach was order'd, and my Lady and Lady *L*——, and Mrs *Brown* went among the Shops as they call it, that is to make all the Tradesmen in their Way pull down their Goods; tell them what Lady bought of such a Pattern, and what of such a one; in fine to hear News, and buy Pennyworths if they meet with any. But this is nothing to my Purpose.—After they were gone, I went up into my Lady's Room, to lay her Night-Things ready, as I always did, against she undrest, and was a humming a new Tune to myself, little thinking anybody was behind me, when turning about, I saw Sir *Thomas* just coming into the Chamber; I was very much startled, but had not time to speak, before he said Mrs. *Syrena*, I have a Favour to beg of you; in anything I can, and ought to do, I shall obey your Honour, answer'd I; it is only to mend a Hole in my Stocking, that is just now broke, return'd he; and then looking round the Room, I see you are alone, cried he: These Words frighted me very much, and I would have given anything to have been out of the Chamber, or that somebody had come up; but he knew well enough the Under-Servants were all at Dinner; and he had left Mrs. *Mary* busy in her Lady's Room, or else he would not have ventured to come into me in that Manner. He saw I was uneasy, and to dissipate my Fears.—Don't be under Apprehensions, said he, I shall do you no Hurt—you don't think I wou'd ravish you sure.—I hope, Sir, answer'd I, you would not harbour any Thoughts of ruining a poor Girl, who has nothing but her good Character to depend upon. No Child, said he, your Character can run no risque with a Man, who would not forfeit his own—and it is on this Head, I want to talk with you.—He then told me, that he liked and loved me above any Woman he had ever seen; that if I would consent to be his, he would put it out, even of his own power to use me ill, by making me a handsome Settlement.—All which Offers I rejected with (I think, I may say without Vanity) a well-affected vertuous Pride.—I told him, I preferr'd my Honesty in Rags, to all the Splendor in the World, when it must be the Purchase of Vice and Infamy; and desired he would desist making me any such Offers; for as I looked upon it, as a Crime even to listen to them, I must be obliged to leave the House.—Well, said he, I will endeavour to conquer myself, if I am able.—But, how is it possible, continued he, sighing, and looking full in my Face, when I see those Eyes.—Then I must hide them, cried I, turning away.—No resumed he, I must not, cannot loose the Pleasure of seeing you—cruel Girl as you are—but still I hope, you will one Day be kinder.—Yes you will.—You must, continued he, catching hold of both Hands, and pressing them between his—then perceiving I began to tremble again, why are you so alarm'd, added he? tho' Opportunities are so scarce, that perhaps, I was a little too precipitate in seizing the first; yet you see I now behave to you in a different Manner. Everything that has a Tendency to corrupt my Innocence, said I, is alike alarming; and I against protest, I will not stay in a House where I cannot be secure.—Well, Mrs. *Syrena*, replied he, letting go my Hands, you judge my Intentions with too much Severity.—I assure you, that the short time you have been in my Family, has made an Impression on me, that would not suffer me to injure you.—Only think on what I have said, and command anything in my power: With these Words he kiss'd me, and left the Room. I presently lock'd the Door to prevent his Return; and was sitting down to consider how I should behave in this Affair, when the Closet-Door behind me open'd, and out came Mr. *L*——. Never was Surprize equal to mine, of seeing him there: I had not Presence enough of Mind to forbear shrieking, which I am since heartily glad, nobody heard. Hush! cried he, or you'll bring my Father back again. For Heaven's sake, Sir, said I, what brought you into that Closet? Not Curiosity, upon my Word, answer'd he, for I little expected the Scene I have been witness of; but whatever Motive induced me to conceal myself here, you ought not to be dissatisfy'd, since by it I have proved your Virtue and Prudence equal to your Beauty. I beseech you, Sir, said I, don't rally a poor silly Girl, who has nothing to boast of, but the Resolution of keeping herself honest. No, Mrs. *Syrena*, reply'd he, I never was more serious in my Life than I am this Moment—I was less so, I confess when I went into that Closet, but my Father's Behaviour has been such a Surprize upon me that—He was going to say something, but a sudden Thought made him break off, and after a little Pause, But sure, resum'd he, you do not in earnest intend to quit my Grandmother? I should think it the greatest Blessing of Life, answer'd I, to continue in the Service of so good a Lady; but the Persecutions I am like to receive from Sir *Thomas*, are of a Nature I neither can or ought to bear, for any Consideration. I am sorry to say, returned he, that amorous Addresses are not very becoming in a Man of fifty to a Girl of your Years; but if ever it should be discover'd, 'tis his own, not your Character, would suffer by it— You may depend, that whatever his Inclinations are, he has too much Honour to make use of Force to gain you; and if you should leave us, you can go into no Family, but where those Eyes of yours will lay you under the same Temptations you receive from him. On this I hung down my Head, and kept looking on the Ground to avoid seeing how he look'd when he spoke. Don't be asham'd, pursued he, taking me by the Hand, I tell you nothing but Truth—So, pretty Mrs. *Syrena*, you must not think of going out of the House, at least yet a while. If I could be safe, said I, nothing could give me greater Pleasure than to continue here—but—You shall be safe, interrupted he, Come, dry those lovely Eyes—(for I was just then squeezing out some Tears) I had something to say to you, but will take another Opportunity, and leave you now to compose yourself: He concluded with giving me a Kiss, accompanied with a most tender Pressure of my Hand, and then went out of the Chamber; but had not been gone above three Steps, before he return'd; I believe, said he, you are too discreet and good-natur'd to expose my Father's Folly? I should be very sorry, answer'd I, to do anything that might create Uneasiness in a Family, for the greatest part of whom I have the most perfect Love and Veneration. Those of us who enjoy that are happy, cry'd he, and methought his Eyes struck Fire as he spoke these Words; but he went on, I have one thing more to desire of you, and that is, that you will let me know from time to time what Sollicitations you receive from my Father—My Advice may be of some Service to you; and such a Mark of your Confidence highly obliging to me. Sir, reply'd I, tho' such a Confidence to a Person of a different Sex, must cover me with the utmost Confusion; yet you seem too good, and too full of Pity to me, for me to refuse. You cannot have too great an Opinion of my Goodwill towards you, said he, and so you shall find. Here he took me in his Arms, and gave me three or four hearty Kisses, tho' with all the Modesty in the World, and then ran down Stairs.

Now, Mamma, what can I think of all this, but that he conceal'd himself in the Closet for no other purpose, than to attempt me in the manner Sir *Thomas* has done; but that my resolute Behaviour to the Father, made a Convert of the Son; and turned the Inclinations he felt for me, into others of a more respectful Nature.—I would be loath to flatter myself too far—but I think I am right—Time will discover— This Morning, after he came down from Breakfast, as he always does, with Sir *Thomas* and his Lady in their Chamber, he tarry'd walking backwards and forwards in the great Parlour, for, I believe, three Hours; and everytime I pass'd him, as I was oblig'd to do very often, there being no other way from my Lady's Room, he gave me Looks which told me, he had the kindest Thoughts of me; and once, no Body being in Sight, came to me and kiss'd me, with these Words, Dear Mrs. *Syrena* be easy. He dined abroad to Day with Sir *Thomas*, so I have seen neither of them since; but I don't doubt now, but I shall have Matter sufficient to employ my Pen to you very often. Dear Mamma, with good Success to,

Your dutiful Daughter,
SYRENA TRICKSY

FRIDAY Morning

Dear Mamma,

I am now eased of the Suspence I was in when I wrote to you Yesterday: Mr. *L——* has broke his Mind to me—I'll tell you in what manner—*Thursday* being what they call my Lady's Visiting Day, there was a vast deal of Company; but I had nothing to do with them, for Mrs. *Brown* and the Chambermaid attend in a little Room within the Drawing-Room, as the Groom of the Chambers and Butler do in one without; so having no Body to converse with, I sat in my own Lady's Room, meditating on my Affairs—I think I mention'd in my former, that the two Gentlemen dined abroad—Sir *Thomas*, after he had quitted his Company, it seems, went to the Play, but Mr. *L*—— came Home—He did not stay five Minutes in the Drawing Room, but knowing how the Family were engag'd, and expecting to find me where he did, came directly up. I rose to pay my Respects to him, but he made me sit down immediately, and placing himself near me, I desire, said he, that there may be no Distance observ'd between us when we are alone, and could wish our Circumstances would admit of an Equality in publick—But Fortune is not always just to Merit. I was about to make him some Compliment in return, but he prevented me by going on—I have a great deal to say to you Mrs. *Syrena*, pursued he, but if you desire I should be a sincere Friend to you, you must be sincere to me in answering a few Questions I shall ask. I should be altogether unworthy of the Honour you do me, Sir, reply'd I, if I should make any Attempt to impose on your Belief—I say an Attempt, for being bred up in a perfect Abhorrence of Lying, and all kind of Deceit, I should go about the Practice of it in so aukward a manner, that a very little Share of Judgment would be sufficient to detect me. But, Sir, continued I, thank Heaven, I yet am conscious of nothing I would wish to conceal from the Knowledge of anybody. (There, I think, I followed your Instructions to a nicety, Mamma.) I dare answer for you to myself, said he, that you have been guilty of nothing that can be call'd a Crime; but Love is not so; and my sweet *Syrena*, have you never yet seen the Man happy enough to make an Impression on you? Never, indeed, Sir, reply'd I, nor do I boast it as a Virtue; because till the dreadful Declaration made by Sir *Thomas*, I never heard the Sound of Love from any Man in the World. Well, resumed he, and was it owing, examine well your Heart before you answer, to a Detestation of his Offers, or a Dislike to his Person and Years, that made you so resolutely repulse him? To a Detestation of his Offers, said I, for I consider'd nothing farther. Then, cry'd he, you would equally hate any other should address you on the same score? I think so, answer'd I; but, Sir, I beseech you question me no farther.—I know my Heart at present, but know not what it may be hereafter.—I have heard of Women, that have an hundred Times my Understanding, and yet made a false Step, as they call it.—'Tis Heaven alone must keep me, and by depending on that only Guard, I hope to be secure. Well, but there is no harm, said he, in indulging a Tenderness, for a generous faithful Lover. No, Sir, replied I, not when his Designs are virtuous and honourable. The World, cry'd he, is not well agreed about the true Signification of those Words, Virtuous and Honourable; but for my Part, I think that what tends to make the Happiness of the beloved Object is both Virtuous and Honourable.—But, we'll leave the Definition to the Casuists: I have one Thing more, my charming *Syrena*, to be inform'd of, and then I have done.—Suppose, continued he, I loved you, and loved you with a Passion, which it was utterly impossible for me to subdue, must I for that Reason, be the Object of your Aversion?—(I expected this, so had prepared myself for it, as you will find Mamma.) Heaven forbid, cry'd I, that I should ever be brought into so terrible Dilemma.—I know what I ought to do—but—(here I seem'd to faulter in my Speech) but I beseech you, Sir, do not talk in this Manner to a a poor silly Creature, that knows not how to answer you. Dear lovely Innocence! cry'd he, pulling me to him, and kissing me an hundred Times, I believe in spite of all my Struggling, I do love you, pursued he; the very first Minute I saw you, I loved you.— But your Wit, your Prudence, your unaffected Modesty, has made me now almost adore you. Here, he began to kiss me again with more Vehemence than before, and I could not get leave to speak for a good while; at last bursting from him, and pretending to weep, Ah, Sir! said I, if you lov'd me, you would not use me in this Manner. By Heaven, I do, said he, and to prove it will—here he stopped, and then, will do almost anything. I was going to reply, but heard somebody coming up Stairs; it was the Groom of the Chambers for a Sheet of gilt Paper out of my Lady's 'Scrutore, for one of the Company to write a Song; he seem'd surpriz'd to find Mr. *L*—— with me, as was he at his coming up; but to take off all Suspicion, I came a begging too, said he, for a Stick of Wax; I happening to be out, and I know my Grandmother is a great Clerk, but Mrs. *Syrena* tells me there is none, have you any in your Charge, for I want to seal some Letters? I think I have, Sir, answer'd the other, where shall I bring it your Honour? Into my Chamber, said Mr. *L*——, and went with him down Stairs. I have not seen him since, nor indeed was there any Opportunity, for the Company taking leave soon after, they went to Supper; and he is not stirring yet;—a thousand to one but this Day will produce something more; if it does, I'll write Tomorrow, for my Lady persists in her Design of taking Physick, and I can't come out on *Sunday*. If you find anything amiss in my Management, let me know it by old *Sarah*, for I would not have you trust the Penny Post;

but if I have behaved according to your Mind, defer writing till a more material Occasion, for I would not have anybody come after me too often. I am, dear Mamma, as ever,

Your most obedient Daughter,
SYRENA TRICKSY

P.S. I had forgot to tell you that Mr. *Groves*, the Groom of the Chambers, has been vastly diligent to oblige me ever since I came into the House; and I am afraid guesses somewhat by seeing Mr. *L——* in the Chamber with me last Night, for this Morning he looks very sullen, and did not speak to me as he used to do.

MONDAY Morning

Dear Mamma,

Friday pass'd over, without anything happening worth acquainting you with; tho' both Sir *Thomas* and his Son were at home the greatest part of the Day; not that I believe it owing to the Inclinations of either; but that the Presence of the one was a hindrance to the other, in any Design they might have of speaking to me. On *Saturday* Morning I saw Mr. *L——* in my Lady's Chamber; as he went out, I happened to be pretty near the Door, and he took the Opportunity of snatching a Kiss from me behind a great Screen, that stands to shelter that part of the Room where my Lady sits from the Air. This was all the Place would give him leave to do, but he afterwards watch'd my coming down Stairs, and said he, that impertinent Fellow (meaning *Groves*) interrupted our Conversation the other Night, before I had told you half what I had to say;—my Father will be engaged for the whole Evening, and the Ladies are to be at the Assembly;—don't be frighten'd if I conceal myself again in the same Closet, nor shun the Place because you know I shall be there. I had no Opportunity of making any Answer, if I had been prepared for one, which indeed I was not, he took me so unawares; for the Moment he left off speaking, he turned upon his Heel, fell a singing an Italian Air, and went up Stairs. Indeed, Mamma, I was very uneasy at this.—I thought to be there would have too much the Air of an Assignation; and not to be there when I knew he was waiting for me, would be an Affront, not befitting one of my Station to one of his, and might turn the Love he had for me into hate; so I resolv'd on the former, but how to carry myself, so as that my complying should not give too much Encouragement, employed my Thoughts the whole Day: But I might have saved myself that Trouble, if I could have guessed what would happen. Sir *Thomas* went out at four o'clock, and the Chariot was order'd for the Ladies at seven; as soon as they were gone, Mrs. *Brown* comes jumping into the Parlour, where Mrs. *Mary* and I were talking of some silly Stuff or another; so, said she, now we have the House to ourselves for one while: Mr. *L*—— is gone out, is he not? pursued she, to Mrs. *Mary*; I believe a good while since, answered she, for I saw him with his Hat on presently after Sir *Thomas* went, and his Man is snoring on the Dresser below. Well then, we'll enjoy ourselves, cry'd the other, I'll treat you two with a Bottle of French and a Seville Orange, and then we'll have a Pot of Tea: What say you, Mrs. *Syrena*? I thank you, Madam, answer'd I, but I have so much Business to do—O you are greatly employed, you would make one believe, cry'd Mrs. *Brown*, but we'll have you for all your Excuses. Well then, said I, I will only put my Lady's things in Order, and come down; with that I ran up Stairs in a great Hurry, not doubting but my Lover was at his Appointment; as indeed he was; for pretending he was going out when they rose from Table, he took his Hat and went into his Chamber, where locking himself in till the Ladies were gone, he slipp'd up the Back-stairs, and so into the Closet. When I came into the Chamber, after he had peeped thro' the Key-hole, that he might not be mistaken in the Person, he opened the Door, and catching me in his Arms, dear Girl, said he, what Pains do I take for a Moment's Pleasure, and that too I fear you grudge me;—but with your Leave, my Dear, I'll shut the Door for fear of Mr. *Groves*, added he, with a Smile, and immediately bolted it. O, Sir, cry'd I, I shall be soon obliged to open it, if I make any Stay here. I then told him of Mrs. *Brown*'s Invitation, and how I had promised to go down; on which he gave her two or three hearty Curses; he had not time to utter much more, for Mrs. *Mary* came up, and finding the Door fastened, cry'd, Hey-day! what have you bolted yourself in;—open the Door, Mrs. *Syrena*, Mrs. *Brown* sent me for you. On this Mr. *L*—— was compell'd to return to his Concealment, and I let in the Intruder;—come said she, what are you doing; I was going, answer'd I, to pin up a Head for my Lady;—pish, return'd the other, you know she does not go out Tomorrow—therefore you may let it alone till another time;—come, come, Mrs. *Brown* is making the Bishop herself, and 'tis ready by now—I'll follow you in a Moment, said I. No, no, cry'd she, I'll have you go with me;—come, who knows but the young Squire may surprize us as he did over the Coffee. If I thought so, answer'd I, you should have none of my Company, for I never was so much asham'd in my Life;—there's no Danger, said she, and pull'd me along with her; when we came into my Lady L——'s Dressing-Room, for it was there Mrs. *Brown* made this Regale, you are so fond of mewing yourself up in that Chamber above, said she to me, that one would imagine you met a Sweetheart there;—I believe, Mamma, that in spight of all the Lessons you gave me to the contrary, I could not quite overcome my Confusion at these Words; but putting on as composed a Look as I could, if no body thought no more of Sweethearts than I do, answered I, the Parsons would have little Business—O! one may have a Sweetheart, resumed she laughing, without having any Occasion for a Parson: Ay, cry'd I; for my part I always thought entertaining a Sweetheart, was in order to make a Husband of him. That's as it falls out, said she, for there are Sweethearts of different kinds. She seemed, methought, to speak this with a sort of malicious Sneer, and what I have since heard, convinces me I was not mistaken. I took no Notice, however, but laugh'd as they did, and we were very merry over our Bishop. At last, I can't remember for my Life how she introduced it, but she cry'd all on a sudden, So, Mrs. *Syrena*, you would have us think you never had a Lover yet; I don't care what anybody thinks, answer'd I, but sure if I had one, we should see one another sometimes, and all the House knows, that since I have been here, I have never been once abroad, nor has any Man or Woman either come to visit me—yes, said Mrs. *Brown*, to my certain Knowledge you have had a Visiter, I won't say a Lover. Me! cry'd I, in some Astonishment; yes, you, for all your demure Looks, resumed she, pray was not Mr. L—— once with you in your Lady's Chamber? Here, Mamma, I had enough to do to contain myself; but I believe I behaved pretty tolerably; Mr. L—— said I, yes, he came up one Evening for a Stick of Wax,—but what of that? Nay, nothing, answer'd she, but I had a Mind to banter you a little; she said no more, but I perceived by this that *Groves* had been tatling, and also, that there was some Suspicion that the Stick of Wax was but a Pretence. I resolved therefore to consent to no more Concealments in the Closet, for fear of a Discovery, which would infallibly ruin all our Projects. When Mrs. *Mary* and I were in Bed, she told me as a great Secret, that both Mr. *Groves* and Mrs. *Brown* imagined Mr. L—— had a more than ordinary liking to me; but said she, she has told my Lady nothing of it yet, nor won't, I heard her say, till she had found all out, and I fancy she made the Treat on purpose to try if she could pump you out of anything;—so, Mrs. *Syrena*, as I wish you well from my Heart, I would advice you to take care, if there be anything in it; for Mrs. *Brown* is a very good Woman, but a little prying, and loves to meddle—you understand me. I do, answer'd I, and thank you for your Caution, tho' I assure you there is no need of it, Mr. *L——* never chang'd ten Words with me in his Life. I am glad of it, said she, for what Designs can such a Gentleman as he have upon one of us, but to ruin us. Very true, reply'd I; she again conjured me to Secrecy, which I as firmly promised, and that put an end to our Discourse; but I was so nettled, that I did not sleep all Night. Yesterday I did not stir out of my Lady's Chamber the whole Day, not even to Dinner, for she made me eat a bit of boil'd Chicken with her: and Mrs. *Mary*, and one or other of the House-Maids, brought up and carry'd down everything that was wanted; among other things Mrs. *Brown* told me on *Saturday*, that there was a talk of going out of Town this Week: My Lady also mentioned something of it to me herself; but on what Day, or who of the Family are to go, I know not as yet; but am very sure I shall be one, whoever is left behind, for my Lady likes nothing but what I do for her. If their Resolution holds of going this Week, I shall ask to come and take my leave of you; but I suppose you will hear from me before that, who am, dear Mamma,

Your Dutiful Daughter,
SYRENA TRICKSY

WEDNESDAY Afternoon

Dear Mamma,

Sunday being fix'd for our Country Journey, I send this to acquaint you, that I hope to be with you on *Friday*, for Tomorrow my Lady dresses early to go out, and on *Saturday* we shall all be busy packing up; but I mentioned *Friday* to my Lady, who has promised I shall have the whole Day to myself. Nothing worthy of writing has happened since my last, except that seeing Mr. *L——* in the Parlour, waiting for a Chair to go out, I ventured to run to him, and acquainted him with what Mrs. *Brown* had said to me, and the Hints given me by the Chambermaid;—he bit his Lips all the time I was speaking, and seemed very much out of Humour; I know not whether at me or the News I told him; for just as he was about to reply, we heard somebody coming, and he cry'd, Curse on it, there's no speaking in this House, and I ran as fast as I could into the Back-Parlour, and so down Stairs; the Person who gave us this Interruption was Sir *Thomas*, as I afterwards found, for my Lady's Bell ringing, I was obliged to return, and saw him talking to his Son as I pass'd the Door. If (as they say) Difficulties encrease Inclination, both Father and Son meet with enough in their Designs on me, to make them grow violent at last. But, dear Mamma, I hope we shall have Opportunity on *Friday* to talk over all our Affairs, and consult what future Measures are proper to be taken by

Your most obedient Daughter,
SYRENA TRICKSY

SATURDAY Morning, Eight o'clock

Dear Mamma,

    You little think by what Means I was prevented waiting on you Yesterday, as I intended, and how greatly your poor Daughter stood in need of all the Admonitions you have given her, to defend the Hope of making her Fortune in this Family, from being totally destroyed at once.—But you shall have the whole History of what has befallen me since my last. My Lady being abroad on *Thursday*, I was afraid Mr. *L*——would take the Advantage of her Absence, to slip again into that dangerous Closet; and as I was resolved not to venture holding anymore Discourses with him in that Place, kept as much as I could below Stairs; but in avoiding him, I fell into Sir *Thomas*'s way, who seeing me pass by the Parlour-door, boldly called me to him, under Pretence of asking, whether my Lady took me down into the Country or not; tho' to be sure he knew well enough. He ask'd me the Question loud enough to be heard into the next Room, if anybody had been there; but then, with the same Breath, said in a low Voice, my Charmer, 'tis an Age since I have touch'd these dear Lips—and kiss'd me violently;—I resisted with all my Strength; still unkind! return'd he, but I don't wonder at it;—you don't yet know the Good I intend for you; but when we get into the Country, I shall have more time to shew—he could say no more, for Mr. *L*—— came into the Room; and I could perceive by his Countenance, was not very well pleas'd at finding me with his Father. As I was going away, don't forget Mrs. *Syrena*, said Sir *Thomas*, very gravely, which I suppose was to make Mr. *L*——imagine he had been speaking to me on some Affairs of the Family: My Lady came home in the Evening, and went directly into the Drawing-Room, which was very full of Company; I kept with Mrs. *Brown* the whole time, and did not go up till I knew my Lady was near coming to Bed. Not but I long'd to hear what Mr. *L——* had to say to me, and believed he waited for me, but durst not run the risque of meeting him there, after what had been said to me—I reflected on what Sir *Thomas* had hinted, that in the Country there would be more Opportunities; and if so, did not doubt but his Son would make his Advantage of them, therefore was determined his Designs upon me, whatever they were, should stand still till then. But he was too cunning for me; tho' as things have happened, I think 'tis better for me that he was so, now I know his Mind.—Yesterday Morning I went into my Lady's Chamber, to know if she had any Commands for me before I went out, for she had given me leave the Night before. She told me she had not, and I might have the whole Day to myself. Mr. *L——* was with her, and I left him there when I went to my own Room to put on another Gown: He hardly looked toward me, and I found he was angry. While I was dressing, Mrs. *Mary* came up for something, and I prayed her to send one of the Men for a Coach, which she promised, and when I came down I found one at the Door; so in I stepp'd, full of Joy to think I should have so much Time with you—but I was not two Streets beyond the Square, when the Coach stopp'd; I look'd out to see if anything was in the way, and the mean time the Door on the other side was opened, and in comes Mr. *L——*; never was Surprize equal to mine at being serv'd this Trick—O! Sir, cry'd I, why do you do this?—he made me to Answer, but call'd to the Coachman to drive to Blackheath, and immediately drew up the Window;—I expected nothing less now than to meet a second *Vardine*, and begg'd, and pray'd and would have thrown myself upon my knees to him in the Coach;—no, *Syrena*, said he, I have you now, and will not part with you, till I have told you all my Sentiments concerning you, and know how far yours are influenced in my Favour.—I waited for you in my Grandmother's Closet three Hours Yesterday, but you took care to avoid me, tho' I found you had not the same Caution with Regard to Sir *Thomas*. I then repeated to him the true Reason that made me act in that manner, and also what Sir *Thomas* had said to me, which put him into a better Humour; but all I could say would not prevail upon him to go out of the Coach, or let me do so;—the Fears of what might happen, and the Vexation of my Disappointment of seeing you, made me burst into real Tears;—He endeavoured to compose me as much as possible, protesting he would offer nothing I should not approve of; and indeed during the whole time of our little Journey, he attempted no greater Freedoms than a Kiss. As soon as he found I seemed a little better satisfy'd, my dear *Syrena* said he, I need not tell you that I love you; the Pains I have taken to gain even a Moment's Sight of you, is the greatest Proof of it that can be given; but there are others not in my power to give, which perhaps you would think more convincing: I mean, continued he, making you the offer of a Settlement for Life, and a handsome Provision for any Children that might be the Consequence of our Intimacy.—This, Sir *Thomas* can do for you; and I believe by what he said to you, is what he intends to do for you, if you'll accept it. But you know, *Syrena*, that while he lives, I have no Estate, and am a meer Dependant on his pleasure, for my present Expences; indeed my Allowance is not so scanty, but that out of it I could support you in a Fashion, that, with a little Love on your side, would make you easy;—what Answer, cry'd he, perceiving I was silent, does my dear *Syrena* make? Alas, Sir! said I what Answer can I make, that will not be displeasing to you? I have already told you I prefer my Honesty to everything, and I hope shall always be of the same Mind. Here he brought all the Arguments, and indeed many more than I thought the cause would bear, to prove, that to resign oneself to a Man of Honour, and who loved one, was no breach of Virtue, brought a thousand Examples of Women in past ages, and in foreign Countries, whose Love was never imputed to them as a Crime; and in fine, left nothing unsaid that he imagined might make me think as he would have me. I did not pretend to argue with him, only cried, as often as he gave me Opportunity to speak, good Sir, don't talk so to a poor simple Creature, that does not know how to answer you—I am very unhappy that you should think on me on this Score and such like; but tho' I feign'd a World of Ignorance, I took care still to let him see I kept up to my Resolution, and that nothing should persuade me out of my Virtue. This Discourse lasted till we came to Blackheath, where we alighted at a House, which I suppose he knew to be a proper one for the Purpose he brought me there upon. We had a very elegant Dinner, and fine Wine; but I remember'd *Vardine*, and drank very sparingly; when the Cloth was taken away, and the Waiters gone, I see, *Syrena*, said he, the Source of my ill Success in all I have urged to you—it is because my Person has made no Impression on you, that my Arguments have fail'd;—but believe me, continued he, taking my Hand, and tenderly pressing it to his Heart, that you will one Day see some happier Man, whom to oblige, you will think nothing a Crime. Indeed, Sir, I never shall I'm sure, return'd I with a Sigh. How are you sure you could refuse a Man you lov'd, cry'd he? were you ever try'd by one you loved?—with these Words he look'd full in my Face: (I saw his Drift was to find out if I had any liking to him, and thought that to seem as if I had, would give him the greater Opinion of my Virtue, in so resolutely withstanding his Offers) so feigned to be in a great Confusion—trembled—set my Breasts a heaving—and in a faultering Voice cry'd, I don't know what you call Love, Sir,—but I am sure I could refuse giving up my Virtue to one that I would give my Life to oblige in anything else—and I would give my Life, return'd he hastily, to be that happy Man you speak of, even tho' you should continue to refuse me the Proof of it; I desire—tell me—tell me, my little Angel, pursued he, throwing his Arms about my Waist, am I so blest to thought well on by you? O! do not, Sir, cry'd I more and more confused, endeavour to pry into the little Secrets of a silly innocent Maid, that knows not how to disguise, nor to confess them as she ought;—but if I were a great Lady, I should not be asham'd to let you see into my very Heart;—but don't, added I, hiding my Face in his Bosom,—don't, Sir, talk to me anymore of Settlements and Provision.—Poor as I am, I scorn the Thoughts of anything, but—Love, interrupted he, in a kind of Rapture, say Love my Charmer; if I were to be won from the Principles I have been bred in, said I, Love, since you will have it so, would be all that could induce me. Now, Mamma, I fancy you'll think I carry'd the Feint too far, and brought myself in a Snare, I should not know how to get out of; but I had all my Wits about me, as you'll find. He called me his Life, his Soul, Cherubim—Goddess, and I know not what.—We'll talk of nothing then, but Love, cry'd he, do nothing but Love—and having me in his Arms, was about to carry me to a Settee at the other End of the Room.—I begg'd him to let me go, but he was deaf to all I said; till at length I broke from him, and throwing myself at his Feet, beseech'd him with a Flood of Tears, not to ruin me; but this proving ineffectual, and he still persisting in his Endeavours to raise me from the Posture I was in; I counterfeited Faintings, fell dying on the Floor, and between every pretended Agony, lifting up my Eyes, cry'd, O! Sir, you have kill'd me—but, I forgive you. This Piece of Dissimulation had the Success I wish'd: He vow'd no more to shock my Modesty—said a thousand tender Things, and, I believe, was truly concern'd to see me in that Condition—by little, and little, I seem'd to recover my Spirits, and when I had; how shamefully, said I, have I betray'd myself.—How dare I encounter the Artifices of Mankind, with my plain simple Innocence:—How could I flatter myself such a Gentleman as you, could have any Inclinations for such a Creature as myself; but such as would demean me more: O! infinitely more, than Fortune has done. You wrong yourself and me, reply'd he; you know very well I could not marry you, without entailing Ruin on us both—but anything else.—I beg you, Sir, said I, let us talk no more of Love or Ruin.—I know the Difference between us in all Respects—I am unhappy, and I must be so—then I began to weep again, and appear'd so wild and discomposed, that he was afraid my Fits would return.—He led me into the Garden for Air, and the whole Time we were together afterwards, which was till quite Night, neither said, or did anything, but what would become the most respectful Lover.

Now Mamma by this, you may see into the bottom of his Heart.— He loves me, but will not marry me: Nor can he make a Settlement till his Father dies, and who knows how his Mind may alter before then; so I think it would be better for me to break quite off with him, and see what Proposals, Sir *Thomas* designs to make me. I send this by a Porter, because the Penny-Post would not be Time enough for your Answer, which pray send directly; for I want your Advice what to do, especially, as I shan't see you, till we come to Town again. I am,

Dear Mamma,
Your ever dutiful Daughter,
SYRENA TRICKSY

The Messenger by whom this was sent brought an Answer to it, the Contents whereof were as follows.

Dear Syrena,

You have very well attoned for the Vexation I suffer'd Yesterday, through your not coming; by the full Account you give me of the Cause that detain'd you: I am highly pleas'd with every particular in your Conduct, and, especially, that you have such just Notions of what is your real Interest; and make no Distinction between Youth and Age, but as either is most advantageous.—As Mr. *L——* can settle nothing upon you, and drawing him into Marriage, seems attended with many Difficulties; I would have you receive Sir *Thomas*'s Proposals with somewhat less Severity, than you have done; but not so much, as to make him too secure of your yielding neither; for as I believe, by all Circumstances, that Mr. *L*—— has a strong Passion for you, there is a Possibility you may have him at last your own Way.—Only, my dear Child, stick to this Maxim, to make nothing of him, if you can't make him a Husband.—I doubt not but before you come back, you'll know what Sir *Thomas* intends to do for you;—till then there is no resolving on anything.—I perceive neither of them have, as yet made you any Presents, which I much wonder at—if any should be offer'd, accept of nothing from the Father; but you may receive any Proof of the Son's Affection, because it will also confirm him in the Hope you have given him of yours; which is the only thing you have for bringing him to the Point we aim at.—I wish you a good Journey, my dear Girl, and safe Return; write as often as anything occurs, to

Your Affectionate Mother,
ANN TRICKSY

Sir *Thomas* and his Family went as they intended to his Country-Seat; where they had not been above seven Days, before *Syrena* had Matter to inform her Mother of, which she did in these Terms.

LETTER I

L—Hall

Dear Mamma,

I won't fill up my Letter with any Particulars of our Journey, 'tis sufficient to tell you, we all got safe down; and that People with Heads, not so taken up as mine is, might find everything here, they could desire for their Entertainment. I dare say you are Impatient to know how my Love-Affairs go on.—As to Mr. *L*—— he behaves to me with an inexpressible Tenderness, mixed with more Respect than before our Conversation at Blackheath; but still gives me not the least room to hope, he had any Intentions of making me his Wife—on the contrary, he rather seems afraid I should flatter myself so far; for being one Day with him in an Arbour a good Distance from the House, after he had said a thousand passionate Things, and taken some Liberties which I permitted with an Air, which seem'd to tell him, I was too much lost in Softness to know what I did, I started suddenly from his Knee, where he had made me sit, and cry'd, O! to what does my fond artless Heart betray me.—Cruel! Cruel Mr. *L*——, can you pretend to love me truly, and use me in this Manner? And then fell a weeping in so extravagant Manner, that he look'd quite confounded— but putting his Face to mine, and wiping with his Cheeks my Tears away: My dear *Syrena*, said he, what can I do in the Circumstances we both are?—I wish to God there were less Inequality between us.—You know I am not Master of myself.—Sir *Thomas* likes you as a Mistress, but would never forgive me for making you his Daughter.—My Mother, Grandmother, and all our Kindred, are full of your Praises as as Servant; but would despise and hate you as a Relation.—In fine, you must be sensible, there is no coming together for us in the way you would approve; and therefore if you lov'd me, would not see me wretched merely for a Ceremony, which sometimes instead of joining Hearts more closely, serves but to estrange them. I said nothing to all this, but kept on weeping and sobbing, as if my Heart would burst; but tho' he said all he could to comfort me, I could not perceive that he receded at all from the Declaration he had made.— Nay did not even pretend, that when his Father died, he would marry me—all he talk'd on was the Violence, and Constancy of his Affection, for me; that when he came to his Estate, I should vie with the greatest Ladies in the Town, in fine Cloaths and Equipage; and that if Duty or Convenience ever oblig'd him to marry, I should still be the sole Mistress of his Heart; but as I knew better than to depend on Promises, I had not any occasion for dissembling to shew my Contempt for them. Company coming into the Garden we were oblig'd to separate, which, indeed, I was very glad of, as our being together had made so little for my Purpose.—He made me promise, however, to meet him the next Day, in a Lane on the back of the House; I kept my Word, but that produced no more than a Repetition of those Arguments he had made use of in the Arbour.—So I doubt Mamma, that all the Advantage I shall make by his Addresses, is a more thorough Knowledge of the Passions of Mankind. As for Sir *Thomas*, according to your Directions, I appear less and less reserved, whenever Chance or his own Endeavours throw him in my Way, which, indeed, is very seldom; for what with Company, and what with his Son's Watchfulness, he can hardly get an Opportunity of speaking three Words to me. I believe he was going to say something very material to me Yesterday, but was interrupted by Mr. *L——* coming into the Room. So, my dear Mamma, this is all at present from,

Your most Obedient Daughter,
SYRENA TRICKSY

LETTER II

L—Hall

Dear Mamma,

I was not mistaken when I told you in my former, that I thought Sir *Thomas*, had something extraordinary to say me; for this Morning he watch'd for me, in a Part of the House that he knew I must pass to go into my Lady's Chamber, and as it was too public a Place to hold any Discourse in, he only put a Paper into my Hand and said, I hope this will convince you, that my Designs are such as you cannot disapprove, without being an Enemy to your own Interest. And then went away directly, without staying for any Answer. I was quite impatient to see what it contain'd, and made haste into my own Room, and lock'd myself in, that I might not be interrupted in reading it. I send you an exact Copy of the Contents; because I thought best to keep the Original in my own Hands, for fear he should ask for it again.

PROPOSALS *offered to Mrs.* SYRENA TRICKSY's *Consideration, by one who would be her faithful Friend.*

I. The Person will engage himself to pay, or order to be paid to her, the annual Sum of One Hundred Pound, either Monthly, Quarterly, or Yearly, as she shall think fit, during his Natural Life.

II. The said Person will enter into Articles, and settle, out of what Part of his Estate she shall chuse, upon her, during her Natural Life, the Annual Sum of Fifty Pounds to be paid her in like Manner, as the former.

III. That in case she shall have any Children, they shall be taken care of, and educated without any Expence to her.

IV. This Agreement to be drawn up by a Lawyer of her own Nomination, and sign'd and seal'd according to Form.

I leave it to you, Mamma, to judge of these Conditions, and will avoid Sir *Thomas* as much as possible, till I have your Answer, which I desire may be soon: Direct for me to be left at the Post-House, in—'till call'd for; because if it should be brought to the House, and I not just in the way, who knows but the Curiosity of Mrs. *Brown*, *Groves*, or even

Mr. L—— himself, might tempt them to open it; and as it is but a little Mile, I can easily go to fetch it.

Nothing worth acquainting you concerning Mr. L—— has happen'd since my last; nor has he been able to get one Opportunity of talking to me in private, tho' I can see he is very uneasy, and and more passionate than ever, since he thinks I love him.—If I am in the Chamber when he comes to my Lady, he talks, indeed, to her, but has Eyes continually on me; and if she does but turn her Back one Moment, I am sure to have a Kiss, or a Squeeze by the Hand— the same in the Gallery, or the Stairs, or wherever we meet—but what signifies all his Love, if he won't make me his Wife, nor can do anything handsome for me.—I take care, however, to look upon him, and receive the Proofs he gives of his Fondness; so as to make him think I have as great an Affection for him as he can have for me— Because who knows how far one may be able to work him up at last, when he is once convinced he can get me on no other Terms—I had a Stratagem come into my Head, but I know not how you will approve of it, and that is to pretend to him, that I could not bear to be continually in the Sight of a Person, whom I could not keep myself from having the tenderest regard for, yet knew never could be mine, but by a way I would rather die than yield to; and that I was determined to quit my Lady's Service, and endeavour by Absence to lose the Memory of him. I'll try what Effect this will have, if you think fit, Mamma; it can be no Prejudice to me at least, and if it comes to nothing, I can accept Sir *Thomas*'s Offers at last. Pray give me your Opinion in full, on both these Affairs; for you may depend upon it, I will do nothing for the future without consulting you. Who am,

Dear Mamma,
Your most dutiful Daughter,
Syrena Tricksy

Letter III

L—Hall

Dear Mamma,

Not hearing from you as I expected was a very great Disappointment and Vexation to me, and the more because I was afraid you were sick or dead, or something extraordinary had fallen out; but we are inform'd that the Mail has been robb'd, all the Bills taken out, and the Letters thrown away; so hope the want of your Advice so soon as I could have wish'd, is all the Misfortune of it; and as things have happen'd, I have the less Occasion; for I shall very shortly be in Town. A Man and Horse came last Night with the News that Lady G——, Sir *Thomas's* Sister, is dead, and having left him sole Executor and Trustee for her Children, he is oblig'd to go directly for London. He talks of setting out Tomorrow, with his Son in the Chariot, and the Ladies in two or three Day's after; so you will hear no more from me till I see you—We are all in a vast Confusion and Hurry here, so have time for no more than to tell you, I am,

Dear Mamma,
Your most dutiful Daughter,
SYRENA TRICKSY

P.S. Since I wrote the above, Mrs. *Brown* told me the Ladies were resolved to follow Sir *Thomas* the next Day.

The Family came to Town as *Syrena* had wrote, and the Mother and Daughter soon after meeting, concerted a Design the most abominable that ever was invented, and which in a short time they carry'd into Execution in the following manner.

Sir *Thomas*, either through Grief for the Loss of a Sister whom he had tenderly loved, or the Hurry of Affairs her Death had involved him in, had no Leisure immediately to prosecute his Amour with *Syrena*; but the young Gentleman, less affected, omitted no Opportunity of testifying the regard he had for her, and she, by a thousand different Artifices, everyday improved it, till his Passion for her arrived at that height, that for the Gratification of it, he would probably have given her the Proof she aim'd at, and become her Husband, had not the Fear of being disinherited, and rendering her as unhappy as himself, prevented him.—Her Mother having told her, she approved of her pretending to quit the House, she terrify'd him with that, and one Day, when he was saying all the tender things that Love could suggest, in order to prevail on her to quit that cruel Resolution, as he call'd it— O! said she, could you, Sir, be sensible how much I shall suffer when separated from you, you would acknowledge, I was much more cruel to myself than you. And gave him, while she was speaking this, a Look, which made him think it might still be in his power to prevail on her. On which he began to reiterate all the Promises he before had made her; adding, that if she would be his, he would use her in all things like a Wife, the Name excepted: She feign'd to listen with less Aversion than before to his Offers; but he fearing to be interrupted, for they were then in the Parlour, begg'd she would give him a meeting in some Place, where it would be less dangerous to converse in; but she would by no means be perswaded to see him abroad; pretending, that since the Adventure of Blackheath she had made a Vow—And, said she, I should think breaking a Vow, tho' made only to myself, the wickedest thing I could do—but, added she blushing, Sir, if you desire to take leave of me, or have anything to say that I ought not to be ashamed to hear, I'll tell you how we might pass an Hour, at least, together without Suspicion: Where, my Angel? cry'd he impatiently. You know, Sir, answer'd she, that Sir *Thomas*, your Mamma, and my Lady, go all to Church next *Sunday*, and it being the first of their appearing since the Death of Lady *G*——, Mrs. *Brown*, Mrs. *Mary*, Mr. *Groves*, and myself are order'd to attend them, to shew our Mourning, and the Men, you know, will be all with them: Now, Sir, I can say, I have got a violent Headache to excuse going; and if you could find any Pretence for staying at Home, I will once more indulge myself in the dangerous Satisfaction of hearing you talk. He was quite transported with this Contrivance, and told her that nothing could have happen'd more lucky; for, my Dear, said he, I am at this Time solliciting a Place at Court, and my Lord *R*——, on whose Interest I chiefly depend, has really order'd me to attend him on *Sunday* Morning: Now, as his Lordships Hour of rising is usually about the time of Divine Service, Sir *Thomas* does not expect me to go to Church, and will suppose I stay to dress for this Visit. Then, cry'd she, I will be in my Lady's Chamber, because of the Convenience of the Closet, in case any of the Maids that are left at home should chance to come up for anything—But, Sir, pursu'd she, don't you think me very forward now? Does not agreeing too soon to see you in private, look as if I were consenting in a manner to everything—if it does, indeed I won't be there; for tho' I love to be with you, and my Heart is ready to break when I don't see you, as you know sometimes I don't, for two or three Days together, yet I won't be dishonest—I will die first. My dearest, sweetest Innocence, reply'd he, time will convince you, that I would not hurt you for the World. They had no time for farther Conversation, nor did they meet again, till the Morning equally long'd for by both, tho' for different Reasons was arrived.

The Family went to Church, little imagining, while they were in this laudable Act of Devotion, what a Scene of Mischief was preparing for them at home, by a Creature whom they took to be the most artless and innocent of her Sex. The young Deceiver was ready in the appointed Chamber to meet her expected Lover, who no sooner found the Coast clear, than he flew to her with all the Raptures of an unfeign'd Affection, after the most vigorous Pressures on the one side, and a well-acted childish Fondness, mingled with a shame-faced Simplicity on the other, he gained the utmost of his Desires, and she the Opportunity to attempt the Accomplishment of her's.

He had no sooner left the Chamber, than she tore her Hair and Cloaths, pinch'd her Arms and Hands till they became black; pluck'd down one of the Curtains from the Bed, and throw'd it on the Floor, and put her self and everything in such Disorder, that the Room seem'd a Scene of Distraction—Then having watch'd at the Window Mr. L——'s going out, she rung the Bell with all her Strength, and the Maids below came running up, surpriz'd what could be the meaning, but were much more so, when they saw *Syrena* in the most pity-moving Posture imaginable—She was lying cross the Bed, her Eyes rolling as just recover'd from a Fit—She wrung her Hands—She cry'd to Heaven for Justice—Then rav'd, as if the Anguish of her Mind had deprived her of Reason.—The Girls were strangely alarm'd at so unexpected a Sight—and ask'd her the Occasion—but instead of giving any direct Answer, she only cry'd, let me be gone—O let me get out of this accursed, this fatal House—O that I had been bury'd quick before I ever set my Foot in it—and then begg'd of them, that they would send somebody for a Coach or a Chair for her, but they refusing to let her go out of the House till the Family came Home, she started up, and snatching a Penknife that lay upon the Table, cry'd she would run it into her Heart, if they offer'd to detain her—No, said she I will never see my Lady, Lady L——, nor Sir *Thomas* anymore—I cannot bear it—let me go—raved she—I am sure I have taken nothing from anybody—My Trunk is here—keep that and search, but as for me I will go—I will—I will, continu'd she; and in spite of all they could do, broke from them and ran down Stairs, and so into the Street, in that torn and dishevell'd Condition, where she soon got a Coach, and was carry'd to her Mother's; who highly applauded her Management in this Affair, and gave her fresh Instructions for the perfecting their most detestable Plot.

Nothing ever equall'd the Surprize that Sir *Thomas*, the Ladies, and whole Family were in, when on their coming Home they were told the Departure of *Syrena*, and the Confusion of her Behaviour—They look'd one upon the other, as not knowing what to think of the Matter— Mrs. *Brown* and Mr. *Groves* shook their Heads, as if they apprehended somewhat they durst not speak—and all of them at once demanded who had been in the Chamber with her? The Maids answer'd, that they knew of no body, and were certain no Person had come into the House since they went out. In fine, as 'twas impossible she could have been in such a Condition as was described without some very extraordinary Occasion, the least Mischief they could think of it was, that she had been taken suddenly mad—This unhappy Adventure engross'd not only their Thoughts, but Conversation also, and on Mr. *L*——'s return from visiting the Nobleman his Friend, and was inform'd of it, all he could do to command himself, was insufficient to prevent some part of the Concern he felt from appearing in his Countenance—He said the least, however, of any of them; and endeavour'd frequently to turn the Discourse on other Subjects—telling the Ladies, that tho' *Syrena* was a pretty modest Girl he believ'd, yet he wonder'd they should be so uneasy about her; that probably some Disorder in the Brain had seized her, which might be removed by proper Remedies; and it was pity they should give themselves so much Trouble about a Servant. But this affected Carelessness, which he Thought so politick, was very prejudicial to himself afterward; and help'd greatly to assist the base Designs form'd against him, tho' at present none took notice of it, or at least seem'd to do so. As soon as Dinner was over, one of the Men was order'd to go to *Syrena's* Mother, to see if she was with her, and learn, if possible, the Truth of this Affair: Mr. *Groves* desired he might be the Person employ'd, and Mrs. *Brown* and the Chambermaid who all had a great Regard for her on the score of her Youth and pretended Innocence, begg'd they might accompany him in this Errand, which was readily granted, and Sir *Thomas* told them they might have the Coach; but before it could be got ready, so industrious is Villany, Mr. *L*—— was informed two Gentlemen desired to speak with him, he went to receive them in the Parlor, where they had been conducted by the Footman, who had open'd the Door. He no sooner was within the Room, than one of them coming up close to him, told him, that he was sorry he was obliged to execute the Duty of his Office on a Gentleman like Mr. *L*——, but had a Warrant against him, on account of a Rape and Assault sworn to be committed by him that Morning, on the Body of *Syrena Tricksy*. Not all the Astonishment Mr. *L——* was in, and there could not be a greater, quelled the Emotions of his Rage at so vile an Accusation, and without considering the Consequences, laid his Hand on his Sword, with Intention to draw it; but both the others seizing him at once, prevented what else his Passion might have prompted him to; and there ensued so great a Scuffle among them, that Sir *Thomas* and the Ladies, who were in the next Room, heard it, and ran in: The Occasion was soon discover'd, and it would be very difficult to describe the Consternation, the Terror, the Grief, the Shame, with which everyone of their Faces was overspread; the Ladies fell into Fits, the Servants who assisted in recovering them, were little better themselves, and all were in the utmost Hurry and Confusion. Sir *Thomas* offer'd to engage for his Son's Appearance; but the Officers said it could not be allow'd in a capital Case: That the Girl had suffer'd Violence, which perhaps might be her Death; but as they knew the Respect due to so worthy a Family, Mr. *L——* should have no reason to complain of the want of anything but Liberty, during the time he was with them; and added, that they hoped things might be made up so with the Plaintiff's Mother, that he would be restored to that also in a short time. Mr. *L——* gave no answer to this Insinuation; but a Look which shewed his Contempt of coming to any Terms with such abandon'd Wretches. In fine, after some little Debate he was compell'd to obey the Order, brought against him, and quitted his Father's House with Company he little expected ever to be among.

This was the Stratagem which these pernicious Creatures had devised, and thus was it executed; the Moment *Syrena* came home, the same Coach carry'd her, in the deplorable Condition she had made her self appear, with her Mother to a Magistrate, who seeing the Youth and seeming Modesty of the Girl, doubted not the Truth of their Accusation, and sent Tipstaves immediately to seize on Mr. *L——*, which being done, Mrs. *Tricksy* congratulated her Daughter in Iniquity, as well as Blood, for the Success of their Enterprize: Now, Child, said she, you will be Lady *L——*, the proud Puppy will be glad to marry you now to save his Neck; and marry you he shall, or come down with a Sum sufficient to entitle you to a Husband of as good an Estate as he will have.

But the Satisfaction they had in this Event, greatly as it flatter'd their presuming Hopes, was short of the Anguish the unspeakable Horror in

which it involved Sir *Thomas* and his noble Family: Dear as Mr. *L*——
was to them all, not one, when they consider'd Circumstances, the
Time, the Place, the still believed Artlessness of *Syrena*, the Confusion
he appear'd in at hearing she was gone, and which he strove to conceal,
but could not—All concurr'd to make him seem as guilty as he was
represented to be, and was rather an Addition, than an Alleviation of
their Sorrows, especially to the Ladies.

As for the young Gentleman in Custody, Rage, Shame, and
Amazement took up all his Mind, and left no room for any Thought
how to disintangle himself from the Snare his Love for an unworthy
Object had brought him into—He never could conceive there was so
much Villany in Womankind, much less in one so young; and was ready
to curse the whole Sex, for the Sake of the perfidious *Syrena*: So unjustly
do our Passions often make us blend the worthy with the unworthy!

Sir *Thomas* in the mean time neglected nothing that might remedy
this Misfortune—The best Councel was consulted in the Affair,
who, on hearing the whole of the Affair, advised to make it up, if
possible, with the Mother of *Syrena*; but that Monster would listen
to no Proposals, and set the Virtue and Reputation of her Child at
no less Price than Marriage. 'Tis impossible for Heart to conceive the
Indignation of the young Gentleman when he was informed of this;
he protested that he would sooner yield to all the Law inflicts in such
Cases, than become the Property of those vile Serpents; for that was
all the Name he could bring himself to call them by. Hard, indeed, was
his Fate, when those who most endeavoured to defend him, in their
Souls believ'd him guilty—His Councel, his Parents, all the Servants
in the Family, even his own Man (who had been the Person who call'd
the Coach for *Syrena*, when she was carry'd to Blackheath, and knew
his Master had a Design upon her) had the matter been brought before
a Court of Judicature, could have said nothing but what must have
tended to prove the imaginary Crime. How false and weak, therefore,
is that Notion which some Men have, that they may do anything
with a Woman, but marry her, and that nothing but a Wife can make
them unhappy; when, in reality, there are often more Disquiets, more
Perplexities, more Dangers attend the Prosecution of an unlawful
Amour, than can be met with, even with the worst of Wives; for if
a Woman cannot be sincere in a State where 'tis her Interest to be so;
what can be expected from her in one where 'tis her Interest to deceive:
Besides, the Artifices practised to gain the Sex at first, gives them a

kind of Pretence for Retaliation afterward; and Men frequently find to their Cost, they but too well know how to be even with them.

Thus Mr. *L*——, who in the Morning thought himself happy in the Possession of a beautiful innocent Creature, that loved him with the extremest Tenderness, found himself before the Sun went down, the wretched Property of a presuming, mercenary, betraying, perjur'd and abandon'd Prostitute—His Friends incensed—his Reputation blasted—his Liberty at the Disposal of the lowest and most despised Rank of Men, and his Life in Danger of the most shameful and ignominious end.

So greatly were all Appearances against him, that what a Day before his Friends would have looked upon as the heaviest Misfortune could have befallen them, they now labour'd with all their Might to bring about, as the only remaining Remedy for the present Evil; and Mr. *L*——, to aggravate the Horrors of his Mind, was compelled to hear every Moment, from all who wish'd him well, the distracting Solicitations, that he would Consent to make the supposed injured Girl his Wife. Whether he would at last have been prevailed upon by their Arguments; or whether he would rather have chose to endure the Sentence of the Law; or whether, to avoid both, he would not have been guilty of some Act of Desperation on himself, is uncertain; Providence thought not fit to punish him any farther, and when he least expected it, sent him a Deliverance.

The Villains who had robb'd the Mail, as beforementioned, after they had taken out the Bills, threw the Bag and Letters into a Ditch; but there happening to be no Water in it, the Papers receiv'd no Damage; but the Post-Man had been so beaten and cruelly used, that he was not capable of telling what had become of them; they were afterwards found by a Country-Fellow, who seeing what they were, carry'd them as directed; there being two for Sir *Thomas L*——, and one for Mrs. *Syrena Tricksy*; the Man delivered them at his Seat, but the Family being come to London that Morning, a Servant took them, and putting them altogether under a Cover, sent them up by the next Post. Those for Sir *Thomas* were nothing to the Purpose of this Story, but everybody agreeing that it would be proper to open that for *Syrena*, they found it from her Mother, and contained as follows:

Dear Syrena,

I Have considered on all you acquainted me with; and have been much perplex'd in my Mind how to advise you in this ticklish Affair;

ELIZA HAYWOOD

but am at last come to a Resolution. Sir *Thomas*'s Proposals are very niggardly; what is an hundred Pounds a Year to a Woman that would appear handsome in the World?—and then if he dies, to be reduced to Fifty—good God! I wonder how he can offer to think of having a fine Girl, and a Maid too, as he takes you for, on such poor Terms;—but it may be it would have been better for his Family, if he had bid higher; for I have a Project in my Head to force his Son to marry you, in Case all your Arts to draw him in should fail—Nay, and to oblige Sir *Thomas* and my Lady, and all of them, to consent to it; and if he should refuse to live with you afterward, the Allowance they must give you as his Wife, will be more than his Father's pitiful hundred Pounds a Year: Besides, when Sir *Thomas* dies (and what I design to do, will go a good way towards breaking his Heart) you will be Lady *L——*, they can't hinder you of that; and a Title will give you such an Air among the young Fellows, that you may make what Terms you will with any of them;—the Contrivance I have formed is indeed pretty dangerous, and requires Abundance of Cunning and Courage too to go thro' with it to Purpose; but I perceive with Pleasure, you have a good share of the one; and as I shall be obliged to act a Part in it myself, I don't doubt but I shall be able to give you enough of the other also;—but nothing of this can be put in Practice till you come back to London;—all you have to do in the mean time, is to heighten the young Squire's Affection, by all the little Stratagems you can invent;—as to the Father, I would have you avoid, if you possibly can, giving him any positive Answer; but be sure not to part with the Proposals he gave you; they may be useful hereafter, in making him fearful of provoking us to expose him;—if he should ask for the Paper, you may pretend you burn'd it as soon as you had examin'd it, for fear of its being found.—My dear Girl, my Head is always at work for thee—be careful to do as I direct; let Mr. *L——* believe you love him to Madness if he will; but be still more and more tenacious of your Virtue, till I inform you the proper time for resigning it—'tis possible as he loves you so well, you may persuade him to marry you, when he finds there's no having you without; but once again depend that I have the sure Means to make him be glad to do it. So no more at present, from

Your affectionate Mother,
ANN TRICKSY

Here Mr. *L——*'s Parents found a full as well as a seasonable Discovery of the wicked Plot, and their Son's Innocence, as to the pretended Rape, cleared. Their Transport could not but be great, tho' somewhat allayed by the Story of Sir *Thomas* and his Proposals; the Confusion of that Gentleman, and the jealous Disdain of his Lady, a while combated with the sincere Satisfaction they would otherwise have felt—some few Upbraidings on the one side, and Excuses on the other were natural on the Occasion, but at length were wholly swallowed up in the Joy for the Deliverance of an only Son. The next thing they had to think upon, was how to proceed for the Punishment of these vile Creatures who had imposed upon them; but when they found that it could not be done without bringing the whole Affair to a public Trial; their Counsel advised them rather to compromise it, and rest contented with the Disappointment *Syrena* and her Mother had met with, and not pursue a Justice which would occasion so much Town-talk of themselves; especially considering that such Practices would infallibly sometime or other, draw on the Authors the publick Shame they merited, where perhaps the Avengers had not laid themselves so open to Ridicule, as Sir *Thomas* and his Son had done. The Letter therefore being produced, and the Person who brought it, detained as an Evidence, in Case they had offered to deny the Hand, the audacious Expectations of our female Plotters, were turned into Submissions; and all their Arts employed only to prevail on the Lawyer, who negotiated between them, that Sir *Thomas* and his Family would not prosecute them for Perjury and Fraud, which he pretended to accomplish with a great deal of Difficulty; and so this troublesome and dangerous Business ended, and was, 'tis to be hoped, a means of preventing both Father and Son from rendring themselves liable to any future Impositions of the same Nature.

Now had the wicked Mrs. *Tricksy* and her Daughter time to reflect on the ill Success of their Stratagem; but instead of acknowledging the Justice of Divine Providence in unravelling this Affair, they only cursed Fortune, and accused themselves for having trusted the Secret of their Design to Pen and Paper: Dreadful Proof that their Hearts were totally void of all Distinction between Vice and Virtue! The best may have fallen into Errors which they have afterwards so truly repented of, that even those Faults have contributed to the rendering them more perfect.—Others again may have been guilty of repeated Crimes, and yet have felt Remorse, even in the Moment of perpetrating them; but the Wretch, incapable either of Penitence or Remorse, one may, without Breach of Charity, pronounce irreclaimable but by a Miracle, and fit for the engaging in any Mischief where Temptation calls.

When our young Deceiver and her Mother had a little recovered from the Emotions occasioned by their Disappointment, they began to consider what they had best do: The Family *Syrena* had quitted, kept so much Company, that for her to think of getting into any other as a Servant was dangerous; as she possibly might be seen, by those she had ill treated, and by that means be exposed: It therefore seem'd most prudent to get out of the way for sometime, and trust to Chance for Adventures. Greenwich was the Place they pitch'd on for a Retirement; and Mrs. *Tricksy* having sold what few Houshold-Goods she had, took a neat, but plain ready-furnish'd Lodging, for herself and Daughter, at a House which had a Door into the Park; as judging not improbable, but that by frequent walking there, the little Harpy might happen on some Prey to her Advantage: The Event in part answered to their wish; her Youth, her Beauty, and seeming Innocence, soon made her be taken Notice of by several Gentlemen, whom the Season of the Year, and the Pleasantness of the Place, had drawn thither; but he that seem'd most affected with her Charms, was Mr. D——, he had often seen her walking in the Park, sometimes with her Mother, and sometimes with a young Lady, who lodged in the same House with them; and had more than once fallen into such little Conversations with them, as the Freedom of a Country-Place allows, without being particular; his Eyes however discovered something, which did not 'scape the vigilant Observation of both Mother and Daughter, and afforded a Prospect they so much wish'd to find.

Mr. D—— was a young Gentleman of about 800*l.* a Year, was contracted to a Lady called *Maria*, and shortly to be married to her, with the Consent of the Friends on both sides; but a near Relation in Lincolnshire, from whom she expected a considerable Augmentation of her Fortune, being taken ill, the young Lady was gone to make her Visit. During her Absence, Mr. D——intended to pass the time at Greenwich, a Place he always liked, but now more especially; the solemn Prospect of the Sea indulging those Ideas, which Persons separated from those they love, are ordinarily possess'd of. The first Sight of *Syrena* struck him with a kind of pleasing Surprize;—he fancy'd he saw something in her Face, like that of her he had for many Years been accustomed to admire: he little thought how much he injured the virtuous Maid, by making any Comparison between her and this unworthy Resemblance; or that the Affection he had vow'd to *Maria*, could ever be diminish'd by an innocent Conversation with *Syrena*; yet so it was, by pleasing himself with seeing her for the Sake of another, he by degrees grew delighted with seeing her for her own—So little do we know ourselves, and so hard it is to preserve Constancy in Absence. As on his first Acquaintance with *Syrena*, he had no manner of Design upon her, he made no Secret of his Affairs, and talked of his beloved *Maria* in the most tender Terms; but afterwards mentioned her Name with less and less Emotions; and from being passionately fond of talking of her, fell at last into an Uneasiness of hearing her spoken of at all.

Mrs. *Tricksy* therefore had some Reason to flatter herself, that the Impression her Daughter had made on him, had erased that of the Mistress he had so long adored; and that he wanted nothing but an Opportunity to confess it to her; on which it was contrived, that she should throw herself in his Way, at a time, when there should be no Witnesses of their Conversation. They knew he was accustomed to walk early in the Morning, on that side of the Park that has the Prospect of the Sea; and there on the side of a Hill did *Syrena* place herself, leaning in a pensive Posture, her Head upon her Hand; she had not waited long before Mr. *D*—— came that way, and felt (as he afterwards called it) a guilty Flutter at his Heart, in perceiving she was alone. He accosted her at first only with the usual Salutations of the Morning; but she, with a modest Blush, downcast Eyes, and all the Tokens of an Innocent Surprize (which she before had practised in her Glass) soon allured him to entertain her in a more tender manner. I am afraid Miss, said he, I have disturbed your Contemplations, and perhaps been injurious to the happy Man who was the Subject of them; for it cannot be that a young Lady like you should chuse this solitary Place, but to indulge Ideas more agreeable than any Company can afford. It is certain, Sir, replied she, that there is a Pleasure in being alone sometimes; but I assure you that is not my Case at present: I love to rise early, the Sweetness of the Morning tempted me abroad, and the few Acquaintance I have here, are all too lazy to partake of it. Then, rejoined he, you will give me leave to be your Companion? provided, answered she gayly, your Complaisance is no Violence on your Inclination; for as you have owned yourself a Lover, it may very well be supposed you come here to indulge those Ideas, you just now accused me of. Perhaps, Miss, said he, I can no where so well indulge them as in your Presence. That's impossible, replied she, unless I had seen the Object of your Affections, and could expatiate on the Beauties of her Shape, her Air, her Face, and Wit; while you shew me your own, cried he, I need no more to inspire me with the most passionate Sentiments.—Sure none, added he, catching her in his Arms, can see the charming *Syrena*, and lose a Thought on any other Object.—Hold!—hold! good Sir! said she, disingaging herself from him, you grow a little too free, and I shall be in Danger of growing too serious—what! continued she, this from a Man in love with another Woman! whatever I may have felt, for any other Woman, replied he, while I see *Syrena*, I can love nothing but her. O fie! rejoined she, what has a Man to offer, that has already disposed of his Vows. His Heart, answer'd he. O! then I find, said she, your Heart is like a ready-furnish'd Chamber, to be let to the first Comer, who must go out at a short Warning, on the Prospect of a more advantageous Lodger.

The Reader will perceive she was here acting the Coquette.—The Reason of it was, that imagining a sprightly Behaviour would be most agreeable to a Man of his gay Temper; and as she could have no hopes of gaining him for a Husband, things having been gone so far with *Maria*, whose Fortune she had heard was to pay off his Sister's Portion, she thought too great a Reserve might deter him from making any Addresses to her; and tho' she could not expect any Settlement, as her Affairs now were, it seemed better to play at a small Game, than stick out.

She continu'd to rally with him for sometime, and her Wit and the little Artifices she made use of, so much inflam'd his amorous Inclinations, that he was ready almost to take the Advantage of that solitary Place, and become a Ravisher for the Gratification of them; but it needed not, she received his Caresses in such a manner, as afforded him a sufficient Cause to hope, she would not be cruel.—She promised to meet him the next Morning, at the same Place and Hour, and let fall, as if unguarded, some Hints that she wanted only to be convinc'd of his Affection, to give him the Proof of hers that he desired.

The Time of their Assignation being arrived, both were punctual, and she allow'd him yet greater Freedoms than before, but kept back that he was most eager to obtain; he was not to seek what 'twas she aim'd at, and presented her with a Diamond Ring, which she accepted on as a Proof of his Love.—The next Day he brought her a Gold Watch, and after that an embroider'd Purse with Fifty Broad Pieces.—All which she took, without returning him anything in Exchange, but the liberty of Kissing and Embracing her, not that she absolutely refus'd him; but pretended she would find a fitter Opportunity, and that her Mamma was to go shortly to London, on some Business that would detain her the whole Day and Night; and that she would then contrive a Way, to get him privately into their own Lodging. This satisfied him for the present, but finding no Effect of the Promises she made him, he began to grow impatient; and was for seizing the Joy he aimed at, in a Place where the seeming Delicacy of *Syrena*, would not consent to yield it him.—She found Means, however, to prevent him, both from having any Suspicion she had a Design to jilt him, or from compassing his Intent, till she thought fit to grant it.

The Motives of her behaving in this Fashion, were two; the first was to get as much as she could of him, before she granted him any material Favour, having an After-game in her Head to play upon him; and the other was, that she had another Lover whom she found her Account in managing.

This was a rich Portuguese Merchant, who having finish'd some Business, which had brought him to England, was on the Point of returning to his Family, when Mrs. *Tricksy* and her Daughter came to Greenwich: He lodg'd at the next Door to them, and being charm'd with *Syrena*, soon got acquainted with them. The cunning Mother soon perceiv'd his Inclination, and to encourage him to discover it, in a proper Manner, was always entertaining him with the Misfortunes of her Family, and the Straits to which they were subjected.—He took the Hint, and gave her to understand, he was ready to contribute to the Relief of the Necessities she complain'd of, provided he might obtain a grateful Return from the fair *Syrena*.—In fine, the Agreement was soon struck up between them—he gave his Gold, and *Syrena* her Person.—As he had begun to visit them at their first coming, there was no suspicion in the House of the Amour, which lasted for about a Month; at the End of which, having fully satisfied his Desires, and the Necessity of his Affairs calling him to Portugal, he took his leave: And *Syrena* had now leisure to prosecute her Intrigue with Mr. *D——*, which she could not so well do, while the Merchant was so near her.

She had met by Appointment this young Gentleman for several Mornings; but she now came not according to her Promise, which did not a little perplex him; but he saw her in the Afternoon in the Park, accompanied by that Lady, who frequently walked with her in the Evenings. He joined them as usual, and discoursed with them on ordinary Things; but perceived a Gloom on the Face of *Syrena*, which he had never seen before, and found that she frequently sigh'd: He long'd for an Opportunity to enquire the Cause, but could find none in that Company. *Syrena* too, whenever she look'd upon him, expressed some Impatience in her Eyes; but for what he was not able to guess; till they turned a Corner to go down a Walk, she let her Handkerchief drop, which he taking up, and returning to her she slipt a Paper into his Hand at the same Time, and he convey'd into his Pocket unperceiv'd by the other. *Syrena* after this seem'd tir'd with walking, and with her Companion took leave of Mr. *D*——, who eager to see what his Billet contain'd, made no Efforts to detain them; and as soon as they were out of Sight, found to his great Surprize these Lines.

Dear Sir,

That I met you not this Morning, was owing to the Misfortune of my Mother's finding the Presents, you were so kind to make me; and which I had conceal'd from her, knowing how scrupulous she is in such Things.—She would needs make me tell her how I came by them, I had no way to conceal the Truth, and was obliged to endure a strict Examination on what had past between us. I assur'd, as I well might, that our Conversation had been perfectly innocent; but was oblig'd to add, that your Addresses to me were on an honourable Foot.—She told me she would believe nothing of it, unless she heard it confirm'd by your Mouth, and had sent for you to Day, if Company had not come from London to visit us, on Purpose to return the Watch and Ring; for the Purse she knows nothing of, and hear what you would say as to your Designs on me.—Therefore, dear Sir, do not contradict what I have said, unless you would forever be deprived of the Sight, and thereby break the Heart of,

Your Syrena

P.S. If you humour my *Mamma* in this Article, you will have leave to Visit me, and we may be together as much as either of us desire. Pray burn this.

Mr. *D*—— was so much shock'd at this Proposal, that for some Moments all the Love he had for *Syrena* was converted into Contempt, imagining it a Trick contrived beween Mother and Daughter, to draw him into a Promise of Marriage; but when he reflected that the Girl had behav'd in a quite contrary Manner, the good Opinion he had of her Sincerity, soon clear'd her from having any share in it. He had great Debates within himself what to do in the Affair: He thought it base to pretend a Thing which he was far from intending; but then the exposing a young Creature who loved him, to the Rage of a Mother, whom he suppos'd she stood much in awe of; together with the thoughts of never see her anymore, out-balanced the Consideration of his own Honour; and he chose, as, indeed, most do, when they are in love; to sacrifice his Character to his Passion, rather than his Passion to his Character, since he found himself in a Dilemma, where both could not be maintain'd.

The next Day, as he expected, the Servant of the House, where Mrs. Tricksey lodg'd, brought him a Letter, which was to this Purpose.

Sir,

I Am sorry to have Occasion to write to desire you will call on me, on an Affair which you ought to have found an Occasion of communicating to me.—I scarce think you can be Ignorant of what I mean, tho' I am as to your real Designs; but if they are of a Nature fit to be acknowledg'd, to a Person in the Circumstances I am in; you will not hesitate to come, and immediately declare to her, who wishes to be with Honour,

Sir,
Your oblig'd humble Servant,
Ann Tricksy

This Letter, and the Summons it contain'd, renew'd his Confusion; but he found himself under a Necessity of giving some Answer; and as he did not care to write, bid the Messenger give his Service to the Lady, and say he would wait on her as soon as he was drest. He was afterwards several Times prompted by his good Genius to break his Word on this Occasion, and go directly for London, without troubling himself about what *Syrena* or her Mother should think of him; but the Presents he had made, and the Happiness which they were to purchase for him, got again the better of the Dictates of his Prudence, or his Consideration for *Maria*; and he went with a Resolution to make the Mother of his new Charmer satisfied.

Few Women knew better how to behave themselves on all Occasions than Mrs. *Tricksy*; and on this 'tis not to be doubted if she exerted all her Artifice: She receiv'd him with the greatest Respect, yet at the same time mingled a certain Severity in her Air, which gave him to understand, she expected to be answer'd with Truth, to the Questions she had to ask him; the principal of which were, on what Score he had made her Daughter such valuable Presents? And when he had told her on the most honourable One: Wherefore his Intentions, and the Courtship between them had been conceal'd from the Person, who as a Parent ought to have been consulted? To this he replied, that he was willing to know how far he could influence the Affections of the young Lady, without the Interposition of a Mother's Commands; and that also as he was contracted to another, it would be highly improper that the World should have any Suspicion he had made a second Choice, 'till he had found some Pretence to break entirely off with the first.

On these Declarations, Mrs. Tricksey seem'd perfectly easy, and telling him she depended on his Honour and Veracity, gave him leave to visit *Syrena*, as often as he pleas'd; and assured him at the same Time, that she would keep his Secret inviolably till a proper Time for revealing it; and that the Family where they liv'd should never know he came there, with any other View than to chat away a leisure Hour, as an ordinary Acquaintance.

Glad was Mr. *D——*, when he was got over this Task: He was a Man who naturally hated all kind of Deceit, and look'd on Lying, as beneath the Dignity of his Specie; he could not therefore utter Words so foreign to his Heart without feeling an inward Shock. Yet so great an Ascendant had the Charms of *Syrena* gain'd over him, that the unhappy Passion he had for her, corrupted even his very Morals; and made him think nothing vile that tended to the Enjoyment of her.

Mrs. *Tricksy*, in the mean time was far from believing what he said, tho' she feigned to do so, nor indeed had not yet formed any Design to draw him in to marry her Daughter; because his former Engagement, and the necessity of his Affairs requiring he should keep it, she had looked on it as an impracticable Attempt. All her Design in obliging him to pretend an honourable Passion, was only to support her own Character, and compel him afterwards to do more for *Syrena*, than perhaps his Inclinations would have excited him to; but I will not anticipate.

Mr. *D——*, had now all the Opportunity he could wish with *Syrena*, which he did not fail to make use of for the Gratification of his Desires; and our young Dissembler so well acted her Part, that he imagined never Woman loved to a greater height than she did: In the midst of this Intrigue, he received a Letter from *Maria*, and another from that Kinswoman at whose House she was: That Lady being recovered from her Indisposition, and loth to lose Maria's Company, made him an

Invitation to come down, telling him as what she imagin'd would be a great Inducement, that he would have the Pleasure of Conducting to London, that dear Person, who was shortly to be his Companion for Life. *Maria* also desired him to come, in Terms as pressing as her Modesty would permit, and the engaging Manner in which she wrote somewhat awaked his former Tenderness; but happening to see *Syrena* the same Evening, and mentioning the Invitation, the artful Creature presently fell into Fits, crying out between her counterfeited Agonies, O! I shall never see you more—you love *Maria*—you will marry her—*Syrena* will be forgot—but I will not live to be forsaken—then run to the Window as tho' she would throw herself out; and on his taking her in his Arms, and vowing never to be ungrateful to her Love, clung about his Waste, bathed his Hands and Bosom with her Tears—then swooned again, and in fine, so well feign'd the desperate half dying Lover, that he thought he should be the most cruel of Mankind, to quit so soft, so endearing a Creature; all he could say or do however could not pacify her, till he gave her the most solemn Assurances not to go to Lincolnshire; and the more to convince her of the Sincerity of what he said, wrote an Excuse to the Ladies in her Presence, for his refusal.

When *Syrena* told her Mother how much he was affected with her pretended Grief, and the Condescention he had made, the old Woman began to be of Opinion that he really lov'd enough to marry her, if it were not for his Engagement with *Maria*, and from that Moment thought of nothing but how it might be broke off—the most feasible Way she could invent was to make that Lady think him unworthy her Affection—She knew very well how far Pride and slighted Love work in the Minds of Women, and without farther delay wrote to *Maria* in the following Terms.

To Miss Maria S——, at Mrs. J——'s House in Lincolnshire

Madam,

The Assurances you have given Mr. *D*—— of making him happy in your Person and Fortune, might justly render any Man highly contented with his Lot; but as our Happiness consists chiefly in the Sense we have of it; I am sorry to inform you Mr. *D*—— is ignorant of his. I beg you will not suspect I give you this unwelcome Intelligence out of any sinister View, for I assure you, Madam, I am a Person who have not the last Self-interest in this Point; and nothing but the Love I bear to Truth and Justice could have prevail'd on me to let you know how void of both Mr. *D——* is now become. You had no sooner left London than he went to Greenwich, in pursuit of a young Girl esteemed very beautiful, but I have never seen her, so take that Character of her upon Trust; I am, however, very certain that she is so in the Eyes of Mr. *D——*; that he makes honourable Addresses to her, and has assured her Mother that he only waits an Opportunity to break with you, and will then avow his Passion for her in the face of the World—I appeal to yourself for one Proof of what I say, if it be true as he gives out that you invited him to Lincolnshire, and he declined accepting that Favour on a frivolous Pretence—if you know this to be real, it is easy for you to convince yourself yet farther, by employing any Person to inspect into his Behaviour, while you are absent—It would be vain to wish you might hear it is such as would merit your Approbation—the next Blessing therefore that can attend you is, that you may be undeceived in your good Opinion before the indissoluble Knot is tied, that would put it out of your power to punish his Ingratitude, which is the sole Motive of this trouble, from

> *Madam,*
> *Your unknown Friend*

This mischievous Letter Mrs. *Tricksy* sent to Lincolnshire by the Post, after having got it copied by a Friend in London, to prevent any Suspicion it was herself that wrote it, in Case *Maria* in a rage should either send it up to Mr. *D——*, or shew it him at her return. The unfortunate Gentleman little guessing what had been contrived against him, continued treating, presenting, and caressing his pretty *Syrena*, till he was sent for to London on the arrival of an Uncle, who had been three Years in Antigua; and whose Absence, he being Guardian to his Nephew, alone had so long retarded the Nuptials of Mr. *D——* and *Maria*, the Friends of that Lady insisting on Accounts being made up between them before Marriage.

Syrena no sooner heard this News, than she had recourse to all her Artifices to retain him; Tears, Complaints, and Faintings were all employed to detain him, while the Mother on the other hand plied him with Remonstrances of the Promise he had made her of breaking with *Maria*, than which she told him there could not be a fitter Time than the present, as he might easily find some way to embarrass the Accounts, so as to render it impossible to make any Settlement on a Wife to the Satisfaction of her Kindred.—To this he cooly answer'd, that she might depend he would act as became a Man of Honour; but tho' he had enough to do between the Mother and Daughter, and had a Heart relenting to the Sorrows of *Syrena*, he began now to be satiated with Enjoyment, and the virtuous Affection he had avowed to *Maria* to resume its former Dominion over his Soul.—He therefore took his leave of them with so ill-dissembled a Concern, that they easily perceived there was a Change in him no way to their Advantage. Mrs. *Tricksy* however, flatter'd herself with some Success in her Plot on *Maria*; she imagined that if it did not absolutely break the Match it would breed a Jealousy and Uneasiness on her side, which in time would create a disgust on his; and that join'd with a Stratagem she had from the beginning intended to put in Practice, would renew his Affections for her Daughter, and cement him to her more firmly than ever.

Mr. *D*—— being got to London, the Pleasure he took in the Society of an Uncle he had not seen in so long a Time, and who he looked upon as a Parent, being left very young to his Care, together with the hurry of settling his Affairs, so took up all his Mind, that there was little room for remembering his Greenwich Amour; he had not however left that Place above ten Days before he was reminded of it by a Letter from *Syrena's* Mother. The Contents whereof were as follow:

Sir,

I am very much surprized that you have not in all this Time found a leisure Hour for a Visit at Greenwich, or at least for writing a Line to let us know you remember'd that you have some Friends here, who have reason to expect that Proof of your Sincerity—I am loth to call your Honour in question, yet as I am a Mother, must beg you to reflect, how cruel it would be, to take so much Pains as you have done to gain the Affection of a poor innocent Girl, for no other purpose than to leave her to despair—I see the concern she is in through all her Care to hide it from me; and tho' I find enough to chide her for, in the course of her Conversation with you, yet I have a Mother's Heart; and cannot but tremble at the Apprehensions to what she will be reduced, if you should prove ungrateful or unkind—Put an end therefore, I beseech you, Sir, to the suspense we both are in, inform us how your Affairs are, and if you have made any Progress towards getting rid of your old

Engagement—*Syrena* would fain have accompanied this with one from herself, but I would not permit it, till I had first heard from you, which I once more intreat may be with a Speed, conformable to the professions you have done her the Honour to make, and your Promises to,

SIR,

Your most Obedient Servant,

ANN TRICKSY

This Letter put Mr. *D*—— into a very ill-humour, he now saw some Part of the ill Consequences attending the Prosecution of an unlawful Flame, and condemned his own Inconstancy as much as any other Person could have done. He was in the utmost perplexity what to do to rid himself of this troublesome Affair, and for a long time could not decide within his Mind, whether not answering Mrs. *Tricksy* at all, or answering her in such Terms as might let her see there was nothing to be hoped from him on the score of Marriage, would most contribute to that End. At length he resolved on the latter, and wrote in this manner.

Madam,

As I have a great Opinion of your Honour, and Sense of Religion, I can scarce think you will blame me, that on mature Reflection I dare not make any Efforts to break an Engagement, into which I voluntarily enter'd.—I have the utmost Regard for your Daughter, and doubt not but she may be much happier with any other, then she could be with one, who to be hers must be perjur'd.—I ask your Pardon for having deceiv'd you; and shall rejoice in any Opportunity that shall put it my power to attone, for what I have done, by any Act of Friendship, that is consistent with the Character of a Person, who is shortly to give his Hand to another. I dare say, you have too much Prudence to make any Talk of this Adventure, which would only create Uneasiness to me, without any manner of Advantage to yourself and Daughter.—Pray make my best Wishes acceptable to her; but at the same Time let her know, that all future Correspondence between us, would be disreputable to her, and highly inconvenient to,

Madam,

Your humble Servant,

D——

He wrote at the same Time to *Syrena*, in these Terms.

Dear Syrena,

I Suppose you are no Stranger to the Contents of your Mother's Letter; and as you very well know, there never was any real Intention of Marriage between us, and that what I said to her, was merely in Complaisance to your Request; I should have taken it kind, if you had saved me the Shock of her Remonstrances, or Upbraidings on that Score; by seeming to think me unworthy of your Affection, and pretending to her that that the imaginary Courtship, broke off wholly on your Side.—Believe, dear Girl, that I shall always retain the most grateful Sense of the Favours, I have receiv'd from you; but as I am now going to enter into a State, which allows not the Continuation of them, our Interviews hereafter must be as private as possible, for both our Sakes.—Therefore, I beg you will make yourself easy—in a little Time, perhaps, you will hear from me, more to your Satisfaction, and be convinced that I shall never cease to love you.

Yours,
D——

Both these he sent by the Penny-Post; but directed that for *Syrena* under a Cover, to the Person at whose House he had lodg'd, while he was at Greenwich, that it might not fall into the Mother's Hands; and betray to her, that her Daughter had been of the Plot to deceive her: Poor Gentleman, little suspecting himself was the only Person impos'd upon, or that the Excursion he had made, would be attended with Consequences, which he soon after dreadfully experienced. But, methinks, I hear many of my fair Readers cry out, that no Punishment could be too severe for the Inconstancy of Mr. *D——*, and that the least inflicted on him, ought to be the everlasting Contempt of the Woman to whom he was false, and the Insincerity of her for whose Sake he was so. It cannot, indeed, be deny'd that he had acted an ungenerous Part; and if we may take his own Word for it, in the latter Part of his Letter to *Syrena*, had no Intention to be more constant to *Maria* after Marriage than before: 'Tis certain, however, that tho' that insinuating Creature had got but too much Possession of his Heart, he had at sometimes his repenting Moments. He was soon after involved in Perplexities from another Quarter; he had wrote three Letters to *Maria*, to none of which he had receiv'd any Answer; and the last being accompanied with one to Mrs. F——, he obtain'd one from that Lady, in which he found these Lines.

SIR,

Your Letters for my Cousin came safe to my House, but she being gone from me, I have according to her Desire, laid them by in order to send to her, when I shall receive Directions from her where to do so; for at Present, I am entirely ignorant of her Retirement.—I know not what has happened, since she left my House, to go to that of a Relation we have Twenty Miles hence; where, she said, she intended to pass some Days; but I have heard went from thence directly in the London Stage.—I am greatly surpriz'd you have not seen her, nor that she not has wrote to me.—She seem'd in a good deal of inward Agitation at her Departure;—but I could get nothing from her of the Motive.—I wish all is well.—I do not doubt now you have this Intelligence, but you will make a strict Enquiry, and beg as soon as 'tis in your power, you will let me know, for I am in more Concern, than I am able to express.

SIR

Your most humble Servant,

K. J——

'Tis a common saying, that People seldom know the Value of anything, till they are in danger of losing it.—Mr. *D——* was not sensible himself how much he lov'd *Maria*, till this Letter. Jealousy, and the Fears that some Accident had befallen her, by Turns distracted him; he sent—he went himself to all the Relations and Acquaintaince she had in Town, to enquire after her; but to no Effect; whoever he spoke to on this Head, seem'd no less amaz'd and concern'd than himself, and the more he reflected on it, the more he was bewildered in his Thoughts. One Evening as he return'd to his Lodging with a Heart full of disturb'd Emotions from this fruitless Search; he was told by the People where he lodg'd, that a young Lady had waited for him sometime; as he then thought of nothing but *Maria*, he imagin'd it must be she, and flew up Stairs with all the Impatience of Love and Curiosity. But how great was his Surprize, when instead of her, he found *Syrena*: A Visit from her seem'd so presuming, and at the same Time so distant from that Modesty she had always counterfeited before him; that on his first coming into the Room, he had scarce command enough over himself, to forbear saying something, that might have been accounted too shocking to a Person of her Sex, and whom he once pretended to love. She gave him not much Time, however, to consider how he should receive her; for rising from an easy Chair into which she had thrown herself, and running to him with a most artfully assum'd Wildness in her Countenance, the Moment he enter'd the Room.—Pardon me, cry'd she, my dear, dear Mr. *D——*, that I come here an uninvited Guest.—'Tis the first and last Trouble I shall give you; but I could not die without seeing you:—All I beg is a kind Farewel, and that you will pity the unfortunate, the too tender *Syrena*. If he was before amaz'd and angry at an Action, which he look'd upon as too bold; he was now more confounded and grieved at a Behaviour, which had in it so much the Appearance of Despair; and demanded hastily what had happened, and what she meant by talking of dying, and Farewell? On which she told him with a Flood of Tears, that her Mother had intercepted the Letter he wrote to her, and finding by it the Truth of their Correspondence, and that she had been of the Party to deceive her; she flew into such an Extremity of Rage, that she turned her out of Doors, with an Oath never to see her more, or own her as her Child.—Thus, added the young Dissembler, I am abandon'd to the World.—Destitute of Friends, of Lodging, or any Means of supporting a wretched Life; and what encreases my Misfortune, I fear I am with Child?—What then can I do but die? And die I will. The Minute I go from you, I will seek out some private Stairs that lead to the Thames, and throw myself in. Mr. *D——*, who believed all she said, thought now of nothing, bur disswading her from so dreadful a Resolution: He made use of all the Arguments he was master of; assur'd her of his everlasting Friendship, and swore that neither she, nor the dear little One, in case it was as she apprehended, should ever be to seek for Support. This being what she wanted to bring him to, her Distractions by little and little seem'd to abate.—He sent his Man to provide a handsome Lodging for her, gave her Twenty Guineas for her Pocket, and promised to bring her Three Pounds every Week, till something should offer more to her Advantage.

Now was *Syrena* a kept Mistress, and being by his Good-nature, settled in a commodious and reputable Lodging, found many Excuses besides her pretended Pregnancy to drain Money from him, more than her Allowance; but not all the Extravagance of Love she pretended to have for him, nor all the liking he had of her Person and Behaviour, had the Efficacy to drive *Maria* from his Mind: Her strange absenting herself from him and from all her Relations, at a Time, when it was expected their Marriage would have been celebrated, gave him Discontents, which it was in the power of no other Woman to dissipate. To aggravate his Confusion, he receiv'd by the Penny-Post an anonymous Letter, the Contents whereof were these.

SIR,

I Am no Stranger to your Engagement with Miss *S*—, nor to the Disquiet you at present labour under on her Account, and am enough your Friend to advise you, not to give yourself any farther Trouble in searching after one, who if found, might occasion you to be guilty of somewhat unworthy of your Character;—in fine, she is in the Arms of a Man, whom an Inconstancy natural to the Sex, makes her prefer to him intended for her Husband;—Chance discovered the Secret to me; nor would I have been so cruel to the Lady, to inform you of it, had I not thought I could not have conceal'd it without Ingratitude, having once received an Obligation from you, which I cannot forget;—I chuse, however, to stand behind the Curtain, till it is known how you relish so disagreeable an Intelligence.—If you have Love enough to forgive this false Step in Miss *S*——, and and make her your Wife, when she thinks fit to be visible, you cannot expect to know the Person, whom you could not look upon without a Blush;—but if, thus warn'd, you take the Advantage she has given you of concealing herself to break off, you shall be made acquainted with the whole Story of her Infidelity, and also the Name of him, who now subscribes himself,

Your Well wisher

Mr. *D*—— believing *Syrena* to be the most disinterested, open and sincere Creature in the World, had been so weak as to entrust her with Maria's having absented herself from all her Friends; the fruitless Enquiry both himself and they had made after her, and also some jealous Sentiments, which ever and anon rose in his Mind, that so odd an Elopement could have no other Motive, than a new and more favour'd Lover; and the artful Hypocrite appear'd always to take the suspected Lady's part, invented Excuses for her having acted in that manner, and apologized for her with so much seeming Earnestness, that Mr. *D*—— was perfectly charm'd with her Generosity, and in some Moments thought he should not be much concern'd to hear the worst that could be of *Maria*, since he had in *Syrena* so faithful a Friend as well as Mistress. He no sooner receiv'd the above Letter, than he flew to communicate it to her, tho' it was then very late at Night, and he had passed all the Afternoon with her; but as if since his unhappy Amour with her, he was to be continually involved in Matters of Surprize, of one kind or other, he met one here he little expected, that of being told she was abroad; as he had left her quite undrest, and she had mentioned no Occasion that should call her out, he knew not what to think of such a nocturnal Ramble; he resolved however to wait till she returned, tho' it should be all Night, and bid the Servant of the House light him up Stairs; for *Syrena* boarding with the Family, had yet taken no Maid of her own; the People durst not refuse him, and he sat down, full of various and disturbed Emotions. He had not long indulged them, before casting his Eye on the Table, he saw a seal'd Letter; he took it up, and finding it directed to Mrs. *Syrena Tricksy*, and as he thought in her Mother's Hand, he broke it hastily open, and found he was, not deceiv'd; it was indeed from Mrs. *Tricksy*, and contained these Lines:

Dear Syrena,

I Was in Town Yesterday, and should have been glad to have given you my Opinion on what you wrote; but durst not come or send for you any where, for fear of Mr. *D*——'s being with you—a little Circumspection, my Girl, may draw the Fool in to marry you at last; therefore I am vex'd you have gone so far with Captain *H*——s; if anything should happen to discover your Intrigue with him, and Mr. *D*—— should turn you off before you have got a Settlement, the other you know has no Estate, but it is too late to advise you now, only be cautious; it is lucky your Keeper depends so much on your Sincerity, as to tell you his Suspicions of *Maria*; I took the hint you gave me, and sent him a Letter as from an unknown Person, which will make him quite confirm'd of her Falshood. That I sent to Lincolnshire I am positive has had a good Effect, for a Person has been at Greenwich since you left it, making great Enquiry concerning you and Mr. *D*——, which could be only by Maria's Orders—I dare believe by this time they heartily hate one another, and as we have contrived it, can never come to a right Knowledge of the Matter; only I once more charge you to take care, that nobody has it in their power to betray your Affair with the Captain; and also, that you will get as much as you can of him soon, for I hear his Ship will sail in a Month's Time;—let your next bring me an Account how Mr. *D*—— takes my anonymous Letter, and whether *Maria* is heard of yet—I think to leave Greenwich soon, and then we may see one another privately, for I must not pretend to forgive your yielding to Mr. *D*—— yet a-while. Adieu, dear Girl. I am,

Your Loving Mother,
ANN TRICKSY

ELIZA HAYWOOD

No Man that has not loved, entrusted, and been jilted, and betray'd, like Mr. *D*——, can have a true Notion of what he felt at this Scene of Villany, so wonderfully laid open to him—he shudder'd to think there could be so much Wickedness in the World; but when he reflected that it had been practis'd on himself, by a Person he had so much confided in, he was all Rage and Madness. Had he follow'd the first Dictates of his Fury, he would have staid till the false *Syrena* had come home, and torn out her beguiling Eyes, and soft dissembling Tongue; but Reason afterward remonstrating, that all he could do, would be but a demeaning of himself, and fall short of what her Hypocrisy merited at his Hands, he took Pen and Paper, and wrote to her in these Terms.

Base Monster,

A Letter from your vile Mother and Accomplice of your Crimes, has fallen into my Hands; I need say no more to let you know, I am no longer a Stranger to your Treachery to me, and the injured *Maria*.— Tremble then, curs'd Deceiver! thou abandon'd Profligate! thou hoard of complicated Crimes, at my just Resentment, and fly forever from my Sight, lest I stamp Deformity on every Limb, and make thy Body as hideous as thy Soul.—'Tis highly probable I am not the first, but am resolv'd to be the last on whom your detestable Artifices shall take Effect—Captain *H*——*s* shall be immediately inform'd what a Viper he cherishes; and after, your Character shall be made Publick, to warn all Mankind from falling into those Snares, so fatal to the Reputation and Peace of Mind of

D——

This Letter he left for her on the Table, and put that from her Mother into his Pocket, as an Evidence of their confederated Baseness; he read it over several times after he got home; but tho' he plainly perceived by it, that *Maria* had been imposed upon and made uneasy, as well as himself, by their Artifices; yet he could find nothing that could give him room to think they knew what Steps she had taken, anymore than that a Person enquiring after him at Greenwich, seem'd probably employed by her; but who this Person was, he could not guess; and his Curiosity in that Point was so great, imagining, that if he could discover this Agent of *Maria*, he might by that means be informed where she was; that he was sometimes tempted to offer old Mrs. *Tricksy* a free

Pardon for herself and Daughter, if she would in the first Place turn her prolific Brain, for discovering the Person that came to Greenwich; and in the second, make a full Recantation of all she had put in Practice, for sowing Dissention between *Maria* and him; but tho' he would have done almost anything to come at the Knowledge of the Truth, yet when he came to consider a second time, he could not yield ever to see or to hold any Conversation more, tho' for never so small a time, with those Wretches, who had so grosly imposed upon and betrayed him.

Much Compassion had been due to the Vexation this Gentleman was involved in, had not his Infidelity, in a manner, merited the Mischiefs it drew upon him; but what the innocent and wrong'd *Maria* suffered all this time, cannot but excite the Pity of every generous Reader.

This Lady loved Mr. *D*—— with a Tenderness, which is rarely to be met with in these times of Gallantry: She had from her very Infancy been taught to look upon him, as the Man who was one Day to be her Husband; and her Virtue and Duty improving the Inclination she naturally had for him, she had never indulg'd herself in those Gaities so many of her Sex are fond of—had never listen'd to the Sound of Love from any Tongue but his, nor had a Wish beyond him. He, for his part, had seem'd to center all his Hopes and his Desires in her, had never given her Cause for one uneasy Moment on his Score, nor did she even know what Jealousy meant; till that fatal Letter from the wicked Mrs. *Tricksy* awaken'd in her that poisonous Passion, and forc'd her, all soft and gentle as she was by Nature, to experience those furious Emotions, which Love ill-treated, and Confidence abused, never fail to excite. The Shock she felt at first reading the malicious Intelligence, was greater than her tender Frame could well sustain—She strove to disbelieve it, but in vain: The racking Idea return'd, in spite of all she could do to hinder it—sleeping and waking the hated Vision of a Rival flash'd upon her Mind—She painted her in Imagination, sometimes kind and consenting to his Vows, sometimes reserv'd and haughty, repaying his Inconstancy with Scorn—In fine, Love, Hate, Curiosity, and what was more distracting than them all, Suspence, made her once tranquil Soul a perfect Chaos of Confusion: Resolving to be satisfy'd, yet unwilling to make any one privy to what she felt on the Occasion of it, she pretended to Mrs. *J*—— that she would visit a Kinswoman at some Distance, and where she knew that Lady would not offer to accompany her, on account of a little pique between them—She went, indeed, but stay'd no longer than one Night, and took the Stage for London. She let no Person into the Secret of her Arrival, but one who had formerly been a Servant in the Family, and was now married and kept a House for Lodgers: With her did the discontented *Maria* take up her Residence: It was her whom she sent to Greenwich, to enquire concerning Mr. *D*—— and *Syrena*, and from her she received an Account which seem'd to confirm the Truth of the Letter; for Mrs. *Tricksy* had taken care to spread through all that little Town, that her Daughter was about being married to Mr. *D*——. Being thus, as she imagined, fully assured of the worst that could have been suggested to her, Curiosity led her to try all possible Methods to gain a Sight of the Face that had undone her: By the Diligence of her faithful Emissary, she obtain'd that too; for Mr. *D*—— being watch'd to the House where she lodg'd, *Maria* afterward went disguised into the Neighbourhood, and saw not only her Rival, but her ungrateful Lover also, with her at the Window—Killing Sight! All the Fortitude she had assum'd for this Adventure, was too little to enable her to endure it.—She fell immediately into Convulsions, and after into a high Fever, which from the very beginning threaten'd Death. The poor Creature who had been her Confidant, now wish'd she had been less industrious in obeying Orders, which were likely to bring on so fatal a Catastrophe; and judging it wholly improper to conceal her any longer, sent to several of her Relations, who immediately came to visit her full of Surprize, to find she was in Town, and had hid herself till her Condition made it necessary to disclose the place she was in: no body, however, question'd her on that Head, believing it might encrease her Disorder; but they fail'd not to enquire of the Woman the Motives which had brought her thither, to which the other pleaded Ignorance, and kept inviolably the Secret committed to her trust; tho' it did not long remain so; for *Maria*, growing delirious, so often mention'd the Names of Mr. *D*—— and *Syrena*, that it was easy to believe that something relating to that Gentleman, had been the Cause both of her strange Behaviour, and the Condition they now found her in. As they were sensible of the Trouble he was in on her Account, they thought it best he should be sent for, which he accordingly was, tho' much against the Will of the Woman of the House, who fear'd the Sight of him would heighten her Fever.

Mr. *D*—— received the News where *Maria* was, and of her Indisposition, the very Morning after he had detected the Treachery of *Syrena*; and not doubting but it was to the pernicious Arts of

Mrs. *Tricksy* that she owed her Illness, flatter'd himself, that his Presence, and a full Confession of what had past, would greatly contribute to her Recovery; but he found altogether the reverse; that unhappy Lady no sooner saw him in her Chamber, than she fell into such Agonies, that he was obliged to withdraw: He imputed it, however, to the Force of her Distemper, and still hoped, that if she came a little to her Senses, she would consent both to see him, and hear what he had to say; so order'd a Bed to be prepared for him in the same House, that he might be near to watch her Intervals of Reason, and endeavour to make his Peace with her. In the mean time, he was inform'd by the Confidant, of the pains *Maria* had taken to convince herself of a Truth, she had better have been eternally ignorant of; and in relating the Steps that had been taken, highly condemn'd her self for having assisted in the cruel Discovery. Mr. *D*—— shook his Head, and told her that he wish'd she had been enough his Friend to have given him a private Intelligence of Maria's Sentiments—Tho', added he, I cannot blame your acting in the manner you did, as Appearances were so much against me.

Two Days had Mr. *D*—— been under the same Roof without being able to speak to her; the Physicians having order'd she should be kept extremely quiet—but at the end of that time, being, as they thought, somewhat better, the Women ventur'd to acquaint her, who was so near her, and his true Remorse for a false Step, which Youth and Inadvertency alone had made him take, and his real Innocence as to the main Point, that of having any Inclination to breaking of with her, or of marrying *Syrena*. The disconsolate *Maria* listen'd attentively to her, without giving any other Answer than Sighs; and when the other alledg'd the Improbability there was, of his having any settled Affection for a Girl, such as *Syrena*, and expatiated on the Vileness of both her, and her Mother; so much the more unhappy is my Lot, cry'd *Maria*, to be the Sacrifize of such Wretches—However, continu'd she, I will see the still dear and guilty Man—Let him be call'd in.

He threw himself on his Knees by her Bedside, and said everything that Love and Repentance could inspire, to assure her, that his Heart had never been but hers; however, an unlucky, as well as criminal Inclination, had for a small time made him act contrary to his Honour and his Vows—I believe Mr. *D*——, answer'd she, you are now sorry for and asham'd of your Acquaintance with *Syrena*; but, perhaps, it is more owing to the Discovery of her Baseness, than to your regard for me; and the next new Face that pleased you, would have the same Influence; at least the Passion you have had for her has destroy'd all the Confidence I had in you—I could not now be happy with you—Nor, cry'd she, in a low Voice, can I live without you. In speaking these Words she fainted away—He was obliged to ring for the People to come to her Assistance; but all they could do was ineffectual, she dying in less than an Hour, and left him, who could not but look upon himself as the Cause, in a Condition little different from Distraction.

The real Affliction Mr. D——was in for this sad Accident, made England and the Sight of all his Friends hateful to him: He embark'd in a short time for foreign Parts; but before he went, wrote all the Particulars of this fatal Adventure, and desired it might be made publick, as a Warning to Gentlemen, how they inadvertently are drawn into Acquaintance with Women of *Syrena's* Character.

Our hypocritical Mother and Daughter had all this time Business enough upon their hands: *Syrena* no sooner came home, which was about six in the Morning, than finding Mr. D——'s Letter, she made no Delay, for fear he should return, and use her as she knew she merited at his hands, but pack'd up her things, quitted her Lodging, and took a Coach immediately to Greenwich. Mrs. *Tricksy*, on being told what had happen'd, thought that Place altogether unsafe for them; so they both return'd the same Day to London, and took Lodgings at Westminister; where, having no Acquaintance, they lived quite private for some Days, to avoid meeting with Mr. D—— or Capt. H——s, to whom they did not doubt, but that the Resentment of the other, had exposed them, as he had threaten'd in his Letter. Between the Liberality of Mr. D——, the Portuguese Merchant, and the Captain, they had made a pretty handsome Purse, which if they could have resolved to be honest, might have put them in some way of getting Bread; but neither of them were of frugal Dispositions, they indulged themselves in everything they liked, and *Syrena* sent for a Mercer, Millener, and other Trades People to equip her in a gay manner, that when she went abroad, her Charms might appear to advantage: By private Enquiries they soon heard that the Captain had failed, and also of Maria's Death, and Mr. D——'s voluntary Banishment from England; on which *Syrena* broke from her Obscurity, drest, and trod the Mall with as great a Grace, and as little Concern, as the most virtuous that frequented that place; she had nothing, indeed, to apprehend; but meeting with some or other of Sir *Thomas* L——'s Family; she had, therefore, her Eyes continually on the Watch, that if she happen'd to see any of them at a Distance, she might turn away, before they came near enough to distinguish her, thus disguised as the Hussy was in Lace and Embrodery. The Season for Park-walking in an Evening being far advanced, it quite past over without her being able to make one Conquest, which was no small Mortification to this fine Lady, especially as her Money was almost exhausted in Cloaths, luxurious Eating, and Chair-Hire. In short, Winter came on, without anything being done.—She durst not go to Plays, Opera's, nor Concerts, because she very well knew, that there was seldom a Night but some or other of that Family she had so grosly imposed upon, were at those Diversions.—The Masquerade was the only place she could go to without fear of being exposed, and even there was in Danger of being accosted, either by Sir *Thomas* or his Son; she flatter'd herself, however, that she should have Penetration enough to find either of them out in any Habit, without their being able to discover her; and she happen'd in reality to be more lucky than she deserv'd on this score. She was not so, however, in her principal Intention, that of being address'd to in a particular manner. She had been there twice without having been accosted with any other than the common Salutations of the Place, as *Do you know me*, and *I know you*, and such like Stuff; or the impudent Freedoms which are used to common Women, and which some who glory in being accounted Libertines, have the Effrontery to practise in the most publick Places. The Expence of her Tickets, Dress, and Chair-Hire thus thrown away, was no small Mortification to her, as Cash began now to run very low: She adventured, however, a third time, and happening to be address'd by a Person, who, on stretching out his Arm to reach at something on one of the Beaufets, she perceiv'd, by his Domine falling a little open, had a Star on his Coat; she resolv'd to encourage a Conversation with him; and keeping her Eye constantly fix'd upon him, had Artifice enough to draw him off, wherever she found he was engaging with any other of the Masks. Her Wit and Manner pleas'd him extremely, and at length he grew very particular with her—She seem'd no less charm'd with his Behaviour; and, after a good deal of feign'd Reluctance, consented he should conduct her to some place, where they might discourse with more Freedom; and he accordingly carry'd her to a Bagnio in St. James's-Street. If she had appear'd agreable to him before, she was much more so now, when she had an Opportunity of revealing those Beauties in full, which in the Ball-Room could but be shewn in Part, and that too, but by stealth.

After a Supper, and some amorous Conversation, he entreated she would stay with him all Night; but tho' she pretended to have been struck with an irresistable Passion for him, the first Moment she saw his Face, and had it not in her power to refuse him anything; yet said, she would sooner die than be guilty of an Injustice to one of her own Sex; so begg'd to know if he were married. He told her, on his Honour, that he was not.—She then insisted on his Name, and he made no Scruple of letting her know, he was Lord *R*——.

They past the Time till Morning in mutual Endearments, and indeed mutual Dissimulation—*Syrena* artfully mingling with her pretended Fondness certain modest Shocks to heighten his good Opinion of her, and he affecting to be possest of a more than ordinary Passion, for the more emboldning her to meet his amorous Desires with equal Warmth. The Night being past, and his Lordship fully gratify'd, he made her a Present of ten Guineas, which she at first refused with an Air of Disdain, telling him that he injured her greatly if he imagin'd she had yielded from any motive but Love. But he forced her to accept this Token, as he call'd it of his Affection; on those Terms, said she, I take it from my dear Lord; but were every Piece a Thousand I would reject them with Scorn if offer'd as the purchase of my Virtue—I am no Prostitute, continued she, and if I thought you look'd on me as such, and having accomplish'd your Desires would never see me more, I would this Instant undeceive you, by running your Sword through my too fond, too easily charm'd Heart. Lord *R*—— smiled within himself to hear her talk in this romantick Stile; but willing to humour her in it, made her as many promises of Constancy as she desired, and assured her in a very small Time, he would write to appoint a second Meeting, and they would then settle Things so as to see each other often.

Thus they parted, and *Syrena* went home somewhat better satisfied with the Effects of this Masquerade than she had been with the two former, tho' she did not flatter herself with securing the Heart of this Nobleman, as she had done those of Mr. *L*—— and Mr. *D*——; she feared he knew the Town too well to be drawn into any serious Engagement with a Woman he had come acquainted with in that manner, but expected however, that he would send to her, and that she should have further Presents from him.

The first Part of her Conjectures she soon found were but too true for her, but the other greatly deceiv'd her; for his Lordship thought little of her after they were parted, and less desired a second Interview: He judged by her Behaviour that if he were to encourage her Expectations by making any future Assignations she would become a troublesome Dependant, and be a kind of Bur not easily shaken off. Beside he had a Mistress whose Love and Fidelity he had for many Years experienced; by whom he had several fine Children, and who was at that Time lying-in at his Seat in the Country. He would have been loth to give any Cause of discontent to a Woman he loved, and had Reason to do so, by any settled Intrigue with another, and tho' meeting with *Syrena* (at a Time when Christians as well as Jews think they may indulge an amorous Inclination without breach of Constancy) he had toyed away a Night, it never entered into his Head to continue an Acquaintance with her.

Four Days being past over, *Syrena's* impatience would suffer her to wait no longer, and having enquir'd where Lord *R*—— lodged, for he kept no House in Town, drest herself in as alluring a manner as she could, and went to make him a Visit.

His Lordship was strangely surprized when his Gentleman told him a Lady in a Chair, who said her Name was *Tricksy*, desired to speak with him; he looked on her coming to his Lodging as a Piece of Impudence altogether inconsistent with the Modesty she affected to be Mistress of; however he ordered she should be admitted, but resolved to behave to her in such a manner as should prevent her from ever troubling him again.

This was certainly a very wrong step in *Syrena*, and what her Mother would fain have dissuaded her from; she told her that none but those who were not ashamed to be thought common, ever went to visit Men at their Lodgings; and that if Lord *R*—— were a Man of Sense, or had but the least Knowledge of the World, he must contemn her for it; but our young Deluder was of a quite different Opinion; she imagined that going to him in that manner, would give him a high Idea of the extreme Passion she had flatter'd him with, and that also it would make her seem to act without Disguise, and that she was too innocent even to know there was any indecency in what she did. So all the Arguments Mrs. *Tricksy* made use of were to no purpose; the pert Baggage told her she was capable of managing now for herself, and would walk with Leading-Strings no longer.

This is a Favour I little expected Madam, said his Lordship, as soon as she was introduced. Then, my Lord, answer'd she, you were ignorant of the Power you have over me; but it is not to be wonder'd at, that you should not expect any Effects of Love from me, when you are so insensible of that Passion yourself—what, continued she, to be four long Days without seeing me or sending to me—I have had Business, return'd he coldly. O ungrateful! cried she, can you have any Business of equal Moment to the peace of one who adores you as I do, who have given you the greatest Proofs of it a Woman can do, and who cannot live without you?—Hush, Madam, interrupted he, we may be overheard—this is not a Place for Expostulations or Upbraidings,— and as I never receive Visits from your Sex, unless those who are known to be nearly related to me; I must beg you will make yours as short as possible for both our Reputations. O my Stars! cryed she, are you then asham'd of me? with these Words she burst into Tears. Fie, fie, said he, with a half Smile, which denoted his Contempt, do not spoil that pretty Face with crying—You were all Gaity when I saw you before, and good Company, and if you desire to pass three or four Hours again in the same Manner, I assure you this is not the way to charm a Man of my Humour.—*Syrena* now burst into a real Rage, and scrupled not to treat him in a Manner little befitting his Quality; on which he bid her leave the House, and learn better Manners. She had then Recourse to Fits, and swoon'd so naturally, that if he had not been well versed in this Artifice of the Sex, he would have taken it to be real; but he immediately saw through it, and instead of calling for any Help, only said—look you, Madam, these Airs won't pass upon me, I see your Drift—you want to pin yourself upon me—but it won't do; and instead of softning me into the Cully you want, you only incur my Disdain, and inspire me with the worst Sentiments for you I can have of any Woman,—therefore put your Face into Order and be gone; for if you continue in this Posture, I shall order my Servants to put your Head in a Pail of Water, which I look upon to be the best Remedy in the World for such Disorders as yours. These Words frighted her, and not doubting by all his Behaviour to her, that he would do as he said; raised herself from the Ground, and flew down Stairs without making any farther Attempts to bring him to her Purpose.

I do not doubt but many of my fair Readers will be highly disobliged at this Nobleman's Behaviour; they will say, he ought to have carry'd with more Complaisance, at least to a pretty young Creature, who had obliged him; and some perhaps may even tax him with Savageness and Brutality; therefore to vindicate his Character from all such Aspersions, I must inform them, that he had before met with Women of *Syrena's* Stamp;—that he had for some few Years of his Life devoted himself so much to Gallantry, that he was perfectly acquainted with every little Art put in Practice by those, whose Business it is to ensnare; and had more than once been imposed upon by the Pretence of a violent Affection, which made him not only presently discern, but likewise abhor those studied and counterfeited Tendernesses; but as to the rest, no Man knew more how to value real Merit in the Sex, nor paid a greater Regard to it.

The Disappointment *Syrena* had met with, made her half distracted: She was ready on her coming home to break and tear to pieces everything that was in her way; then her Mother remonstrated to her, that she could expect no better Usage, when she pretended to pursue a Man to his Lodgings, and reproach'd her for not taking her Advice; But the other, instead of acquiescing with what she said, or acknowledging she had been to blame, flew into a greater Rage than before, and told her, that all her Misfortunes had been owing to the Rules she had prescribed. You were always preaching up Softness and Tenderness, cry'd she, but I dare swear if I had been sawcy, and given myself an Air of Insolence, as indeed is more to natural to me, I should have fared better. You are a poor ignorant Fool, reply'd the Mother, if you are not used well by the Man who thinks you love him, you never will by the Man who thinks you do not.—Softness is the most prevailing Arms we have; Beauty may attract, but that alone secures the Heart. A great Argument on this arose between them, and at length terminated in a Quarrel, in so much, that *Syrena* went directly and took a separate Lodging, and vowed she would henceforth follow no Direction, but her own Humour; but this Quarrel did not last long, each found she had need of the other, and their mutual Interest reconciled them; it was judged proper, however, they should live apart for sometime; *Syrena* having embark'd in an Adventure, which could best be carry'd on without the Appearance of a Mother.

She remember'd that in the time she was kept by Mr. *D*——, happening to buy some Silk for a Short-apron, at a Shop in Covent-Garden, the Mercer had seemed to look upon her with an Eye of Admiration, pulled down several pieces of fine Brocade, under the Pretence of tempting her to buy; but in reality, only to have the Pleasure of detaining her as long as he could; and tho' she bought only such a Trifle, would fain have sent one of his young Men home with it. All this she thought testify'd a Desire of being acquainted with her, if he could find any Means to bring it about, so she contrived it for him in this manner.

She made it her Business to walk for several Evenings by his Shop, just in the close of Day, when they were preparing to shut up; and the first time she saw him there, ran in a vast Hurry and seeming Fright up the Steps, and cried, I beg a thousand Pardons for this Trouble, Sir, but for God's Sake give me House Room for a few Minutes—for I am frighted to Death. He immediately reach'd a Chair, and having made her sit down, enquired the Cause of her Disorder—O! said she, this Covent-Garden is a wicked Place—I hope I have not the look of an ill Woman—but a Gentleman has followed me I know not how far—I could not get rid on him for my Life; and he swore I should either go with him to a Tavern, or he would see me home.—O! what a Terror he has put me in—so I took the Liberty to run into your Shop to avoid him. The complaisant Mercer told her she was extremely welcome, and perceiving she grew pale, and ready to faint (which she could counterfeit whenever she pleased) ordered a Glass of Water, and bid his Man ask his Wife for some Drops; the good Gentlewoman hearing of the Accident, ran down, and assisted in recovering the Hypocrite from her pretended Illness, exclaiming all the time against the Vileness of Mankind; who, tho' there were so many fit for their Purpose, could not suffer civil Women to pass. *Syrena* having created a good deal of Bustle, began at last to come to her Senses, and then made a great many Apologies for the Trouble she had given, but begg'd they would add to the Obligation, that of letting one of the Servants call a Chair for her; this was readily granted, but not till they had made her drink a Glass of Sack, and eat a bit of rich Cake; she assured them she would endeavour to return their Favours, by buying everything she wanted in their way, and recommending the Shop to all her Acquaintance. As she was going into the Chair, she took care to give the Men Directions where to carry her, loud enough for the Mercer not to be mistaken in the Place, in case he should take it into his Head to visit her, as she imagined he would do, by some tender Looks and Pressures he gave her, while he supposed her not in a Condition to be sensible of them.

She was not deceived, indeed, for the amorous Mercer was quite charm'd with her, and the next Day came to her Lodgings, under the Pretence of enquiring how she got home, and found herself after her Fright;—she had dress'd herself in Expectation of him in a loose and most becoming Dishabillee, and received him full of Sweetness and affected Modesty. Every Look she gave him, and every Word she spoke, was new Fuel to the unhappy Flame she before had kindled in his

Heart;—he thought there never was so perfect, so beautiful a Creature born, and wish'd himself unmarry'd, that he might have endeavoured to gain her Affection, which he now durst not presume to attempt. He thought however he might indulge himself in the Pleasure of seeing and conversing with her, without any Injury either to her or his Wife; but the Consequence proved (as indeed it always does) how fatal it is to give way to Inclinations of that sort, which, by not being nipp'd in the Bud, at length grow too sturdy to be bowed down, and extend themselves to the most dreadful and enormous Size. She asked him to drink Tea, which he too gladly complied with, and after that a Bottle of Wine; among other Chat, she led him into that of his Business, and of the Fashions, asked him many Questions concerning what Colours, and what Patterns were most in Vogue; and then told him, she should soon be his Customer for three or four Suits of Cloaths; for, said she, I have been out of Town for a considerable time, and am quite out of Gowns and Petticoats; but I must stay, continued she, till I receive a Remittance from my Husband. Husband! Madam! interrupted the Mercer, are you married then? Yes, cry'd she, with a deep Sigh; you Answer, Madam, added he, as tho' you were not so happy in that State, as I am sure you deserve to be; where Hearts are not united, replied she, there can be no solid Felicity—however, he is my Husband, and absent, neither is it owing to him if I am miserable; in speaking these Words she let fall some Tears, which gave him a Curiosity to know the Motive; and tho' he thought it would be too great a Freedom to ask it, yet he could not help dropping some Expressions which testify'd his Desire, and gave her an Opportunity of telling him a long Story that she had invented to amuse him.

As she found he was married, and that there could be no hope of drawing him in for a Husband, she thought it best, for many Reasons, to pass for a Wife; so said, that being courted very young by a Gentleman, who was Heir to a great Estate, her Mother had compelled her to marry him, but that his Friends were so enraged at it, that they had sent him to Venice, where he now resided; and added she, must do so till Heaven shall turn their Hearts, which I see little hope of; they allow him a very handsome Income, however, out of which he sends me sufficient to support me, in the little way you see me in—as we lived together but three Days, I do not chuse to be called by his Name, till I can appear in a Fashion more befitting his Rank in the World; and also, because I have been privately informed, that if they can bring him to consent to it, they will give me a handsome Sum of Money to renounce all Claim to him. Thus, Sir, said she, I am a Wife, and no Wife—have lost my Peace of Mind and Character, with those who know not the Truth of my unhappy Marriage, and all thro' the mistaken Care of a too covetous Parent.

The Mercer seemed much affected with her Misfortunes, but gathered more Courage for his Love, thinking there was more hope at least of being listened favourably to by a Wife in such Circumstances, than there would have been by a young Virgin of a handsome Fortune, as he at first took her for.

He made her a great many Compliments on her Beauty and Merit; highly blaming her Husband's Friends for their inexorable Behaviour; and saying, that in his Opinion, such a Woman as she would become the highest Rank of Life. He told her moreover, that as she had said she wanted some Silks, she was extremely welcome to whatever his Shop afforded, and begg'd she would come the next Day, and order what she would have sent in.

She thank'd him for his kind Offer, but seemed loth to accept it, till he press'd her over and over, and assured her, with the tenderest Air he could put on, that having it in his power to oblige her, was the happiest thing could befall him. At last she promised to come, and he took his leave, rejoiced at this Opportunity of continuing an Acquaintance with her.

She, who was perfectly sensible of the Ascendant she had gain'd over him, resolv'd to manage him, so as to command everything he had: She went the next Day according to Appointment; and became his Customer for three rich Suits and two Night-gowns—which she carry'd away with her in a Hackney-Coach, after having invited him and his Wife to drink Tea at her Lodging, the first Time their Leisure permitted.

It is not to be suppos'd he fail'd waiting on her; and his Wife taking her to be a Lady of strict Modesty, was so much charm'd with her, that nothing but the fear of being troublesome, kept her from being almost continually with her. She never thought herself so happy, as in her Company, and was forever inviting her to dine and sup at their House.—*Syrena* accepted her Kindness, as often as Prudence would admit; and the Intimacy between them encreasing everyday; the Husband took the Advantage of their Familiarity, to grow more so also. He told *Syrena* that if she were a Man, he should not approve of the Affection his Wife had for her; and as she was a Woman, he thought he merited something from her in Compensation, for robbing him of so much of his Wife's Company.—The sly Deluder answer'd, that she look'd upon him and his Wife as one, and therefore desired when she could not have them both, that she might not be without One.—Your Business calls you so often my Way, added she, with a most bewitching Air, that, methinks, I need not miss the Sight of you once or twice everyday.—This with someother kind Expressions she let fall, whenever she had an Opportunity, by Degrees dissipated the Awe his good Opinion of her had inspired him with; and he at length took Courage to discover his Inclinations. Never had *Syrena* given a greater Proof, how perfect a Mistress she was in the Art of Dissimulation, than by the Amazement she put on at hearing him talk to her in the Language of a Lover—a half Resentment, and a half Compliance were blended with it, so as not to dash his Hopes too much, nor lessen herself with him by approving too easily of his Addresses. In fine, she behaved in such a Fashion, as made him think her an Angel of Virtue, and at the same Time, a Woman not a little attach'd to him by a secret liking of his Person.—He was not, however, long held in Suspence, he was one Night at her Lodging—they were alone—had drank a Glass of Wine pretty freely.—He was bolder than ordinary, and she sunk into his Arms at once, and gave herself up entirely to him, without seeming to know what she did.

Never Man thought himself happier than the transported Mercer; and *Syrena* was perfectly content with what she done; not doubting but she should henceforward have the command of his Purse; as indeed, she had; he lov'd her too well to refuse her anything, and she had so little Conscience in the Expences she brought him into, that in three Months, there was a frightful diminution of his Substance. His lavish Love bestowed so much upon her, that had she liv'd in any frugal Decorum, she might have sav'd sufficient to have made her easy for a long time; but having nothing now to think on, farther than indulging every Luxury, she became exceedingly leud; and the Mercer not being able to give her enough of his Company, and, besides, had something of a Sobriety in his Nature, not agreeable to her present Way of thinking; she fell into an Adventure which was not a little Expensive to her.

Living in good Lodgings, appearing always rich in Dress, and conversing with none who were any Blemish to her Character, for her Intimacy with the Mercer's Wife, took off all Scandal on his Account; she visited, and receiv'd Visits from several Ladies in the

Neighbourhood; with them she us'd frequently to take a Morning's Walk up Constitution-Hill, as it is call'd, in the Green-Park. She was seldom there without seeing a Man of a genteel Appearance and agreeable Person; she was struck at first Sight of him, with something she had never felt before, and which made her uneasy to become acquainted with him. As she found he was pretty constantly there; she went one Morning alone, and had, what she thought, the good Fortune to meet him—as they drew pretty near, she tript her Foot purposely against a little Pebble, and fell down as if by Accident, as he was just by her; he ran and rais'd her, but she pretended to have sprain'd her Ancle, and was not able to walk without Support, so she lean'd upon his Arm till they got into the lower Park, where they sat down on the first Bench. As she had no farther Designs on him, than entring into an Amour, she shew'd herself without Disguise, and was all the Libertine. On his proposing to go to a Tavern, she immediately consented, and yielded herself up to his Embraces, without the least Reserve or Scruple.—If such abandon'd Inclinations can be call'd Love, she might be said to love this new Gallant to a very great Degree.—She stay'd with him the whole Day, and encroach'd some Hours on the Night; nor parted without telling him her Name and Lodgings, and exacting a Promise from him, of coming to see her the next Day.

She had no reason to doubt his Punctuality in this Point. He was of as amorous a Constitution, as her vicious Desires had made her languish for.—He was at that time free from all Engagements, and thought himself lucky, in having so young and beautiful a Mistress thrown in his Way; but what extremely added to his Satisfaction, in the Enjoyment of her was, that he was pretty secure, both by her Appearance and Temper; for she would not suffer him to pay the Reckoning, that she would be no manner of Charge to him; but on the contrary, he should be able to render his Acquaintance with her serviceable, as well to his Interest, as he had found it to his Pleasure.

Their second Interview was no less full of Rapture than the first; and they were so highly satisfied with each other, that both swore eternal Constancy, and, perhaps, at that Juncture intended to preserve it. From this time they were seldom asunder; he breakfasted with her at her Lodgings, then they went together to the White-Eagle in Suffolk-Street to dine; and parted not till the Hour, in which she expected the Mercer, or his deluded, injur'd Wife; she always defraying the Expence, tho' he complain'd he was asham'd of it; but that being a young Fellow of a small Fortune, he had it not in his power to behave towards her in that Respect, as he could wish. She told him she had enough for both, and begg'd he would make himself easy, for his Love and Constancy, was all she expected from him; and withal told him, that he might command whatever she was Mistress of, with the same Freedom as his own. Nor was she backward in the Performance of this Promise; whenever they went abroad, she took care to put more Money in his Pocket, than the Charges of the Day could possibly amount to. So that never any Man, who could content himself with receiving Obligations of that Nature from a Woman, had more reason to be satisfied.

The Passion she had for this young Gallant, however, did not make her negligent in preserving her Interest with the Mercer. She was never out of the way, when he appointed to be with her, and received him with such an Infinity of Tenderness, that he would almost have doubted the Testimony of his own Eyes, had they told him she was false.

But being willing to prevent any Accident that might discover her Intrigue, or render it even suspected by the People of the House; she consider'd that it would be proper, he should not be much seen at her Lodgings: She had past him at first, as a Country Kinsman just come to Town; but as a Continuance of such frequent Visits, might occasion Enquiries, she henceforward met him at her Mother's; and for this Reason it was she submitted herself to her, and was reconciled. But knowing well that Mrs. *Tricksy*, being past the Pleasures of Love herself, was solely devoted to Interest; she carefully conceal'd from her the Truth of her Sentiments for her new Lover, pretending to her that he was a Man of Fortune, and allow'd her Five Guineas a Week; and to gain Credit for what she said, gave him wherewith, to make her very handsome Presents. Thus was the Instructress in Deceit, deceived herself; and tho' she did receive some Profit from her Daughter's Vices, yet it was little in Comparison of what she might have got, if the other had been as sincere to her, and to her own Interest, as she pretended. But it is generally speaking, the Fate of Prostitutes to lavish on some Indigent Favourite, who, perhaps, despises them, what they gain by the Folly of the deluded Keeper.

The Mercer at length finding her grow exorbitant in her Demands upon him, and beyond what he cou'd continue to grant without ruining his Family, began to feel some touches of Remorse for the wrong he did his Wife and Children, but the artful *Syrena*, whenever she found him slack either in his Embraces or Presents, knew so well how to win him to her Purpose, and disperse all Thoughts, but those of the Pleasures he enjoyed in her Arms, that he could not find in his Heart to refuse anything to so lovely, so endearing, so faithful a Creature; much less to abandon her entirely; and had certainly kept on his Correspondence with her, till his Destruction had been inevitable, had not an Accident happened to open his Eyes to her Perfidy and Ingratitude.

Early one Morning she receiv'd a Letter from her beloved, acquainting her, that he had been arrested the Night before, by his Taylor, for the Sum of an hundred Pounds, and desiring she would forthwith oblige him with the Money; for he had no Bail to offer, and had other Debts, which, he fear'd, would come upon him and fix him in a Gaol for Life, if not discharg'd immediately. This News gave her the utmost Concern, she had been too profuse to have half that Sum by her, and could not bear the Loss of a Lover, so well qualify'd to please her. She, therefore, sent directly to the Mercer, begging he would come to her that Moment, on a Business of equal Moment with her Life: He had too much real Tenderness not to obey so pressing a Summons, and found her lying on her Bed, half drown'd in Tears. She told him her Mother was going to be carry'd to Prison for a Debt of an old standing, and that tho' there had not been a very good Understanding between them of late, on account of her unhappy Marriage; yet she could not live and see her Parent die in a Gaol, as she must do, if the Money was not paid—It would be highly improper, both on your own Account and mine, said she, that you should appear in the Affair, either as to bail her yourself, or send any other Person to do it; and besides the Money must be paid at last, so that if you have any Love, Friendship, or Pity for the poor *Syrena*, let me have the Sum required, that I may fly to save from Misery, the Person to whom I owe my Being.—I would have pawn'd my Jewels, and what little Plate I have, added she, rather than have given you this Trouble; but I know not which way to go about such a Business, and also fear they would not raise so much. How moving are the Griefs of those we love; had she ask'd him for his Soul he would have given it, and tho' at that time he could very ill spare it, being going to pay a Bill drawn on him by one of his Weavers, yet he immediately took out of his Pocket-Book two fifty Pound Bank Notes and gave her, bidding her dry her Tears, and go instantly to remedy the cause; with these Words, accompany'd with a thousand Kisses, he took his leave, and she order'd a Hackney Coach to carry her to the Place where her Lover was confined. As the believing Mercer was going home, he met a Taylor, with whom he had been long acquainted, and was a Customer; this Man seeing him so opportunely, told him he was going to a Spunging House, to hear what Offers a Person he had arrested, had to make him: The Mercer comply'd, and they went together. On their coming to the Officer's House, they were told a Lady had just gone up to the Prisoner, and desired to wait in the Parlour till she was gone: Accordingly they did so, but the Door not being shut, what Astonishment was the Mercer in, when the Lady passing by to go into the Coach that waited for her, he saw it was his, till then, suppos'd faithful *Syrena*: She had pluck'd her Hood pretty much over her Face, not that she suspected in the least who was there, but that her Face might not be known hereafter, by anyone who should have seen her in such a Place: Her Cloaths, however, being the same he had just left her in, and which had come from his own Shop, her Shape, her Air, and and her Voice in speaking to the Coachman, discover'd *Syrena* too plainly, to one who had so much Cause to know her, for him to be mistaken. He was scarce able to dissemble his Confusion, before the Person he was with, but their being that Moment desired to go up to the Prisoner, prevented the other from taking Notice of it. On going in he receiv'd a dreadful Confirmation of *Syrena's* Baseness, had he doubted of it—He saw the two fifty Pound Bills he had just given to her, and the Number of which he knew, paid as so much Money to his Friend, and on the Prisoner's Finger a Diamond Ring he presented her with, and which she pretended to have lost.

Those of my Readers who have sometime or other in their Lives, found themselves in the Mercer's Case, need not be told what 'twas he felt at so amazing a Proof, how greatly he had all along been imposed upon by the Artifices of this wicked Woman; and those who have never been so unhappy to experience such Deceptions, ought to be warn'd by the Despair this poor Man afterwards fell into, how they enter into any Engagements with Women, whose Principles they are not acquainted with; and not like him be beguil'd and ruin'd by a fair Face and seeming affection; but, as the Poet says, *Shun the dangerous Beauty of the Wanton*—. For in corrupted Morals no Sincerity can be expected, and the sacred Names of Love and Friendship are but prophan'd and prostituted for the basest ends.

The Mercer thought every Moment an Age till the Business on which his Friend had brought him there was ended, that he might go to *Syrena*, and vent some Part of his Rage in those Reproaches which her Behaviour had merited from him. He found her at home, and was received by her with such a Shew of Love and Gratitude, that his Astonishment at her Dissimulation was so great, he had not presently the power of uttering what was in his Heart; but he gave her a Look, and, at the same time push'd her from him, as she was throwing her Arms about his Waste, as sufficiently inform'd her somewhat very extraordinary was labouring in his Mind—She trembled inwardly, but disguis'd it with her usual Artifice, and ask'd him tenderly, what had disorder'd him? As soon as he could speak there was nothing opprobrious, that he omitted saying to her; he call'd her every vile Name that his Passion could suggest, and on her having recourse to Protestations of Innocence, and falling into Faintings, he let her know he was not to be again deceiv'd, and flung out of the Room, leaving her in a pretended Swoon.

The loss of so great a Support vex'd her to the Heart; but perceiving he was not to be recover'd, and that the Proofs of her Infidelity were too plain for her to aim at any Justification of her Actions, she consoled herself with the Reflection, that he would not dare to expose her, for the sake of his own Character; and that she had Youth and Beauty enough to attract someother, who might be as much devoted to her Interest as he had been.

The Mercer after this examining into his Affairs more heedfully than he had done during the Hurry of his Passion for the infamous *Syrena*, found himself in very bad Circumstances, and that he was no less than thirteen hundred Pounds a worse Man, for his Acquaintance with her, tho' it had not lasted above four Months—The Injury he had done his Wife and Family now glared him full in the Face, and together with the Thoughts how impossible it was for him to retrieve this false Step, made him grow extremely melancholy: His Wife perceiv'd it through all his Endeavours to conceal it, and often with the greatest Tenderness, urg'd him to reveal the Cause; but could get no other Answer from him, than that he had of late had some Losses in Trade, which hinder'd him from being so punctual in his Payments as he had been accustom'd to be; but that he hoped he should recover it in time. This he said, to keep her from the Knowledge of her Misfortune as long as he could; but finding his Creditors grow impatient, and no visible way of making things easy, but by a Statute of Bankruptcy, his Pride would not suffer him to consent to that, and, therefore, resolved to put a Period to his Life and Troubles at once. To this end he shut himself one Day in his

Counting-House, and clapp'd a loaded Pistol to his Ear, with an Intent to shoot himself through the Head; but Providence averted his Aim, and by a sudden shaking of his Hand just in that dreadful Moment, directed the Bullets another way, and they but graz'd on the back part of his Head, and lodg'd in a Shelf behind him. The Report of the Pistol drew all the Family to the Place; the Door was immediately broke open, and they found him with that Instrument of Death in his Hand, about to charge it for a second Attempt—His Servants by force wrested it from him, and his Wife having made them carry it away, and leave the Room, threw herself upon her Knees before him, and conjured him, for the sake of his own Soul, and for the sake of those dear Babes, who must be left Orphans, not to harbour Thoughts so contrary to Religion and to Nature—You know, said she, that my Fortune is by our Marriage-Articles settled on me, I will give it you up entirely; dispose of it as you please to make you easy—If that is not sufficient, take all my Jewels, my Cloths—And should all be ineffectual, I will go to my Father, prostrate myself before him, and never leave his Feet, till I have obtain'd wherewith to retrieve your Circumstances—It was now he found the Difference between a virtuous and a vicious Woman; and having naturally very tender and grateful Sentiments, was quite overcome with her Generosity—He could not resolve to abuse it, nor suffer her to remain longer in Ignorance.—The wrong he had done her, was a Burthen on his Soul, which he could not sustain—O cease this Goodness, said he, to an unworthy Husband—I have been base, been unfaithful, and deserve the Punishment my Crime has brought upon me.—I will not involve you in my Ruin—Live, my dear virtuous Wife, continu'd he, and enjoy what, I thank Heaven, my Creditors cannot dispossess you of; and do the best you can with it for yourself, and our unhappy Children—for me, I am determin'd either not to live, or not to live in England. The poor Gentlewoman was ready to die at these Words; but insisted, as well as she was able, on his accepting her Offer. O, said he, you little imagine what a Villain I have been—but you shall know—Then after some small Struggles between Shame and Generosity, he made her sit down by him, and related the whole Story of his guilty Commerce, concealing not the least Article of what he had done for *Syrena*, nor the Ingratitude with which she had return'd his too sincere, tho' criminal Affection—concluding with these Words— Now my injur'd Dear, said he, judge if a Wretch like me ought to live, much less to receive any Marks of Goodwill from you, whom I have so much abus'd and deceiv'd? It was impossible for a Wife to hear such an Account of the Cause of their Misfortunes, and from a Husband's Mouth, without being seized with many different Emotions, all violent in their turns; but Jealousy, Resentmeat, Pride, all subsided, and gave way to Tenderness and Pity—She was a few Minutes without being able to give him any Answer for Tears, but a kind Embrace supply'd the want of Words, and when she spoke, it was in these Terms: My dearest Love, said she, I look on your making me the Confidant of your failing, as a full Attonement for it—had I been told it by any other, I could not, perhaps, so readily have forgiven it; because I cannot but think, that the Heart still takes Pleasure in a Crime which it cannot bring itself to acknowledge as such, and that there is no true Penitence without Confession.—But your having told me all, obliges me in return to pardon all, and to do all in my power to contribute to your ease—I now, more than ever, insist on your commanding my Fortune; and if you refuse taking it up, I will do it myself, and distribute it among your Creditors, as far as it will go. The Husband was confounded at a Sweetness, so rarely to be found in a Woman wrong'd in so tender a point; and the Pleasure he took in having thus eas'd his aking Heart, mingled with the just sense of Shame, for having injured a Goodness and Excellence of Nature, superior to all he ever heard of, render'd him in a manner beside himself—He could say nothing but what a blind Wretch was I?—How insensible of what was truly valuable—How could I slight the real Diamond, and set my Heart upon a common Pebble, fit only to be trod upon, spurn'd, and kick'd into the Sewer!—Come, come, no more of this, my dear, cry'd she, throwing herself upon his Breast, many Men like you, have erred where there was less Temptation to excite them; but few Men like you, have honour enough to own they have done amiss—if you think me worthy the return of your Affection, oblige me by speaking no more of this matter than I shall do, to whom it shall be as it had never happened; and let us study how to recover our little Affairs from the Perplexity they are at present involved in.

It was with the utmost Difficulty however, that she at length prevailed on him to call in her Fortune; and just as he was about to do it, News arrived of the Death of a Brother he had abroad, who left him more than ten times what was necessary for the retrieving of his Credit;—to make what Reparation he could to his Wife, he settled upon her all that remained after paying his Debts; he soon after left off

Trade, and retired into the Country, where no People live more happy in each other; she blessing his Return to Virtue, and he the Goodness that had reclaim'd him.

Syrena in the mean Time soon began to feel the want of his Purse, and as her power of treating and presenting declined, found also her Favourite's Inclinations declined in Proportion: He talk'd of nothing now in her Company but the want of Money, and on her reproaching him with the change she found in him, he told her that Love was the Child of Plenty, and that for his Part he could think nothing charming that was indigent—this so enraged her that she gave him a Blow on the Face, which he, who neither loved nor regarded her, but for Self-Interest, return'd with Interest, and there was a perfect Battle between them—as she found her Strength inferior to such Sort of Combats, and liking him too well for his Ingratitude to extinguish, she fell into abject submissions, beg'd his Pardon for doing what indeed he deserved from her, since vile as she was to others, she had been generous to him even to Excess; and did everything in the Power of Woman to engage a Continuation of their Acquaintance, which however lasted not long, Debts came upon him; and she not having it in her power to discharge them, he was oblig'd to quit the Kingdom to avoid a Prison.

She was now destitute of either Friend or Lover, and having expended and made away with all had been given her by the Mercer, fell into extreme Poverty, and had nothing for her Support but the Credit, which having laid out a great deal of Money in the Neighbourhood; had given her, on this she lived some little Time, but the Shop-keepers beginning to send in their Bills, she was thinking to remove privately to someother Lodging, to prevent one being provided for her, she could by no Means approve, when Chance threw an offer in her Way, which her Industry had for a good while in vain sought after. Happening to be looking at some Lodgings at a Tradesman's House in the Strand, she perceived as she was going home a Fellow in a very rich Livery followed her till she came home, and as soon as he had seen her enter, go to an opposite Neighbour's; she could not guess the meaning, but was informed by that Person soon after, that a Footman had enquired there her Name. And the next Day receiv'd a Letter to this Effect.

Madam,

I saw you Yesterday at one of my Tradesmen's Houses where I call'd to pay a Bill, and at the same Time lost my Heart; if you will permit a

Visit from me this Afternoon, I shall endeavour to convince you that I think you deserve a better Situation than his House can afford—favour me with your Answer by the Bearer, and believe me,

Your sincere Admirer,

M——

This was indeed wrote with the freedom of a Man of Quality, to one he thought honour'd with his Addresses; but she was not at present in a Condition to stand upon Forms, and therefore answered him in these Terms, after being informed by his Servant by what Title she should address him.

My Lord,

I am extremely oblig'd to the Honour of your Lordship's Notice, and know too well what is owing to your Rank and Character, not to receive the Favour you are pleas'd to offer with all Submission; but must take the Liberty to acquaint your Lordship, that tho' under Misfortunes, I am a Gentlewoman, and have hitherto preserved my Reputation; so flatter myself, your Lordship has no other View in this Visit than Commiseration for the ill Fate that perhaps may have reach'd your Ears of the

Unhappy

Syrena Tricksy

Having dispatch'd this Epistle, the remainder of the Day was taken up in setting herself forth to the best Advantage, and consulting in what manner she should behave; as she thought it might give him an ill Opinion of her Sincerity afterwards, if she pretended to put herself upon him for a Virgin, she resolved to tell him the same Story she had done the Mercer, only with this Addition that her Husband died abroad, and by that Means she was cut off from any Hope of future Support from that quarter.

About six in the Evening came the expected Guest, who, struck with her Beauty and seeming Innocence by seeing her only *en passant*, was now quite ravish'd with her Charms; as he knew well enough however that she could not be ignorant of the Intention of the Visit, he made no great Ceremony, but came directly to the point; and she seeing his Humour was not to be dallied with, practised none of those Artifices to keep him in hand, which she had made use of to others: All she insisted upon was a Settlement for Life, but he stop'd her Mouth, by telling her he was under an Oath to the contrary, having been deceived by some, who after that Engagement had ill-treated him; and, said he, you, Madam, have much less Occasion than any of your Sex to desire it, since you may be certain your Charms will secure me constant while you continue to be so. Finding that nothing was to be done that way, she gave over all Speech of it, and told him she would then depend entirely on his Love and Honour. So a Bargain as it might truly be call'd, was struck up between them the same Night. He made her a Present of 50 Broad Pieces, and the promise of 10 Guineas per Week to defray common Expences.

Now was *Syrena* in high Spirits again, and her Lord was so fond of her, that she might have brought him almost to anything, if the Warmth of her Inclinations could have permitted her to content herself with his Embraces alone; but publick Affairs, or Pleasures of a different Nature took up so much of his Time, that she wanted a Companion in his Absence; and by keeping a great deal of Company, and those not of the best Sort, she soon enter'd into Intrigues in which her usual Cunning had not the least share: In fine, she became so free of her Favours, that she at length got the Disease common in such Cases, and without knowing it, made a Present of it to his Lordship: As Persons of his Quality cannot feel the least Disorder without having immediate recourse to their Physicians, he was soon informed from what source his Ailment proceeded; and as he had no Gallantries with any Woman since the Commencement of his Amour with *Syrena*, had no room to doubt if it were she who had done him this unwelcome Favour: He accused her with it in Terms, which made her know he was convinced of her Inconstancy, and tho' she here made use of every Stratagem to perswade him she was Innocent, all her Vows, her Tears, her Imprecations were of no Force, he quitted her, and told her, if it were not more for demeaning himself than any remains of regard for her, he should resent the Injury she had done him in a severer manner.

One would imagine she should, in so terrible an Exigence, have look'd back with Shame and Confusion on her past Conduct, but she appeared rather harden'd than abashed, when her Mother, who soon discovered the Truth, remonstrated to her the Folly and Madness of her late Behaviour—'tis possible the old Woman now began to repent the having train'd up a Child in that manner; but if she did, it was of no Service, since the other was too opinionated and too obstinate to take any Advice, but such as was agreeable to her own Inclinations. 'Tis certain, that tho' she at first taught her to ensnare, to deceive, and to betray, her Aim was to enable her by those Arts to secure to herself someone Man, by whom she might make her Fortune; and never imagined she would have run such Lengths, meerly for a precarious Dependance, or to gratify Desires, which when once indulg'd, bring on inevitable Destruction; but it was too late to reflect on what was past, and she forbore saying much to her, seeing the Violence of her Temper, and unwilling to come to a downright Quarrel, hoping she might still make some Conquest, that might be of greater Service than those she had lost; and her Condition now requiring Medicine rather than Reproof, she bent all her Cares for her Cure in the most private Manner; for which Reason she made her leave the Lodging she was in, and come to hers; where, by the Assistance of a skillful Surgeon and good Nurse, she was perfectly recovered in a short time.

But her Circumstances were not so easily repair'd as her Health had been; the Expences of her Illness had so reduced her, that she had scarce a change of Garments to appear in; in such as she had however, she took little Rambles about the Town, in hope of captivating some admiring Fool; but nothing offering answerable to her Expectations, she grew very much mortify'd, and began to fear she had lost the Power of pleasing, tho' not yet seventeen. No Necessities could almost be greater than what Mother and Daughter were now in, yet would neither of them think of betaking themselves to any honest way of getting a lively-hood. Those Relations who had formerly been kind to them, having heard something confusedly of *Syrena's* Conduct, had for a long time withdrawn their Bounties, so they were entirely destitute of all Assistance.

In this melancholy Posture of Affairs *Syrena* went one Day into the Park, not with the view of meeting any Adventure to her Advantage, for she was now quite hopeless, but meerly to indulge her Vexation—she sate down on one of the most remote and unfrequented Benches, and no body being in Sight, vented her Spleen in real Tears, mingled with Sighs, and ever and anon an Exclamation—What shall I do?—what will become of me? did she frequently cry, without being sensible she did so;—such was the Agony she now was in, she neither saw, nor heard the Tread of any Person approaching, till all at once she turn'd her Head, and found a grave old Gentleman, sitting by her on the same Bench. If it would not be an impertinent Question, pretty Lady, said he, I should desire to know what occasions such excessive Grief in one so young and beautiful? Overwhelm'd with Sorrow, as *Syrena* had been, she felt her Heart spring with Joy, at being accosted by a Person, who looked as if he had it in his power to redress her Grievances; so drying her Eyes, and assuming all possible Sweetness in her Countenance, alas, Sir, answered she, my Misfortunes are too great to be conceal'd; and as they are not fallen upon me through any Fault I have been guilty of, I need make no Scruple of declaring the real Cause, especially to a Gentleman, who tho' a Stranger, seems to have a Heart relenting to Distress. She then told him, that she had been married very young to a Gentleman, whose Friends having been disoblig'd on the Account of her having no Fortune, had sent him to Venice; whence, out of what they allowed him, he had always sent her something; but that being now dead, all her Support was lost; she having no Friends but a Mother, wholly unable to help her—adding, that she was a Gentlewoman, and had never been bred to any Business.

He seemed very much affected with her Story, but persuaded her not to give way to Despair; telling her, that the Ways of Providence were mysterious, and that frequently when things had the worst Appearance, good Fortune was nearest at hand—he talked to her in this Fashion for a considerable time, and asked her many Questions, to all which she answered with so much Sweetness and seeming Sincerity, that he grew very much taken with her; and among other Particulars, having enquired of her where she lived, and her Name, told her, he would make her a Visit, if she would give him leave; for, added he, it may be that I may think of something that will be to your Advantage.— You seem, Sir, replied she, too much the Gentleman and the Man of Honour for me to apprehend you have any Motives for this Offer, but meerly Pity for the Calamities you see me involved in; therefore shall think myself honoured in your Acquaintance. I assure you, returned he, I shall never give you any Reason to repent this Confidence; and when I see you next, and acquaint you who I am, I flatter myself the Character I bear in the World, will entirely rid you of all Scruples on my Account—in the mean time, continued he, you shall promise me to be chearful, and attend with Patience a Lot which may be happier than you at present see any Cause to expect. She replied, that she would do her Endeavour to follow the Advice of so worthy a Person—he then took his leave, and she went home a good deal more at Ease than she went out—her Mother was rejoiced at hearing what had befallen her, and cry'd out in a sort of Transport, *Syrena*, this is the Man will make you happy! not one Woman in an hundred makes her Fortune by a young Fellow—a young Fellow thinks himself upon a Par with any of us, be we never so handsome; but when once an old Fellow takes it into his head to fall in love, he will do everything, give everything to render himself agreeable—there is indeed a kind of boyish Love, which begins about sixteen or seventeen, and lasts till twenty or something longer, but then it wears off, and they commonly despise the Object afterwards, and wonder at themselves for having found anything in her to admire— from twenty to thirty they ramble from one to another, liking every new Face, and fixing on none—after thirty, they grow more settled and wary; and if they love at all, it is commonly lasting; but a Passion commenced between forty and fifty, is hardly to be worn off—'tis certainly strange, but true of that Sex, that amorous Desires grow stronger, as the power of gratifying them grows weaker, and an old Lover is the most doating fond Fool on Earth, especially if his Mistress be very young; for it is remarkable, that when a Woman is advanced in Years, I mean about Forty, she shall look more lovely in the Eyes of a young Man, than in those of one of her own Age, who at that time begin to grow fond of Girls, in so much, that I have known some forsake very agreeable Women, and take up with, nay, have been ready to ravish Creatures that have been Blear-ey'd, Hump-back'd, had pimpled Faces, and all for the Sake of dear Eighteen—so that while you are young, my Girl, chuse a Lover old enough to be your Father, and as you grow older, one who might be your Son.

With these learned Maxims did the old Jezebel entertain her Daughter, who stirr'd not out all that Day nor the next, in hope of the old Gentleman's coming; but he deferr'd his Visit till the third Day, either thinking it unbecoming to his Character to appear too hasty, or perhaps not altogether determined within himself how he should act when he did come.

At last he came however, and *Syrena* seeing him from the Window, ran to tell her Mother, on which they both took up a Work-Basket: *Syrena* seem'd darning a Cambrick Apron, and her Mother altering an old Velvet Mantelet. These Marks of good Houswifry and Frugality were very engaging to the old Gentleman; to find them thus employ'd gave him an advantageous Idea of their Modesty and Virtue, and he did not fail to give them those Praises he thought they merited.

After some few Compliments and preparatory Discourses; I have been thinking, said he, to Mrs. *Tricksy*, on the Account your Daughter gave me of her Misfortunes, and have been ever since very much affected with them.—I should be glad, methinks, to have it in my power to alleviate them; but the way I have to propose may not, perhaps, be agreeable to either of you. O! Sir, reply'd she, I dare believe you are too worthy a Person, to offer anything we should not approve of with Joy. You might think it an under-valuing of your Family, which I hear is very good, rejoin'd he; for your Daughter to undertake the Charge of a House, I do not mean the servile Offices of it; but to overlook the Servants, and see that they did their Duty.—She seems, added he, to have a Prudence above her Years, and I imagine would be very fit for such a Trust in every Respect. I am sure she would endeavour to be so, cry'd her Mother, if you, Sir, would do her the Honour to recommend her. She needs no other Recommendation than her own, answer'd he, since it is myself, who would put the care of my Family into her Hands. He then told them, that he was call'd Mr. *W——*; that he was formerly a Merchant, but having acquired sufficient for his Contentment, he had retir'd from Business, and took a House in an airy Part of the Town; that he was a Widower, had but two Sons, one of whom was married, and settl'd in the City, and the other a Student at Oxford.—So that continued he, I live alone, and should be glad of a Gentlewoman to eat with me, play a Game at Picquet in an Evening, and, in fine, be a Companion as well as Housekeeper.

Both the Mother and Daughter seem'd very much pleas'd with his Proposal, and left it to himself, what Consideration she should have for the Trouble she was to take; telling him that he should reward her as he found she merited. This he thought was acting like real Gentlewomen, and the Confidence they placed in him highly oblig'd him. It was agreed that she should come into his House, in the Station he mention'd, the ensuing Week, and he then made a Present of a Twenty Pound Bank Note to Mrs. *Tricksy*, for hers and her Daughter's Use till that Time.

After he was gone, *Syrena* communicated to her Mother some Fears she had, that he intended her for no other than a real Housekeeper; but Mrs. Tricksey told her there was not the least Reason for such Apprehension.—Thou silly Girl, said she, would any Man, take a Stranger like you into his Family without having a more than ordinary liking to her Person; and will not that liking produce Offers of a different kind, when he becomes more acquainted?—Perhaps, he has a mind to try how you will behave before he will discover his Inclinations; therefore it behoves you, indeed, to be very cautious—to keep a strict guard upon every Word and Look, and above all things to strengthen the Opinion, he now has of your Innocence and Virtue. But said, *Syrena*, if I should seem too rigidly honest, it might deter him from any Attempt upon me, and in time extinguish all amorous Inclinations, if he now has any for me. Not at all, reply'd her Mother; Men, especially rich Men, are apt enough to think their Wealth will conquer the most stubborn Virtue—beside have not I instructed you how to play at fast and loose, as I call it, with the Men—sometimes kind, sometimes reserv'd.—Coy when they're free, and Tender when they seem more cold; and all as if by Accident, and as if Design had not the least share in your Conduct?

Between Lessons for her Behaviour, and preparing things necessary for her Departure, the time was taken up till the appointed Day; on which he came in his Chariot, and conducted her himself to his House; where they no sooner arrived, then he had all his Servants call'd into the Parlour, and told them he had brought a Gentlewoman to be in the Place of their Mistress, and they must follow her Directions in everything. The Keys of all the Plate and Linnen were then deliver'd to her, and she took Possession of all, as tho' she had been Wife, or Daughter of the Owner of the House. As it was not thought proper her Mother should come often to visit her anymore, than when she was at Sir *Thomas L*——'s; they agreed *Syrena* should write whenever anything material occur'd; and that her Mother whenever it requir'd any Answer should send it by old *Sarah*, who still liv'd with her, and not trust to the Penny-Post. In three or four Days she wrote as follows.

Letter I

From G—Square
Thursday

Dear Mother,

I Cannot yet tell what to make of the old Gentleman's Designs: He uses me with more Respect than I could look for as a House-keeper, and with all the Freedom of a Relation; but speaks not the least Word of Love. He approves of everything I do, and has never found the least Fault; tho' God knows I am ignorant enough how to order the Affairs of a Family. I do my best, however, to please him; and every Morning as soon as I get up, write a Bill of Fare, and shew it him when he comes down to Breakfast; and I assure you he has told me more than once, that I have an elegant Taste; whether he is earnest or not, I don't know; and I am sometimes afraid he should think me too delicate, but I bring myself off: For Yesterday having set down Green Pease, are there any yet said he, pretty hastily, as I thought? yes, Sir, I reply'd, I saw some Yesterday, but they are dear; I set them down only to shew you, that I know they are to be had, if you should have a Fancy to any; for you see the second Course is full without them, and they may be omitted. You are very obliging, answer'd he, and I think may spare yourself the trouble of making any Bills of Fare hereafter, since you are so good a Judge yourself, of what would become my Table. I told him that I could not be easy, unless he saw how his Money was to be laid out: Well, said he, if it must be so; but, I believe, you'll seldom find me either add or diminish to what you shall contrive for me. I play'd at Cards with him last Night, till Twelve o'clock, and he had a Bowl of Rack Punch made, and set by us on a Dumb Waiter; but tho' he prest me very much to drink Glass for Glass with him; yet I begg'd to be excus'd, telling him I had a weak Head, and had never been accustom'd to drink anything strong.—Indeed, I could have drank the whole Quantity, myself; and you know how well I love that Liquor; but I tell you this, to shew you what a Command I have over myself—if he intends to make me either a Wife or a Mistress, I find 'tis necessary to give him a very high Opinion of me; for he is devilish wary and observing; so I must lead the Life of a Vestal, tho' cruelly against my Inclinations, till I have got the upper Hand of him; and then—but I won't build Castles in the Air.—

As soon as I know anything farther, I will write again, and am,

Dear Mother,
Your dutiful Daughter,
Syrena Tricksy

P.S. Just as I had finish'd the above, he sent for me to tell me Tomorrow is his Birthday, and he shall have his Son in the City, and his Wife, and several other Relations to dine with him; so bid me order a Dinner accordingly. I wonder whether I shall sit at Table or not, or what he will say of me to them.—Pray Heaven none of them know me.

ELIZA HAYWOOD

LETTER II

From G—Square
SATURDAY

Dear Mother,

Yesterday was, as I expected it would be, a very hurrying Day, we had a vast deal of Company indeed, and a very noble Entertainment I provided for them. A little before they came, the old Gentleman sent for me into the Parlour, and said, Mrs. *Tricksy* as I shall have so many People here to Day, and your Youth and Beauty may possibly occasion some Raillery, or if not some Conjectures at least that I dare say your Modesty would not willingly excite; I hope you will not take it ill, if I desire you to dine alone,—I say alone, for I will not have you dine with the Servants by any Means—I am sorry I did not think of bidding you invite your Mother to keep you Company—but it is too late now—when any other such Occasion falls out I shall be more considerate. I told him nothing could be more agreeable to my Inclinations than to avoid being seen by so many Persons to whom I was an utter Stranger, and not at present in a rank of Life to entitle me to such Conversation. As to that, replied he, you are Company for anybody; and when you have been here a little longer, it may be, I may introduce you; in the mean time you must be content. I made him a low Curtesy in token of being perfectly satisfied with his goodness, and was going out of the Room, but he called me back and said, I had like to have forgot to tell you that I insist upon it, that you order a Part of whatever you like best to be carried into your own Chamber, and not let anything come to your Table after it has been on mine—I have my Reasons, continued he, for this Injunction, and shall not be pleased if you do not observe it. I made him all the Acknowledgements so great a Mark of his Respect deserved from me, but would have declined accepting it till I found he was resolved upon it.

At Night after they were all gone, which was not till almost 12 o'clock, I went in to him to ask if Things had been ordered to his Satisfaction: Nothing could be more so, my pretty Manager, said he, with a Look that I thought had something very amorous in it, but I perceived he had been drinking pretty freely; so I asked a great many Questions on purpose to give him an Opportunity of opening his Mind, and I imagined he was going to say something two or three Times, but whatever it was he restrained himself, only as I was taking my leave he gave me a gentle pull by the Gown, and said, I must not omit making you a small Acknowledgement for the Care you have taken to Day, and put 5 Guineas into my Hand, and at the same Time kissed me with a good deal of Eagerness three or four Times, then push'd me from him as it were, and cried go your ways, you little Temptation you! I neither seemed frighted, nor yielding all the time, but affected a little Confusion, and once more wish'd him a good Repose: He did not call me back again, as I was in hopes he would; and this Morning at Breakfast he behaved to me no otherwise than usual; so whether he has forgot, or repented of the Freedom he took with me last Night, I know not, but it vexes me that he comes on no faster—I hate Suspence of all Things, and begin to grow weary of this dull insipid Life, yet I am resolved to endure it a little longer—I long to see you and have some talk about this Matter—I have never stirr'd out since I have been here, and I find it pleases him wonderfully to think that I love home so well—I am sure it would not be improper for you to come to see me some Day next Week, so if you don't hear from me before I shall expect you, who am,

Your Dutiful Daughter,
SYRENA TRICKSY

Her Mother came as she desired the *Wednesday* following, but *Syrena* having nothing of Consequence to inform her their Conversation is of no moment to the Reader. But on the *Monday* following she wrote a third Letter to this Effect.

LETTER III

From G—Square
MONDAY

I Have now the Satisfaction of acquainting you, part of the Secret which we so much wish'd to know is at last reveal'd—I will tell you how it came out.—Last *Saturday* Night I was sitting in the Parlour reading the Play call'd the *Conscious Lovers*, when the old Gentleman came home—I laid down the Book as soon as I saw him enter, which he perceiving, cried, don't let me disturb you—pray what is the Subject of your Entertainment, and then looking into it—O! the *Conscious Lovers*, continued he; this is accounted a very good Play—pray what's your

Opinion? I told him I was no judge, but it pleased me. So it does most People, said he, and indeed is a good Performance, but yet, methinks, there is somewhat in the Characters of Bevil and Indiana not quite agreeable to Nature.—The Gentleman is very generous, Sir, cried I; ay, replied he, and less self-interested than we Men are capable of being to the Object we love. I could not help looking a little surprized at these Words, and cried, I thought, Sir, that Love had inspired Generosity. Yes, answered he, it does inspire what is commonly called Generosity, we are ready enough to give everything, and do everything for the Person we love; but then that Passion that makes us so liberal, makes us also desire something in return—we cannot content ourselves with rendring happy the Object of our Affections, but languish for something more than Gratitude.—Indeed, pretty Mrs. *Tricksy*, continued he, taking my Hand and pressing it, these are all Romantick Notions; and as charming as you are, you will never find a Man who loves you for your own sake alone. I cannot expect it Sir, said I, without I had as much Merit as Indiana: You have as much, and perhaps more, replied he, at least in my Eyes, than ever Woman had—yet sweet Creature, my Heart is far from feeling any Platonick Sentiments for you.

Here I pretended to be in a vast Confusion, and hung down my Head as ashamed to hear him talk so—don't blush, said he, whatever Liberty I may take in thought, my Actions shall never be such as shall give you cause to fear me—I am an old Man now, and cannot hope to make myself anyway equal with your Youth and Beauty—then perceiving I made no reply, but seemed more and more ashamed—is not what I said too sad a truth for me, pursued he? I know not what you mean Sir, answered I, but I am sure the Goodness you have been pleased to shew me, deserves all the regard I can pay you. Well, well, resumed he, that's all I expect at present—But it may be that in time I shall grow more covetous and over-rate my Services in hope of greater reward—but come let us go to Cards, for I find you are more at a loss in Conversation of this kind than any other. I made him no Answer, but rung the Bell for a Servant to set a Table, and we went to play—I won every Game, for I found he lost to me on purpose, and was a gainer above 50 Shillings—when we left off, you know how to conquer me every way, said he, but I must have a small Revenge, and kissed me with an infinity of warmth—I cannot help loving you, hc cried, two or three times over, but you must not be angry, then went up to his Chamber without staying to hear what I would say. I went soon after to Bed, but could not sleep all Night for thinking of his odd Behaviour—yesterday Morning at Breakfast he look'd more than usually earnest upon me, and after being silent sometime, ask'd how long it was since I heard of my Husband's Death; the Question a little startled me lest he should happened to have been told something of me that had made him suspect the Truth of what I had said; but I disguised my Confusion well enough, and answered about eighteen Months. I wonder, said he, you have not been tempted to make a second venture: On which I replied with a Smile, that it must be something very extraordinary indeed, that could tempt me to enter again into a State which had cost me so much disquiet. Indeed, pursued he, there are so manythings requisite to make a happy Marriage, that if Passion did not get the better of Reason much fewer would engage in it than do. These Words were uttered with a Sort of Coldness, which I knew not to what Cause to attribute: Nor has he since spoke to me but on ordinary Things—I very plainly see he loves me, but for what End I know not, and fancy that he has also a kind of struggle within himself what he shall do concerning me—I wish therefore that there could be something contrived to put him in fear of losing me.—I would have him think I had some offer of Marriage much to my Advantage, if such a Thing could be artfully brought about—I wish you would consider of it, and help me out—it would certainly make him declare what he would be at sooner than he seems willing to do at present; and my Patience is almost worn out I assure you. For tho' I live well, want for nothing, and am treated with the greatest Respect; yet you must be sensible, my Youth and Inclinations are not to be satisfy'd with such a sort of Life; besides I should be glad to be at some certainty—I shall not fail to acquaint you with everything that happens, but in the mean time think of my Request, and believe me,

Dear Mother,
Your dutiful Daughter,
Syrena Tricksy

Letter IV

From G—Square
Thursday

Dear Mother,

My old Spark comes on a little, tho' not so fast as I would have him.—He both din'd and supp'd abroad Yesterday, and did not come home till very late—I would not go to bed, thinking he would take it as a Mark of my Respect; and so, indeed, he did, and seem'd mightily pleas'd with it, tho' he said he was sorry to have been the cause of breaking my Rest—He was in a very gay Humour, and I found had been drinking pretty hard, tho' he was not what one may call fuddled neither: He told me, they had been very merry with him upon my account, and will need have it, said he, that I should not have made choice of so young a House-keeper, if I had not lik'd her for the Management of other Affairs besides those of the Family—So, continued he, I am at a loss what Reparation to make you for the Scandal the living with me is like to bring upon you. O, Sir, answered I, putting on a very troubled Countenance, I fear these are People who envy me the Happiness of your Favour, and invent this Ridicule on purpose to make you part with me.—No, no, no such matter, said he, they rather envy me.—But let their Designs be what they will, if you ever leave me, it shall not be my Fault—I am only afraid you will grow tir'd of an old Man's Company, and I shall lose you by your own Inclination. I then assured him, with an Earnestness that came pretty near to Tenderness, that I thought my Lot extremely blest in being with him—that I looked upon him as my good Angel—that nothing could be more perfectly satisfy'd than I was with my Condition; and would not quit his Service, for any Consideration whatever. He was so much transported with what I said, that he catch'd me in his Arms, and held me there for some Minutes, then kiss'd me, and cry'd, My dear Creature, you shall never quit me—I could not live without you.—Good God! what a Neck, what Breasts are here! added he, putting my Handkerchief back with one Hand, and laying the other upon my Breast—I drew a little back—but he pull'd me to him, and forc'd me to sit by him on a Couch, where he took me about the Waste, add kiss'd me till my Breath was almost gone; I struggled, and begg'd him to desist; but he pursuing what I found gave him an Infinity of Pleasure; I fell a weeping, and cry'd, O, Sir, do not compel me to call back the Words, I just now said, and make me fearful of the Lot I so lately blest—I am unhappy, it is true; but I am virtuous, and will be always so. He seem'd very much affected with the counterfeit Terror I was in, and wiping away my Tears with his Handkerchief, forgive me, said he, I told you there were times when we Men could not command our Passions—but I will never do anything to your real Prejudice—I love you too well for that—indeed I do—love you much more than you imagine—and—here he stop'd, and after having paus'd a while—But

I won't keep you any longer from your Repose, goodnight, my dear Creature, permit me one more Kiss, in token of Forgiveness, with these Words he gave me another tender Embrace, tho' less vehement than the former, and so retir'd.

Now, my dear Mother, I think this looks as if he had kind of Inclination to make me his Wife, only the Fear of the World's Censure, and the Dissatisfaction it would be to his Children, hinders him from coming to any Resolution about it.—I am almost sure, if he could be made to believe I refused some good Offer for the sake of living with him, Jealousy and Gratitude would spur him up to a Determination in my Favour—'Tis worth trying for, at least—so I beg you'll think on't—I know you have a good working Brain, and can do anything when set about it. Consider that if I get him for a Husband, we are both of us made forever—but I won't urge you any farther, I dare say, you will not neglect what shall be as much your own Interest, as that of,

Your Dutiful Daughter,
SYRENA TRICKSY

To this her Mother return'd the following Answer by old *Sarah*.

FRIDAY

Dear Syrena,

I Have been considering of what you wrote, of hastning the old Gentleman to come to a Resolution, ever since your first Letter.—There are several Stratagems; but that which seems most likely to prevent Suspicion, is my writing to you, concerning some Person that has been in love with you a long time, and has a good Fortune; if you can anyway contrive that my Letter might fall into his hands—but this is a nice point, and must be manag'd very delicately, or it would Ruin all.—Old Men are naturally wary, and apt to think everything has a Design in it; and if he should once imagine you went about to deceive or trick him, he would never endure you more—So without you can order it so, that he may see what I write, without your knowing he does so, I would not advise you to attempt it—I cannot but say, if it could be done cleverly, it would bind him very much to you, and also oblige him to declare himself sooner than, perhaps, he otherwise will—Therefore weigh the matter well, and when you have resolved, let me hear from you again, and you may be sure of all the Assistance in the power of,

Your affectionate Mother,
Ann Tricksy

Letter V

From G—Square
Monday

Dear Mother,

I Have been racking my Brains ever since I received yours, for some expedient to assist my Project; but can think of nothing, but what may give room for Suspicion, and I am of your Mind so far, that the least doubt of my Sincerity would ruin all: However, I would have you write in the manner you speak of, and send it to me. Some Opportunity may happen, that I do not yet foresee—In the mean time I must acquaint you, that he now makes no Scruple of telling me he loves me, whenever we are alone; but he has never yet put the Question to me, and all his Words are so ambiguous, that I cannot, for Soul of me, discover what he would be at; nor dare I ask him for fear of offending him.—If he means honourable, it would be making myself cheap to seem to imagine he could have any other Designs upon me; and if he intends me for a Mistress, to give any Hints that I thought myself deserving of being his Wife, would look too presuming, and perhaps at the same time, hinder him from making any Proposals at all; so that I am in a strange Dilemma.—However, since my last to you, I have met with something that a little sweetens the tastless insipid Hours I used to pass here—I mean, the Thoughts of one of the most agreeable pretty young Fellows I was ever acquainted with—Don't be alarm'd; for I have taken such care, that the old Gentleman can never come to the Knowledge of the matter—I met with him by accident the other Day, when I went to buy somethings for our Cook, who had begg'd that favour of me—It happen'd to rain while I was abroad, and believing it would be but a small Shower, I stood for shelter under a Porch, my Spark came there also, we fell into a Chat, and a mutual liking of each other carry'd us into a Tavern—We pass'd two or three Hours as agreeably as any two young People equally gay, could do—In fine, this one Interview made us know we were fitted by Nature for each other, and, I hope, we shall always continue to think as we now do.—I told him I was a young Widow, had a small Fortune, and an unblemish'd Reputation.—Swore he was the first Man, with whom I had ever made a false Step, and that I liv'd with my Mother.—So 'tis to your Lodgings I have appointed him to direct a Letter; which pray let me have the Moment you receive it, and only say to the Messenger that brings it, that I am abroad; but you will deliver it to me as soon I come home, and for the rest leave it me; I know how to order it, so that if he sends never so often, he will never find out, that I do not live with you. Now, methinks, I see you all in a tremble, for fear this Intrigue should undo me with the old Gentleman; but I beg you will make yourself easy, for I will engage it shall never be discover'd, and as for anything else you ought not to blame me; consider I have liv'd like a Nun for three Months, including the time I was sick.—So dear Mother don't think of chiding my Pleasures; but do your best to help forward my Interest: Let me have the Letter I mention'd, and wrote with as much Artifice as you can; if I can find no plausible Occasion to make use of it, it will be only a little Labour lost, which I flatter myself, you will not grudge to

Your obedient Daughter,
SYRENA TRICKSY

P.S. If any Letter comes from my dear new Gallant, I beg you'll send it me the same Moment, for I am half mad with Impatience to see him again.

This Epistle was answer'd as soon as receiv'd by Mrs. *Tricksy*, with another inclos'd, which on first opening, *Syrena* flatter'd herself had been from her young Spark; but her Conjecture this time deceiv'd her: They were both from her Mother, the one for her private Perusal, and the other for the old Gentleman's, if it could be brought about. That which contain'd her real Sentiments was to this Purpose.

Dear Child,

You see I have not been idle in complying with your Desires: I had wrote a Letter, such as I think proper to excite the old Gentlemen to be more hasty in his Resolution, before your last came to my Hand; and will add nothing to the Cautions I before gave you on that Score; because I think you do not seem to stand in need of it. I wish there were no greater Danger of your Inadvertency on another Score; and that the Inclination you have for the young Lover, may not be fatal to our Designs on the old One.—However, if any Letter or Message comes from him, *Sarah* shall bring it directly.—I neither blame, nor wonder at your liking a pretty Fellow; I would only have you keep it ever in your Thoughts, that you never were in so fair a Way of making your Fortune as at present, and not do anything that might even give a Possibility of reversing it.—Remember the Mercer who was so good a Friend to you; and Mr. *D*——, who I don't know but might have married you, if the Discovery of your Amour with Capt. H——, had not ruin'd you with him.—'Tis true that was an Affair of my own promoting; but, however, it should be a Warning to you.—Nothing has contributed more to establish you in the good Opinion of Mr. *W*—— than your staying so much at Home; and if your Passion for this new Gallant, should take you too frequently abroad, who knows what Jealousies, such a Change in your Behaviour might occasion.—He might send to watch where you went, and with what Company; or if he should not go such Lengths, may you not chance to be seen by some Person or other who may inform him of it.—A thousand Accidents may happen, which is not in the power of Prudence to prevent. But I am very sensible, who reasons with a Person in love, talks to the Wind. So I shall say no more than to remind you, how much it behoves you to be upon your guard.—I am far from being an Enemy to your Pleasures; but would have you a true Friend to your Interest; and that you may be so, is the sole Aim of,

Your indulgent Mother,
ANN TRICKSY

The enclos'd contain'd these Lines.

Dear Syrena,

I Have for these three Weeks been strangely persecuted with the Importunities of Mr. *Smith*; I would not have you vain; and you know very well, have always caution'd you against putting too great a Faith in Mankind; but I think that I may venture to say, he loves you with a Passion rarely to be found in one of his Sex, especially in these Days. He behav'd like a Mad-man, when he first heard you had left me; but when I refus'd letting him know where he might see you, or direct a Letter, his Desperation encreas'd to such a Degree, that I trembled for the Consequence. He would not believe but you were married, and on my protesting you were not, seem'd more outrageous than before;

whether it was that he was under some Apprehensions you had dispos'd of yourself a worse Way, or that he thought I deceiv'd him, I cannot tell: He is still extremely melancholy, and I could not forbear letting you know the Proofs he gives of his Sincerity; tho' I don't expect you will ever be perswaded to reward it. Yet after all, *Syrena*, 'tis strange you should be so blind to your own Interest.—If ever you design to marry again, 'tis not to be expected you should have a better Offer as to Fortune; and as to Character, 'tis unexceptionable.—His Person is agreeable enough, I think for any Woman to love; and you know very well, he might have had Wives long ago, who are accounted pretty Women, and handsome Portions.—But if you would not resolve to have him, when you were under such Distresses as you have been; I can neither flatter him, nor myself, that you will do so now, when you want for nothing, and have such a good Master. However, Child, Service is no Inheritance, a thousand Accidents may happen to throw you out, and our Friends who you found were weary enough of assisting us before; will do nothing at all if you persist in this obstinate denying the good that Providence seems to point out for you.—I dare answer even Mr. *W*—— himself, would very much blame you if he knew the Story; and as he has pity'd you, and been so kind to take you into his House, would rejoice to see you have one of your own; which tho' mean in Comparison with his, is yet what no Gentlewoman need be asham'd to call herself the Mistress of—therefore, *Syrena*, I would have you consider seriously of it—'Tis very childish and silly in you, to cry you can't love him; such an honourable and constant Affection as his for you, would bring you to love him in time, especially, if it be true as you say, that your Heart is not prejudic'd in Favour of any other Man: But I have so often press'd you on this Score, and with such small Success, that I think 'tis lessening my Character, as your Mother to say anything farther; nor had I done it now, but the poor Gentleman extorted a Promise from me to write.—I wish you never may have Cause to repent the Ingratitude, you are guilty of to him, or the Injustice you do yourself; which, with my Blessing, is all at present from,

Your affectionate Mother,
ANN TRICKSY

P.S. Your Aunt longs very much to see you, I believe, to talk to you concerning Mr. *Smith*; so if you continue resolv'd to refuse his Offers, it will be best for you not to go.

ELIZA HAYWOOD

Syrena had scarce time to consider on these Letters, before old *Sarah* return'd with another, which had been left for her by a Porter, at Mrs. *Tricksy*'s Lodgings, while she was abroad. This was the dear expected Billet, she had entreated her Mother to be so careful of, and contain'd these Lines.

Dear Creature,

You must be too sensible of the Pleasure your Conversation affords, not to believe whoever has once enjoy'd it, must languish for a second Interview.—You told me other Engagements would detain you for some Days, so have deferr'd Writing as long as my Impatience would permit; but, now I hope my charming *Syrena* will no longer hold herself from me. I shall be at my Cousin's Tomorrow about four; and earnestly entreat nothing may disappoint me of a Pleasure, I till then shall live in the most eager Expectation of, who am,

Lovely Widow,
Your sincerely devoted
Friend and Admirer,
HARRIOT MANLY

The Reader will doubtless be at a loss for the meaning of this Epistle; but never had *Syrena* given a greater Proof of her Cunning, than in the Management of this Intrigue; to prevent his making any Enquiry after her at Mr. *W——*'s; she had told him, that being left a very young Widow, without any Children, she lived with her Mother, and to give him a good Opinion of her Mother's Virtue, and Care of her, as well as to hinder him from knowing she had deceived him in the Place of her Abode, she told him he must never visit her; and when he wrote, as she desir'd he would often do, to appoint a Meeting, it must be in a Woman's Name, whom she said she would pretend to have commenced an Acquaintance with, at the House of some female Friend. She made him believe also, that whenever he desired to see her, he must send the Day before at least, for that Mrs. *Tricksy* was so fearful of her entring into any Correspondence with a Man, that she made her be denied to all that came, unless Relations, or such as she had an Intimacy with herself, nor ever gave her any Letter till she had first open'd it, and examin'd the Contents; so that, said she, you must not be surprized, if the Messenger you send with your Billets, never finds me at home; but when she reads them, and supposes them wrote by a Woman, which I shall take care to mention before, as a mighty agreeable young Lady, who has taken a Fancy to me, she will make no Scruple of permitting me to come out.

Thus having settled everything, as she thought, beyond a Possibility of Discovery, she flew to the Rendezvous, his Cousin's as he term'd it, which indeed was no other than a common Bagnio, with a Pleasure which attends the Gratification of any Passion whatever; but more especially that which more or less is inherent to all animated beings, and for that Reason called the most natural.

To keep Mr. *W*—'s Servants from suspecting anything by old *Sarah's* coming twice in one Day; she pretended her Mother had been taken suddenly ill, after she sent the first Message; and that the second was to desire to see her immediately; she back'd this Excuse with so much seeming Grief, that nobody had the least doubt of the Truth of what she said; and the old Gentleman coming home before her, and being told the Story, was very much concerned at the supposed Indisposition of so good a Woman.

After passing four or five Hours in a manner perfectly agreeable to her Inclinations, she came home in a Hackney-Coach about Eleven o'clock, with a Countenance, conformable to the melancholy Visit she pretended to have made. Mr. *W*—— not being gone to Bed, enquired concerning her Mother's Condition, in a most tender and obliging Manner; and the Hypocrite dropping some well dissembled Tears, answered, that she had found her so ill, that she had ventured to intrude on his Goodness so far, as to promise to go again the next Day; by all Means, cried the worthy Gentleman, and I will send a Physician with you. I most humbly thank you, Sir, replied she, but my Mother has one, who has always attended our Family, and is acquainted with her Constitution. Well then, resumed he, I desire she may want nothing else proper for her;—you shall go to her as early as you please in the Morning;—and pray, continued he, give her this, with my best Wishes for her Recovery; with these Words he put five Guineas into her Hand. *Syrena* affected to receive this Favour with an equal share of Gratitude for his Goodness, and Grief for the Danger of a much esteemed and lov'd Parent. Their Conversation, till he retir'd to his Chamber, was that Night wholly taken up with Mrs. *Tricksy*; Mr. *W*—— imagining any gayer Subjects would be little pleasing to a Person, under the Affliction *Syrena* seemed to be.

She went early in the Morning in reality to her Mother's, and gave her the five Guineas, with a full Recital of the Occasion of that Present; Mrs. *Tricksy* was very well pleased with her Management of his Intrigue, and they both laughed heartily at the ease with which a Woman beloved, could impose on a Man of the best Understanding. They breakfasted together, and then *Syrena* took her leave, and went to the Bagnio, having promised her young Lover to dine with him there, in Confidence, that the Story she had to tell Mr. *W——* would render it no Difficulty for her to come out.

In fine, she carry'd on the Deception of her Mother's Illness, for above a Fortnight; so that in all that time, she never miss'd seeing her Gallant one Day; nay, staid with him two whole Nights, under the Pretence that her Mother being expected to expire every Moment, she waited to pay the last Duties of a Child. Mr. *W——* was always extremely indulgent, sent her ten Guineas more, and some Phials of rich Cordials, which they drank together with a good deal of Mirth and Ridicule on the Donor.

But now Mrs. *Tricksy* began to think it was high time for her to be on the mending hand, lest a too long counterfeiting, might at length raise some Suspicion; and also, because that while she was supposed to continue in this dangerous way, *Syrena's* Affair with Mr. *W——* seemed to stand still, that Gentleman having forborn his amorous Chat, out of Decency to her Grief; but the young Wanton would scarce have been prevailed upon by her Mother's Remonstrances, to have given any Intermission to a Conversation so pleasing to her, had she not been compelled to it by the young Gentleman, who told her a Business of the most urgent Nature called him into the Country. Her Grief at parting with him was really sincere, and she omitted nothing that she thought might detain him, but tho' he had an extreme Compassion for the Agonies she threw herself into, yet there was a Necessity he should quit her at least for a time; she made him swear to write to her, and urged to know the exact Place to which he was going; but it being highly inconvenient for him to comply with either of these Requests, he yielded not to the one without a mental Reservation, and wholly deceiving her as to the other; and told her a County as distant as North from South, from that he went to, which, together with his having passed with her by a feign'd Name, render'd it altogether impossible for her to hear anything of him, tho' on finding he did not write to her, she afterwards strenuously endeavoured.

Well, Mrs. *Tricksy* recover'd, and *Syrena* at home as before this Adventure; the old Gentleman began to renew a Conversation, which with a good deal of Pain to himself, he had so long stifled in his Breast, what he said to her on the first Opportunity, will be seen in the following Letter, wrote by her to her Mother.

Letter VI

From G—Square

Dear Mother,

My old Gentleman, tho' I allow him to be the most compassionate and best natur'd Creature in the World, had certainly a great Share of Self-Interest in the Concern he express'd for your imagin'd Sickness; in the first Place it deprived him of my Company for the most part, and when I was with him, the Sorrow that it was necessary for me to assume, obliged him to restrain the Dictates of his Heart; but now he thinks you out of Danger, he seems to give a loose to his gayer Inclinations. I never go out, nor come into the Room, without being saluted by him in the most tender manner, which I suffer as a Person who has no Aversion to such a Behaviour, but what proceeds from my Modesty; and also, as one who thinks herself too much obliged to his Bounties, not to refuse any Freedoms that are consistent with Virtue; so that by behaving to him in a tender affectionate manner, I give him room to think I am far from having any dislike to his Person; and by a seeming Struggle within myself, and half Sentences thrown in a propo, whenever he takes any extraordinary Liberties, to think my Gratitude alone hinders my Resentment.—I can see he is more and more charm'd with me, and I flatter myself will soon break his Mind to me—that is, let me know what it is I am to expect from him;—Yesterday at Breakfast, as I was going to fill the Tea-pot, the Man being out of the Room on some Occasion, he snatch'd the Kettle from my Hand, no, my Dear, said he, tho' I am an old Man, I know better the Regard that ought to be paid Persons of your Sex, especially such a one as you, to suffer that. O! Sir, cried I, you are too good, and forget I am but your Servant—I never have treated you as such, replied he; and should be sorry you should ever think of me as Master—methinks it is more natural, pursued he, smiling, for you to look upon yourself as my Mistress, than my Servant. God forbid Sir! cried I, I do not mean naughtily, rejoined he, but as the Mistress of my Affections; and indeed if you imagine I can place them on any other Woman you do me wrong. He had perhaps added something more which might have explained what he meant by the word Mistress, but the officious fool of a Footman came unluckily in and prevented any farther Discourse on that Head. I saw him no more till Night, for he dined abroad, and then at Supper, as I was helping him to a Bit of Rasberry Tart; I think, said he, these same Pies are a kind of an Emblem of the Passion of Love, where the sweet and sour seem to strive with each other, and both together are so grateful to the Palate that one cannot wish to be without them; what do you think, pretty Mrs. *Tricksy*, is not the comparison just. Indeed Sir, answered I, the little Experience I am Mistress of, does not qualify me to form any Sort of Judgment on that Passion; and as for Tarts I seldom eat any: Yet you have loaded my Plate, cried he, and may I not also infer from thence that you would wish to see me taste all the Sweets and Sours alone, while you are unmoved at either? I carried on the Raillery, and affected not to conceive he had any other meaning in what he said than meerly literal. But he soon obliged me to be more serious, by telling me, that he would have me henceforward look upon him as a Man whose very Soul was devoted to me. These Words so uncommon with Men of his grave and sober Deportment, and utter'd with the greatest Vehemence, made me regard him with some Astonishment, and indeed render'd me incapable of replying for some Moments. During my Silence he took hold of my two Hands, and pressing them between his, said with a deep Sigh, O! that there were less disparity between us! I then perhaps might have been happy! I know not, Sir, answered I, anything that can be wanting to your Happiness; but this I know, that I should be very miserable if anyway the cause of giving you one Moment's Pain—you are, Sir, my Patron, my Friend, my Benefactor, my Guardian Angel, and when I cease to acknowledge your generous Goodness, may my Ingratitude be punish'd with some dreadful Mark.—Hold, dearest Creature, interrupted he, I know thy sweet, thy tender, grateful Soul— but—but what cried I, for Heaven's sake, Sir, inform me in what I am wanting—in nothing, said he, that's in your power—yet I could wish there were a possibility of—don't ask me what—it is irremediable, and becomes me not to mention—I cannot do it yet at least—goodnight— with these Words he rose from the Table, called his Man, and went immediately to Bed.

Now Mother to what can this Inconsistency of Behaviour be imputed, but to an excess of Love and to some Obstacle within himself that makes him fearful of indulging it—'tis strange he conceals it in this manner, but there is no getting it out of him, till he pleases himself—

something sure extraordinary will be the Event, but what I know not; when I do, you shall not be a Moment in ignorance. I am

Your Dutiful Daughter,
SYRENA TRICKSY

LETTER VII

From G—Square

Congratulate me, my dear Mother, congratulate your happy Daughter—all my Fears and my Suspence are over—Mr. *W——* has at last brought himself to confess an honourable Passion for me—He will soon come to acquaint you with it, and then make me his Wife—O! how I shall roll in Riches and Plenty—How I shall indulge every Wish—enjoy every Pleasure, and despise all Restraint—The very thought of what I shall be is Extasy and Transport—O! that the joyful Time were come—I'll make him settle a Jointure upon me, get possession of his Plate and Jewels, turn them all into ready Money, that the Heirs may not come upon me, and then break the old Fool's Heart, and shine out the Belle of the Town—but I must tell you what brought this fortunate Catastrophe about, and of what infinite Service your Letter concerning the imaginary Mr. *Smith* was to me—you know 'tis more than a Week since I wrote to you, nor indeed had I anything pleasing to acquaint you with—Mr. *W——* after the Conversation I repeated in my last grew more than ordinarily thoughtful—spoke but seldom, and when he did, it was either on Family Affairs, or other Subjects altogether foreign to Love—I was very uneasy in my Mind, but appeared before him as usual, tho' indeed I began to imagine I had small Hopes, not that he either gave me any Words or Looks that testified he had conceived the least disgust against me; but his whole Carriage seemed to tell me, he had conquer'd himself so far as not to make me any offers of being in a better Situation with him than he had placed me in at first. But when I thought my good Fortune farthest removed from me, it happened to be nearest—as you shall hear—He came home last Night about an Hour before the Time of lighting Candles, and asking for me; one of the Servants said he believed I was in my own Room, and was coming to call me; but Mr. *W——* told him it was no matter, he was going up, and would speak to me above. He found me in a musing Posture, leaning my Head upon my Arm, and indeed discontented enough at his late Behaviour: What, Melancholly, pretty Mrs. *Tricksy*! said he, as soon as he came into the Chamber. I was a little surprized at seeing him there, tho' very well pleased, especially as he seemed more chearful than he had done for several Days. Not at all, Sir, answered I, but there are Times when one cannot help being more than ordinarily serious. There are so, resumed he, nor am I sorry to see you so now, because I am come to talk with you on a very serious Matter. With these Words he made me take my Seat again, which I had quitted on his coming in, and placing himself in another Chair as close to me as he could, I have been reflecting for some Days past, said he, on the Pleasure your agreeable Company has afforded me ever since you came into my House, and how forlorn I shall be whenever you leave it. I hope, Sir, said I, that I have been guilty of nothing that should lay you under a Necessity of obliging me to leave it? No, no, cried he, far from any such Thing—I have already told you, and I now repeat it, that it will be yourself alone can ever take you from me—but, my dear Creature, I should be unreasonable to desire a young Person like you, to live always in the manner you now do—there is no doubt but you will have offers of bettering your Fortune—and you will marry—here he ceased; and I took the Opportunity of telling him that I preferred the Honour of living with him as I now did, to being the Wife of any Man in the World: And on his seeming to question my Sincerity in that Point, as he well might; I endeavoured to convince him by all the Asseverations befitting a modest Woman to make; but he stopped my Mouth with a Kiss, and told me, that tho' what I said was vastly obliging, yet he could not think I could be so much an Enemy to myself. I then thought I had a fine pretence for shewing him your Letter, and running to the Buroe brought it in my Hand, and presenting it to him, Sir, said I, tho' I should die with blushing to make you the Confidante of such an Affair, yet I cannot help doing it, to clear myself from all Deceit—so beg, Sir, you will give yourself the trouble to read this—He made no reply, but did as I desired, and I could see while thus employed a good deal of Impatience in his Eyes. As soon as he had finished the perusal—he gave me the Letter again, and ask'd me several Questions concerning Mr. *Smith*; to all which I gave him such ready and natural Answers, that he had no room to imagine I was amusing him with a fictitious Story. After he had nothing farther to inform himself of, he told me he should be extremely happy if he could be sure that I refused Mr. *Smith*, meerly because I chose to live with him, to which I replied to give him still a greater Opinion of my Sincerity, that I could not say I had refused

Mr. *Smith* altogether on his Account, because I had resolved not to marry him before I ever had the Happiness of living with so excellent a Master, but that since I had enjoyed so great a Blessing, and had the Experience of his Goodness; not only Mr. *Smith*, but all Mankind beside were perfectly my Aversion—He seemed overjoyed to hear me speak in this manner—kiss'd me, and embraced me a Hundred Times I believe, before he was able to make me any Answer; at last, well but, my dear Love, cried he, there yet remains one Proof of your preferring my Society above all others of my Sex, and if you deny to give me that, you must give me leave to disbelieve all others?—in fine, you must consent to put it out of either of our Powers to part—you must be my Wife. Judge, my dear Mother, how much I was transported at these Words, but I concealed it under a modest Surprize, and hanging down my Head, said, you are pleas'd to sport, Sir, with your unworthy Servant. No my Dear, reply'd he, the Offer I make you is not only serious, but well weigh'd, the Result of a long Consideration—the first Moment I saw you, I entertained a Thought of it, but was willing to wait till some Proofs of my Friendship had in part compensated for a Disparity of Years—what say you then?—Is it possible for you to yield that Youth and Beauty to the Embraces of an old Man, without Reluctance?—Can you love me as a Husband? answer me, continued he, with your usual Sincerity; if you can love me as a Husband (I again repeat it) I shall be happy—if you cannot, I will endeavour to make you so, either with any other more agreeable to your Years; or if you chuse a single Life, by settling an Annuity upon you; on this I replied, that his excessive Generosity had entirely overcome all my Timidity and natural Bashfulness; and that since he was so good to make me three Offers, the first, and infinitely the best, must be my choice. It would be endless to repeat what he said on this Occasion; had I been a Queen, and he my Subject, rais'd by me to a Throne, he could not have express'd greater Joy. I did not fail, however, to represent to him, the Fears I had, that his Sons and his other Relations, would not be satisfied with our Marriage; but he seem'd to slight all I urg'd on that Head, and told me, he had not liv'd so long in the Word, to place his Felicity in other People's Opinions; and as for his Children, they were too well acquainted with their Duty to repine at anything he thought fit to approve.

Thus is everything agreed between us, and we shall come this Afternoon or Tomorrow to acquaint you with the Affair, and ask your Consent for our Marriage, which he intends to solemnize as soon as a new Coach and Liveries can be got ready; for he resolves it shall be in as much Splendor, as if I brought him a Fortune equal to his own. Well, after all, he is very good to me, but 'tis all to please himself; and I shall follow his Example, in doing everything to please myself—O! I shall live a rare Life—but I must conclude, for I expect him to Dinner every Moment. Dear Mother rejoice for the good Fortune of

Your happy Daughter,
Syrena Tricksy

P.S. I send this by a Porter, for fear the Penny-Post should not have come time enough to apprise you of our coming, for you to get everything in order—once more, farewell.

Mr. *W*—— having determined, and indeed desired nothing more than to make *Syrena* his Wife, fulfill'd the Contents of her Letter to her Mother, in going to ask her Consent in form, which it would be needless to say was readily granted; after this he made no Secret of his Intentions, but declared to everybody that he was going to alter his Condition—accordingly he bespoke a fine new Coach, ordered rich Liveries for his Men, and made some Additions to his Furniture—omitted nothing that he thought might shew his Regard for his designed Bride, who he took abroad with him in his Chariot almost everyday, either for the Air, or to buy things for her Appearance as his Wife.

His eldest Son, tho' doubtless not well pleas'd in his Mind, was oblig'd to treat her with all imaginable Respect; and his other Relations contented themselves with condemning his Conduct among themselves, and did not pretend to dissuade or to argue with him on a thing, which they found he was absolutely bent upon.

Mr. *W*—— resolving however to make all his Family as easy as possible, in this unexpected Change of his Condition, sent for his Son from Oxford, in order to settle a handsome Fortune upon him before his Marriage; and thereby prevent any Apprehensions he might otherwise have had, of being a Sufferer by a future Issue.

By some Accident the Letter was delayed at the Post-House, so that the young Gentleman came not so soon as expected, and arriv'd at his Father's but the Evening before the Day prefix'd for the Wedding; but happy was it for the whole Family he came when he did, as will presently appear.

The old Gentleman happening to be at home when he came, took him directly to his Closet, and entertained him there a considerable time, telling him, that tho' he was about being married a second time, as it was to a Woman, whose Virtue and Good-Nature would rather make her an Advocate for his Children, than the contrary; none of them ought to repine at his Conduct in this Affair. The Son assur'd him with a great deal of Submission, but how much Veracity I cannot take upon me to determine, that he did not think it became a Son to call his Father's Actions in Question; and that whoever he had made choice of, he, for his part, should not have the least Reluctance, in paying her all those Duties she could expect from a Son of her own, if it should please Heaven to favour her with any; which, added he, I sincerely wish. Well said, my Boy, replied Mr. *W*——, I assure thee, thy Disinterestedness shall lose thee nothing—I sent for thee to Town, for no other Purpose, than to make over to thee now, what I intended for thee at my Death; and as near as my Marriage is, thy Settlement shall be made before it—I will immediately send for my Lawyer, and the Writings shall be drawn Tonight—in the mean time you shall see the Lady, I shall make your Mother Tomorrow Morning, and who has been sometime in my House—so that, my dear Boy, continued he, it is not one whose Humour I am unacquainted with, that I am going to make my Partner for Life; but one, whose uncommon Virtues and Goodness I have experienced, and am perfectly convinced of; with these Words he led him the way to *Syrena's* Chamber, who rose to receive them with her accustomed Sweetness, and well affected Innocence. But on his approaching to salute her, presented by his Father, never was so odd a Meeting—the young Gentleman started back as if he had seen a Gorgon, nor could the reality of that Fiction have been more shocking to him. *Syrena* lost all her Presence of Mind, and gave a great Shriek— Mr. *W*—— seem'd thunderstruck at seeing them so—in fine, never did three People appear in a greater Consternation—all of them were in a profound Silence for some Minutes—during which time, the Father cast his Eyes from *Syrena* to his Son; then from his Son to *Syrena* again, as expecting to be inform'd either by the one or the other, of what at present seem'd so mysterious. At last, is this the Lady, Sir, you intend for my Mother? said the young Gentleman, with a faultring Voice: Yes, answered Mr. *W*——, I told you so before I brought you here; have you anything to object against my Choice? or have you, *Syrena*, continued he, turning to her, any Motives for being dissatisfied with this young

Man? No, Sir, reply'd she, by this time having recollected what was best for her to do, but he is so very like a Brother I once had, that the first Sight gave me a Surprize, I could not presently overcome; and you, Madam, cry'd the young Gentleman, are so like a Mistress of mine, and I doubt not but of half the Town beside, that I could not with Patience look on you as the Person intended for my Father's Wife. How! cry'd Mr. W——; with an angry Tone! your Pardon, Sir, reply'd his Son, putting one Knee to the Ground; that I presume to own before you the Folly of my Youth—on any other Occasion I could not hope Forgiveness; but here 'tis absolutely necessary—yes, Sir, I confess, that without your Permission I came about a Month past to London, indeed to give a loose to some Extravagancies, which I will never henceforward repeat—in my Rambles I met with this Woman—we fell into Conversation—she affected in Words to appear a modest Woman; but her Actions were altogether the reverse—in fine, Sir, she is no other than a common Creature—he was going on, but *Syrena* had now no Card but one to play, and interrupted by saying—O! barbarous Aspersion! O! that I had died, rather than lived to hear my Reputation thus cruelly traduced—and to my Face—by one I never saw before, Heaven is my Witness, tho' the likeness of Faces at first deceived me—with these Words she fell into Fits, nor could all the old Gentleman's Endeavours bring her to herself;—the Servants were called in to assist, but she no sooner seemed to recover from one Convulsion, than she fell into another; insomuch, that all present, excepting the young Gentleman, who had experienced her Artifices, imagined she would die.—Mr. W——, who yet knew not what to make of what his Son had said, was too generous and humane to let her perish for want of proper help, even tho' she should be proved guilty of all she was accused of; order'd the Maids to take care of her, and sent immediately for a Physician. Having given these Directions, he withdrew into another Room, taking his Son with him; he questioned him very closely concerning the time of his Acquaintance with *Syrena*—the Places where they met, and every Particular that he thought might inform him of the Truth; for tho' he could not entertain so bad an Opinion of the young Gentleman, as to imagine he had forged this Story on Purpose to break the Match; yet he could not tell how to bring himself to think he could have been so grosly imposed upon by a Woman, whose Temper, Inclinations, and Conduct, he had observed with the utmost Strictness, ever since she came into his House.

I believe the Reader by this time guesses the Truth, and that the Son of Mr. *W*—— was no other, than the last Gallant she had; and for whom, to meet with the greater Freedom, she had pretended her Mother's Indisposition. This Article it was, which more than anything convinced the old Gentleman, that the seeming modest *Syrena*, was the infamous Wretch his Son had described her; for not only her Name, and the young Gentleman's positiveness as to her Person, but the times of their being so frequently together, agreeing exactly with those of her pretended Visits to Mrs. *Tricksy*, at length opened his Eyes to the Villany of both Mother and Daughter; and tho' he had loved the fair Deceiver, with too much Tenderness to endure this Detection without Pain, yet he thought himself bound to thank Heaven for so timely a Discovery of her Guilt; which, had it happened but a Day after, had made him from the most happy, the most miserable Man on Earth. The Frailty of his Son also deserved his Pardon; not only because of the Temptation that had misled him, but likewise, because he could no other way have received a Confirmation of her Crimes. After much Talk upon this Head, Mr. *W*—— burst out into an Exclamation, Good God! cry'd he, what a Fiend must this be under an Angel's Form! She knew herself a Prostitute to the Son, yet would have marry'd the Father! Monstrous incestuous Strumpet! Hold, Sir, interrupted the Son, compound as she is of Leudness and Deceit, let us not wrong her—She knew not till this Hour, I was your Son; for the better to conceal my being in Town from you, I pass'd with her, and wherever I went, by a different Name. But she is now no longer ignorant of that Secret, reply'd the Father, yet would she have persuaded me, you either had mistook her for someother, or had Malice enough to asperse her without Cause.—O what Punishment is great enough for such a Wretch! The Physician that Moment came in and broke off their farther Discourse, by telling them the Lady was dangerously ill—that he had prescrib'd for her, but much fear'd the Success. Young Mr. *W*—— shook his Head in token of Contempt, and after he was gone could not forbear saying, some severe things on the Gentlemen of that Profession; but in this he was guilty of some little Injustice; for the Truth was, that tho' *Syrena's* Fits were only counterfeited, yet the Surprize she had been in, and the Apprehension which immediately follow'd of losing that great Fortune, she had but a few Minutes before thought her self secure of, gave her real Agonies, which put her whole Frame into such Disorders, as, joyn'd with the artificial ones she put on, might well puzzle the Physician's Skill.

The old Gentleman, however, not being able to suffer so vile a Creature under his Roof, made her be told she must quit his House; and that if she were as ill as she pretended, her Mother was the most proper Person to take care of her; and if she were not, it would be doing her a good Office, to send her where she would no longer have any need of feigning.—She begg'd with Floods of Tears to see him, protested her Innocence, and left nothing undone to deceive him once more, and throw the Odium of all upon his Son's Dislike of their Marriage; but he was now too well assured of her Baseness, and remain'd inexorable to all her Messages; so that with a Heart full of Rage, and a Tongue full of Imprecations, she took an everlasting leave of a House she was so near being Mistress of, after having been obliged to resign all the fine Jewels that had been presented to her when intended for a Bride.

It would be needless to repeat the Distraction that both Mother and Daughter were involved in at this sudden turn in their Fate; neither could it be pleasing to a virtuous Ear to hear those shocking and prophane Exclamations, which 'tis easy to suppose Persons of their abandon'd Principles make use of, when anyway cross'd by Providence in the Pursuit of their wicked Designs. It must be confest, indeed, that *Syrena* had very ill Luck in being so often on the very Point of compassing all her Avarice, Ambition, or Pride could aim at; and then, by the most unforeseen Accidents, thrown from the height of all her Hopes. And here, methinks, it is worth remarking, how the indulging one Vice, destroy'd all the Success she might have expected from the other; for had she been less leud, her Hypocrisy, in all Probability, had obtain'd its end, at least, in this last Pursuit it had done so: But it is generally the Fate of such Wretches, who, while they go about ensnaring and deceiving all they can, to be themselves ensnar'd and deceived, either by others, or their own headstrong and ungovern'd Appetites.

In a short Space of time they again began to feel the want of what before they had profusely lavished. *Syrena* was not idle in spreading her Nets; but none as yet had the ill Fortune to fall into them, and the first that did, proved little to her Advantage, as well as to his own.—Their Acquaintance began in this manner.

She was walking one Day through the Strand, equipp'd for Adventures in a modish Dishabillee, with a little Hat on her Head, and a Cane in her Hand, when she saw at a Bookseller's Door a Gentleman, whom she no sooner cast her Eye upon, than she imagin'd fit for her purpose: He was in the prime of his Age, well proportion'd, genteel, and had somewhat in his Looks that denoted him to be of a more than ordinary amorous Constitution: She perceived he had his Eye upon her as she past, and the Street being pretty dirty, and the Kennel of a great breadth just in that Part, she either had, or seem'd to have an Occasion to cross the way—The Coaches driving backward and forward very fast, it being Term time, made her often obliged to stop, and return, then go on again, and all this opposite to where the Gentleman stood; so that he had a full Opportunity of seeing and admiring all the pretty Airs she put on; the Distress she affected, in not being able to prosecute her little Journey, gave him a Pretence of offering to assist her—He step'd hastily to her, and taking her under the Arm with one Hand, and with the other extending his Cane to keep off the Horses, like a true Knight-Errant, lifted his Dulcinea over the muddy Brook, and safely bore her to the farther Shore—when arriv'd, she made a Curtesy, and thank'd him with so bewitching a Softness in her Eyes and Voice, as wholly compleated the Conquest she desired.—He entreated Permission to attend her to the Place where she was going, and telling her it was altogether unfit a Lady of her Appearance should walk the Streets, without some Person who might guard her, both from the Insults of the undistinguishing Populace, and the Dangers also, such uncommon Charms might lay her under, from Men of more elevated Rank—To these obliging Offers and Compliments, she made him such Answers, as gave him an Opinion she had been brought up in high Life, and had conversed only with People of the greatest Fashion; but seemed to decline accepting his Protection, any farther, saying there was no need of his giving himself that Trouble, since she was only going home, and there were no more such ugly Places to pass over in her way thither—adding, that she was already under too great an Obligation to his care to consent to receive any Addition; since conscious there was nothing in her Conversation capable of compensating for his Loss of time. This naturally drew a great many fine things from him; nor would he be perswaded to quit her, tho' she often desired he would; but how sincerely the Reader may imagine.

They walk'd on together talking in this manner, when just as they pass'd by a Tavern, he perceiv'd her Colour change, and a sudden Trembling seize all her Limbs, which, as I have in many Instances explain'd, she could bring on herself whenever she found it necessary for her purpose—He was surpriz'd and troubled at this Alteration, and was about to ask the Cause, when she catch'd hold of his Arm, as if to save her self from falling; roll'd her Eyes with a half dying Languor, then closed them, and appear'd quite fainting.—He little suspecting all this for Artifice, was extremely frighted, and supporting her as well as he could, led her into the Tavern, where having call'd for Hartshorn and Water, she soon became reviv'd, but seem'd not presently to recollect her Senses enough to know where she was, or what had happen'd to her; but when she did, O Heaven! cry'd she, how strange an Accident is this!—Bless me, how can I answer to myself or the World, being in a Tavern with a Gentleman, I never saw before!—or how, Sir, can I ever retaliate the Favours I have received from you this Day! Besides the common Compliments on such Occasions, as thinking it an Honour to be anyway serviceable to a Lady who seem'd so much to deserve it, he being a Man of great Wit and Gallantry, added a thousand infinitely more elegant and obliging;—his natural Complaisance and Respect to the fair Sex, being now heighten'd by a Passion he had never felt before, tho' frequently what is called a Lover, he expressed himself in a manner, which might have charm'd a Woman less susceptible than her he now address'd—'Tis certain she was transported with him, and had no need of feigning to make him see his Behaviour had made an Impression on her.—All her Subject for Dissimulation, was to pass it on him for the first, which she was too perfect a Mistress of, not to succeed in.

On his asking her if she had been accustomed to these Faintings?—No, Sir, answer'd she, calling to her Cheeks a most becoming Blush, I never before knew what it was to lose my Senses, even for a Moment—few Women, I thank Heaven, are blest with a better Constitution, or a more easy and chearful Mind.—I know not what to think of the Accident that has just now happen'd, nor to what Cause to impute it—and were I inclin'd to be superstitious, should be apprehensive it was the Fore-runner of some very extraordinary Event. If we pay any Regard to History or Tradition, said the Gentleman, whatever happens out of the common Course of Nature, as your Disorder, Madam, seems to have been, has ever been look'd upon as a Presage of some unexpected Change in Fortune.—But you have not the least Reason to imagine it an ill Omen; since it would be calling in question the Justice of Providence, to suppose it had created an Excellence like yours, for anything but to give and receive the highest Good this World at least can bestow.—But I suspect, continued he, with a Sigh, that as so many Charms cannot be without an adequate Number of Adorers, it was the Commiseration for Woes, you cannot bring yourself to redress, that overwhelm'd your gentle Heart, and for a Moment depriv'd you of yourself.

Here he ceas'd, and look'd stedfastly on her with a kind of enquiring, yet imploring Eye; and she who easily saw into his Thoughts, and found with Pleasure the Influence she had gain'd, made no immediate Reply; and when she did, assuming a half Smile, by the manner of your talking, said she, I fancy you take me for a Maid—but, Sir, I have been married, and as I was so without feeling for him who was my Husband, much less any other Man; those Emotions, Lovers talk of, I can not have much Compassion for what I always look'd on fictitious, and meer Words of Course.—How, Madam, cry'd he, have you been married, and are so long a Widow, as to be out of Mourning, at your Years? On this she told him the same Story, she had done her former Lovers; only with this Difference, that as she knew not his Circumstances, it seem'd most proper to keep him ignorant of hers, till time should discover, if it were best to affect Poverty or Riches.

After having past about two Hours with him; she thought it time to pretend being perfectly recover'd; nor could all his Persuasions, nor her own secret Inclinations, induce her to stay longer.—She could not now, however, refuse giving him leave to go home with her, which he did; and on her telling her Mother before him, the Civilities she had receiv'd from him; he was treated with the utmost Respect and Gratitude, by the seemingly good Mrs. *Tricksy*. And from her as well as *Syrena*, had Permission to wait on them again.

When he was gone, and these Ensnarers had Liberty to consult together, judging by his Garb and Appearance, that he was a Man of a Fortune sufficient to maintain her as a Wife; they set all their Wits to work to make a Husband of him; for in the way of Discourse to them both, he had declar'd himself neither married nor under any Engagements of that kind.—Schemes were therefore contriv'd between them to delude him; which they afterward had but too much Opportunity to put in Practice; and which his own Temper and Circumstances contributed to assist in.

He was a Gentleman whose Father had been possess'd of a plentiful Estate, but by giving too much into the Gallantries of the Times had dissipated it so far, that at his Decease he had not an Acre to bequeath; and young Mr. *P—* was only left with small a Fortune in Money, for which the last Acre had been dispos'd of: His Education had been the best for a Man of an Estate, but the worst for a Man of

Business: He had too much Pride to descend to anything for Bread, which he thought unbefitting his Birth; and tho' he had many powerful Friends, whose Interest might have procur'd him a Place at Court, or a Commission in the Army, either of which he would glady have accepted, whenever such a Thing was in Agitation, some cross Accident interven'd, and disappointed his Hopes; when they seem'd nearest the Accomplishment.—Several Years having past over since the Death of his Father; and nothing succeeding according to his Expectations, his little Stock of Money almost exhausted, and Years coming on, for he was now turn'd of Thirty; he could think of nothing to retrieve himself but Marriage.—He was, therefore, on his Acquaintance with *Syrena*, looking out for some elderly Widow or Maid, whose Substance might support him in the Eve of Life, in a decent manner; and as he was a Man perfectly agreeable both in his Person and Conversation, 'tis not to be doubted, but he might easily have succeeded in that View, had he not unhappily met with this fair, and more base Deceiver, whose Arts engross'd his whole Attention, on herself, and render'd him incapable because unwilling, to apply where his good Genius call'd him.

He imagin'd by *Syrena's* Appearance, and the manner in which her Mother and she liv'd, that she must have either a good Fortune in her own Hands, or a Jointure; and tho' he was enough infatuated with her, to have marry'd her without a Shilling, could his Affairs have admitted of it; yet the Belief, that she had sufficient for them both, was no small Spur to his Inclinations. With the view therefore of making his Addresses to her, did he visit her the next Day; where everything he saw, serving the more to confirm him in the good Opinion he had conceiv'd of their Circumstances; for they took care to put on the best Outside; he after two or three Visits more declar'd himself a Lover. *Syrena* receiv'd his Suit with the greatest Shew of Modesty; but blended with a certain Languor in her Eyes, which gave him to understand, as if against her Will, that she felt the highest Satisfaction on it.—Everytime he entertain'd her on this Topick, she grew less and less reserv'd, and at last confess'd, that she lov'd him from the first Moment she beheld him; and that it was wholly owing to the Emotions he had occasion'd in her; that she fell into those Disorders which gave Rise to their Acquaintance. How pleasing are the Thoughts of being belov'd by one who seems worthy of being lov'd! Mr. *P——* thought himself the happiest of all created Beings; blest in the purest and tenderest Affections of the most beautiful, most engaging, and most virtuous of her Sex; and one who had also a handsome Competency at least, to make smooth the rugged Road of Life. Tho' he was by Nature a Man of very warm Inclinations, and had been the Destruction of many fine Women's Virtue and Reputation; so great was the Respect he bore *Syrena*; that tho' he had unnumber'd Opportunities he never took the Advantage of any of them, or approach'd her with Liberties beyond a Kiss, which considering her Constitution, and the real liking she had to him, was not, perhaps, so agreeable to her as he imagin'd.— He all this time, however, never came directly to the point, and tho' he courted her on honourable terms, and she had acknowledged the greatest Passion for him, he had not press'd the Consummation of his Happiness; had not entreated her to fix the Day that should give her forever to him.—This very much surprized both Mother and Daughter, and made them begin to fear there was some Mystery in his being so silent on that head; and having consider'd on what means would be best for obliging him to explain himself, Mrs. *Tricksy* one Day, when *Syrena* on purpose had left the Room, took an Occasion to tell him, that as she found he and her Daughter had settled their Affections on each other, she hoped he would not think it an improper Question if she desir'd to be inform'd of some Particulars relating to his Fortune. On which he seem'd a little confounded; but answer'd, that his Estate at present did not exceed four hundred Pounds per Annum; but that he expected more on the Death of a Relation. Well, resum'd Mrs. *Tricksy*, four hundred Pounds a Year frugally manag'd, may keep a little Table for a time—Mr. *P——* thought he had now an Excuse for expressing a Desire of knowing in what manner *Syrena* was left in her Widowhood; his Ignorance of that having been, indeed, the cause he had not been more eager for the Knot being ty'd; for tho' he lov'd her with an Extremity of Passion, he had no Notion of living with a Wife in a mean and penurious manner. Madam, said he, in answer to Mrs. *Tricksy*'s last Words, my Estate is much too small to maintain your Daughter in a fashion worthy of her, and I should be asham'd to be too much indebted to a Wife's Purse: I would, therefore, indeavour to bring my Kinsman to add something before his Death to what I at present enjoy. If you can do so it will be well, reply'd Mrs. *Tricksy*, but if not, you must be content—perhaps when you are marry'd and Children come, he may be prevailed upon.—In the mean time, you may make some small Settlement out of what you have upon my Daughter.— Gladly, Madam, cry'd he, and whatever the young Lady is possess'd of, shall also be settled on herself. This was enough to let her see he expected a Fortune with her, and as it was impossible to deceive him in that point, thought best not to attempt it; but to seem entirely open in what could not be conceal'd, that he might the more readily believe those things in which she had it in her power to impose on him. Sir, said she, what I have to tell you will be a certain test of the Sincerity of that Affection you profess.—I do assure you, *Syrena* has at present no Fortune; but lives dependant on me who have a tolerable good Jointure, and is all that is preserved out of a large Estate her Father once enjoy'd; but which, at my Decease goes also to an eldest Son—Not that she will always be a Beggar—she is set down six thousand Pounds in the Will of a rich Cousin, who by the Course of Nature cannot live many Years, being now more than Ninety.—Several others also of our Kindred have promised to leave her handsomely; so that, as I observ'd before, if you both live frugally for a while, you may hereafter indulge what want of Fortune, at present, will not suffer you to enjoy with Prudence.

Mr. *P*——found a shivering at his Heart from the time Mrs. *Tricksy* had said her Daughter was no more than a Dependent on her; but he conceal'd the Shock it gave him as much as possible, and told her, he was only concerned, that he had not more to lay at *Syrena's* Feet.

Notwithstanding all his Efforts to behave with the same Gaiety as usual, he could not conceal from the piercing Eyes of *Syrena* and her Mother, his inward Discontent; and reasoning upon it after he was gone, they both were of Opinion he would not marry without a Portion, which was not a little Disappointment to them both, as they doubted not the Truth of his being possest of some Estate, if not altogether so much as he pretended.

He, on his part, when the Hour came in which it was proper for him to retire, went home to his Lodgings with an aking Heart: He loved *Syrena*, too well to be able to live without her in any tollerable degree of Peace, and the Impossibility of maintaining her as a Wife, made him pass the Night in the most grievous Aggitations—He curs'd Fate and his Friends, whose Endeavours to get him a Place had been unsuccessful; for as he doubted not the Truth of what Mrs. *Tricksy* had told him concerning the six thousand Pounds, and other Legacies, he thought if he could anyway have supported her till that time, he might very well venture to marry her—but as things stood now with him, that was entirely out of the Question, and how to proceed he could not determine.

He went to visit her the next Day, however, and several succeeding ones as before this Eclaircissement had been made; but tho' he could not forbear talking to her as a Lover, he mention'd not the least Word of Marriage, which confirming *Syrena* and her Mother in their Conjectures, that he intended no such thing, made them resolve to push the matter home; but in what manner they could not yet determine; and were thinking of various Stratagems, without being able to fix on any, when Fortune presented *Syrena* with an Adventure, which furnish'd her with one, that, besides being agreeable in itself, promised Success.

She was walking cross the Park one Morning, after having breakfasted with a Friend at Westminster, when she saw a Gentleman go before her, whose Shape and Air she fancy'd she was not unacquainted with—She, therefore, mended her Pace, and tho' he went not slow came up with him, and pulling her Hat as low as she could to conceal her Face, if it should chance to be any of those she had reason to avoid, look'd full on him as she past, and found it was *Vardine*, the Man who had triumph'd over her Virgin Beauties, and betray'd her Innocence, if a Creature so early bred up in Wiles, can be said to remember she ever had any. It presently came into her Head, that he might be of Service in her Designs on Mr. *P——*, and accosted him with a Tap on the Arm with her little Cane.—He started and turned to her taking her at first for one of those Ladies of Pleasure who frequent that Place; for he knew her not immediately, being grown fatter and somewhat more plump, tho' far from fat; but she soon by her Voice, and discovering her Face more fully, let him see who she was—He was a little confounded at first, and was beginning to make Excuses for his Behaviour; but she would not suffer him to go on, telling him she had forgot and forgiven all that was disagreeable to her in his Conduct—that she was now glad to see him, and had a Favour to ask of him, which it would cost him nothing to grant—He took this as a sort of Reproach for the little he had done for her; but made her no other Answer, than that he should rejoice in an Opportunity of obliging her with anything in his power. After some Conversation relating to their former Intimacy, they adjourned to a Tavern, where finding by him that he was still but a Lieutenant, and had as little Money to spare in matters of Gallantry as ever, she attempted not to impose on him in any Shape, affected not Virtue, nor refused, on his desiring it, a renewing of those Endearments he before had experienc'd from her, tho' then given with more Artifice than she now took the Trouble to put in practice—She told him she was endeavouring to draw in a Gentleman to marry her, and that if he would assist her, he should command her in everything.—He readily comply'd to do anything she desired on that Score, and thought he owed her a greater Service, if in his power, for the Favours she had conferr'd on him.—She carry'd him home to Dinner, and having presented him to her Mother, and told her his Name, soon reconciled her to him, by informing her also, what he was to do for her; they then all three enter'd into a Consultation, and as he was a graceful young Fellow and well dress'd, it seem'd probable, that the very sight of him would create a Jealousy in Mr. *P*——, that might serve to quicken his Love; it was, therefore, agreed upon, that he should stay till the other came, which was generally about the Hours of six or seven—and then take his Leave with a seemingly dejected Air.

Vardine acted his Part as naturally as they could wish, and Mr. *P*—— made no doubt but he had a Rival, which, as he truly loved her, was no small Addition to his Inquietudes—He complain'd of it to *Syrena* in the most tender Terms, and she confest, blushing, that indeed that young Officer had made Pretensions to her almost ever since her Widowhood; but that he was always her Aversion, and that having been oblig'd to go into the Country to his Regiment, she had hoped to have been rid of his Importunities, and was sorry to find he still continued his Passion for her; but, said she, I had not seen him today, if by Chance I had not been at the Window when he knock'd, and am resolved to be deny'd to him henceforward, if he comes ever so often—be easy and satisfy'd, therefore, continued she, for as I loved him not when my Heart was wholly unengaged, 'tis impossible to endure him now, so full as it is of your Idea. The believing Lover appear'd transported with Joy and Gratitude; and had it not been for the Thoughts of not being able at present to make so excellent a Woman his own, his Extasy had been beyond all Bounds.

Some few Days after this they contrived it so, that when Mr. *P*—— was in the Dining-Room with Mrs. *Tricksy* and her Daughter, a great Sound of Voices was heard below, and the old Deceiver feigning a Surprize, open'd the Door, as to listen what it meant, having stood a Moment, Heavens! cry'd she, 'tis Capt. *Vardine*! he is quite outrageous on your being deny'd to him—I must go down myself, and put a stop to the Clamours of his Despair—With speaking this she ran hastily out of the Room, and the Door being purposely left open, Mr. *P*—— heard him say—I have nothing wherewith to accuse the cruel Charmer, nor the happy Gentleman I am told she has made choice of—I only would beg once more to see her—to take my last Farewel, and die before her Eyes. Mrs. *Tricksy* seem'd expostulating with him; but he continued his Exclamations for sometime, and *Syrena* pretended the utmost Terror, lest he should force his way up Stairs, and there should be a Quarrel between him and Mr. *P*——; at length, however he departed, and Mrs. *Tricksy*, return'd, full of a well-counterfeited Concern for his Condition.

To refuse a Man who lov'd her with such an Excess of Passion and unweary'd Constancy, they thought would lay a kind of Obligation on Mr. *P*——'s Honour, as well as his Love to make her his Wife; but to strengthen her Claim to him they also had recourse to another Artifice, which was this:

They had several worthy and good Relations, as has been before mention'd, who had formerly been very kind and beneficent to them; but some Whispers concerning the Conduct of *Syrena*, which the manner in which she was supported without following any Business, served to confirm, having reached their Ears, they had not seen either her or her Mother for a long time; but on this Juncture, that crafty Woman ventur'd to approach them, saying, that her Daughter was now about being married to a Gentleman of an Estate, and that there wanted nothing to hasten the Marriage, but their vouchsafing to own her as a Relation, without which, continu'd she, he may imagine she has been guilty of some Mismanagement, and break off. To retrieve the Character, therefore, and settle in the World a young Person ally'd to them, the greatest Part of them consented to visit her; and now there seldom past an Evening, without his seeing some or other of his intended Wife's Kindred: They all approved highly of his Person and Behaviour, and he was invited to all their Houses by turns, which, not knowing how to avoid accepting, he went with *Syrena* and her Mother: The Fashion in which they lived, and the Entertainments they made for him, would have convinced him, if he had not been so before, that she was no mean Person. But all this served only to make him more unhappy, by reflecting, that he had acted dishonourably, by pretending to have what he had not; and that he appear'd guilty of Ingratitude, by not doing what, as his Affairs were, he had not power to do, without bringing to the utmost Misery, both himself and the Person he loved.

No Offers yet being made by him, of bringing the Matter to a Conclusion, Mrs. *Tricksy* and her Daughter began to despair of ever compassing their point; but to ascertain themselves of the Truth, if possible, they try'd one more Expedient in the following manner.

Pretty early one Morning as he was dressing to go out, the Servant of the House where he lodged, told him, a Lady desired to speak with him. He was a little alarmed, imagining it a young Creature with whom he had commenced an Amour, before he saw the fatal Face of *Syrena*, and who he knew was with Child by him; as his new Passion had render'd him wholly neglectful of her of late, he doubted not but she was come to reproach him, and endeavoured to prevail on the Servant to say he was not at home: How can I do that, Sir, said she, when I have already told the Lady you were? Pish, cry'd he, can't you pretend you were mistaken, and that I went out without your seeing me—as they were arguing, *Syrena's* Impatience at being made wait so long, with a little mixture of Jealousy, that someother Woman might be with him, made her fly up Stairs without being ask'd; he was agreeably surpriz'd to find it was she, and begg'd a thousand Pardons for not coming down to receive her. I have no Reason, said she, to be offended at your want of Ceremony; for as I did not send up my Name, I believe I was the last Person you could think of, that was come to disturb you. He was beginning to make some Compliments on the Favour she did him, but she put a stop to them, as soon as the Maid had left the Room, by saying, the Affair I come upon deserves not these civil things.—I am come, continued she, bursting into Tears, to forbid you our House—you must see me no more—my Mother has resolved it, and is prepared to tell you so at your next Visit—I thought the News would be less shocking from my Mouth; and therefore in spite of all the Considerations that might have restrained me, am come to take my everlasting leave;—and to tell you, that tho' I cannot think you love me with that Tenderness you have profest, you are too dear to me, for me to be able to resent anything you do, and that you ever will be so to the last Moment of my wretched Life.

These Words, and the manner in which they were spoke, touched him to the very Soul,—he was ready to keep her Company in Tears; and tho' he did not absolutely weep, his Eyes were full, and it was not without great Difficulty he withheld the swelling Grief from falling down his Cheeks;—ah, Madam, cried he, what is it you tell me?—what can have made this sudden Alteration in your Mother's Sentiments? that, replied she, which ought to have had the same Effect on mine—your Deceit in pretending to love me only for my Person and Mind, when in reality you regarded nothing but the Fortune you supposed me Mistress of. Here he made a thousand Asseverations to the contrary of what she accused him of; and that no Woman in the World, though endowed with all that could glut the Avarice of the most sordid Man, could have the power to alienate his Affection from her; and concluded what he said with a solemn Vow, never to marry any other, unless she first should lead the way; to this she made no Answer, but Sighs, and he resumed his Protestations; had I Millions, said he, I would devote them all, with myself, to the Service of the charming, the adorable *Syrena*; but as the little, the very little I am at present Master of, is insufficient to give her even ease in Life, is it not a greater Proof of Love, to restrain the burning Wishes she has inspir'd me with, and delay my Happiness till Fate shall put it in the power of one of us, to make Marriage comfortable, than to desire she should be Partaker of my abject Fortune?

Syrena was too penetrating not to see into the Fallacy of this Argument, but as she was resolved to pin herself upon him anyway, she forbore to urge the Matter farther, and said, I should readily agree with you; that it is better to wait till the Death of this old Impediment of my Happiness, shall make me Mistress of my Fortune, but my Mother will never be brought to think as we do—she presses me to marry the young Officer, and though I am resolved never to yield to that, and could sooner die than suffer the Embraces of any but him, to whom I have given my Heart; yet I must, terrible as it is to me, forbear your Sight and Conversation, till better times—if you can be constant in Absence— and preserve your Heart for me, as I shall do mine for you, we may hereafter find a Recompence for our present Pains. This Mr. *P——* was ready enough to consent to, but could not tell how to bring himself to think of not seeing her till the Time should arise, of claiming the Performance of her Promise; and he expressing the impossibility there was for him to live without her Society, she aimed not to render him more satisfied on that Head, but pretended that whatever she had said, she doubted not but he would soon hear she was no more, when she no more enjoyed his Presence.

Nothing could be more tender than their Conversation; but he still persisting in his first Resolution of not marrying yet a-while, she fell into violent Fits, the People of the House were called up, but as she seemed a little recovered, withdrew—she then wept, and hung upon him with Agonies, such as threatned Distraction;—he kiss'd, embraced, said all he could to comfort her, and these Endearments continuing for a long time, rendered both, according to all Appearance, in the end forgetful of themselves, and sinking into each others Arms, they enjoyed the Pleasures of Matrimony without the Ceremony. But *Syrena*, whose every Word and Look during the whole time of her being with him, was studied Artifice, and before concerted with her Mother, seemed so shocked at what she had done, that she begg'd he would that Moment run his Sword through her Heart; for Life after the Loss of Honour, cried she, would be a perfect Hell—he endeavoured to reconcile her to an Act, which he said could not be criminal between two People, whose Souls were already married, and who had resolved never to receive any other Idea, than those with which they were at present fill'd—she began by Degrees to seem convinced by his Reasons, but told him, that after what had happened, she could not think of being absent from him even a Day—that she now looked upon him as her Husband, and conscious of her own Integrity, regarded not what Opinion the World might have of her Conduct—and in fine, said she would live with him as a Mistress, till Circumstances should admit of her being made a Wife.

An Offer, such as this, from a Woman of her supposed Modesty, could not but surprize him—he took it however as a Proof of the most exalted and disinterested Passion that ever was—but when he reflected, that to support her as a Mistress, would be little less inconvenient than maintaining her as a Wife, it very much puzzled him—but he loved her, and that overcame all other Considerations; she staid with him at his Lodgings—shared the same Bed, and they lived together in every Respect, as if they had been married.

So full an Enjoyment did not in the least abate his Tenderness; and tho' after she had been with him some few Days, he was told by Persons who happened to see her at his Window, that she was a Woman of an infamous Character, and made up of Deceit, he looked upon it all as Malice or Envy, and even quarrelled with the dearest Friend he had on Earth, for but seeming to doubt of her Sincerity.—Have I not Proofs both of her Love and Honour, cry'd he, such Proofs as never Woman but herself ever gave, nor never Man but me was ever bless'd with?—O! she is all Charms, both Mind and Body! till I knew her, I knew not what real Happiness was, and vainly searched for it in various Pleasures; but in my dear *Syrena* is all that's excellent compriz'd.

Those who loved him, pitied and lamented his Infatuation; and those to whom he was Indifferent, ridicul'd it—all who knew his Circumstances stood amazed, that a Man of so fine an Understanding in other things, should neglect all Opportunities of making his Fortune, dissipate the little Substance he had left, and devote his whole time to a Woman, who, had she been as much an Angel, as she was really a Devil, had it not in her power either to serve him or herself.

In the mean time, *Syrena* was not idle in providing against a Change, or more properly speaking, for a Change; she liked Mr. *P*—— indeed, but liked Interest better; and frequently pretending to go to some or other of her Kindred, where till they were married, it was improper he should accompany her, went abroad in hope of meeting with something more to her Advantage, than she now began to suspect he could ever be; and continued with him but till she could be better provided for.

Her expensive way of living, and the Pleasure he took in indulging her every Wish, together with the Shame he found in himself, whenever he attempted to let her know how ill he could afford it, had exhausted his little Stock of Money in a short time—he then borrowed of all who would lend—and went in Debt wherever he could—so that soon he found himself without either Money, Friends, or Credit; shunn'd by his Acquaintance, and in Danger of a Gaol—this made him very melancholy, but did not make him love the less—he cursed his Fate, but bless'd the Wretch who had undone him—she took Notice of the Alteration in his Countenance, and press'd him in so endearing a manner to let her know the Cause, that he at last confess'd his Misfortunes, concealing nothing from her of the Truth; she hid the Vexation it gave her, with her accustomed Artifice, and said, well my Dear, be as patient as you can—I love you not the less for having no Estate; and this old Creature of a Kinsman cannot live forever, and my six thousand Pounds will at least procure you a Place.

From this time, however, she thought of nothing but how to get a new Gallant; but none offering their Service, she chose rather to remain with him, till he had made away with the last things, that would even purchase a Dinner, than go home to her Mother, where she must have been put to those Straits herself, which he alone at present sustained.

A Gentleman who had been an old Friend of Mr. *P*——'s Father, hearing of his Misfortunes, made him an Invitation to his House, which he told him should be to him as his own, till he could get into some Employment; but this unhappy and deluded Man refused to accept so kind an Offer, on *Syrena's* falling into Fits, when he but barely mention'd it; and chose rather to starve with her, than forsake her without her own Consent; and sure a greater Act of Barbarity and Ingratitude was never practis'd, than by this base Wretch in still hanging on a Man, who to support her was obliged to be guilty of Meanesses which his Soul on any other Occasion would have abhorred; and Heaven only knows to what Extremes, he might have been driven, had not Providence discovered to him her Perfidy in too full a Manner for all her Dissimulation to evade, had she attempted it; but indeed having now run in a Manner, the last length she could go with him, she took not any Pains about it.

As he was taking a solitary Walk one Afternoon in Chelsea-Fields, indulging his melancholy Contemplations, he met an Acquaintance, who would needs make him go into the next House of Entertainment; where being seated and discoursing of ordinary Affairs, their Conversation was interrupted by the loud laughing of some Persons in the next Room; and their being only a Wainscot Partition between them, they heard distinctly these Words, by G——d, my Dear, if ever Fortune throws a rich Fool in my Way, you shan't want a better Commission. This was a Woman's Voice, and sounded so like *Syrena's*, that Mr. *P——* could not forbear growing as red as Scarlet; not that he imagin'd it could be she, whom he had left at Home undrest, and hard at Work, for she pretended to be a good Housewife; but he was enrag'd that any vile Woman, as he perceiv'd this was, by other Words he heard her say; should have anything in her like his dear modest Creature. The Gentleman, who knew not his Emotions, cry'd, we have got a loving Couple near us, I find.—Prithee, let's try if we can see who they are. In speaking this, he went to the side of the Room, and found a Crevice large enough for the Eye to take in all that was done within—the fond Pair by this time were silent, or what they spoke was in a lower Accent, and, indeed, they were otherwise employ'd, as Mr. *P——* who going also out of Curiosity, saw to his Confusion.—He not only found the Voice, but the Cloaths and Person of the Woman, were the same with *Syrena's*, in fine, 'twas she herself; and in a Posture such as he would have stabb'd anyone, who should have told him, she could have been in with any other Man than himself.

He was naturally of a warm and sanguine Disposition, impatient of Injuries, and incapable of Reflection in the first Moments of his Passion: He made but one Step from the Room he was in to the next, burst open the Door, which tho' lock'd gave way to the Violence he us'd; drew his Sword, and had certainly destroy'd them both in the Act of Shame, had not his Friend been quick enough to prevent him, by catching hold of his Arm behind.—*Vardine*, for it was he, was ill prepar'd for a Combat of this kind, but snatch'd up his Sword which lay in the Window, and stood on his Defence.—The People of the House hearing the Noise, by this time came into the Room, and with the Assistance of Mr. *P*——'s Friend secur'd both their Swords, and prevented the Mischief which must otherwise have happen'd; with much-a-do they got Mr. *P*—— out of the Room, tho' not till after he had loaded the vile Wanton with all the Reproaches her Treachery merited.—*Vardine* and she went out of the House together; and she return'd no more to Mr. *P*——'s Lodgings—a happy Riddance, and a Day which he has since vow'd to celebrate every Year, as the most fortunate One, that he had ever seen.

The next Morning he receiv'd a Letter by a Porter, the Contents whereof were these.

SIR,

Tho' I think it little worth my while to to demand any Satisfaction on the Score of the Woman you found me with Yesterday; yet it would ill become my Character, to put up with your forcing into the Room where I was, and disturbing my Pleasures.—I shall therefore expect you will meet me Tomorrow Morning in the Field behind Montague-house, to decide with the Points of our Swords, which of us has been to blame.

J. Vardine

The Gentleman who had been with Mr. *P*——, at the discovery of *Syrena's* Falshood; came to see how he did after this Disorder, and was at Breakfast with him when this Letter was brought. Mr. *P*—— would have conceal'd the Contents, but the other guessing the Business, would needs see it; and having read it, you shall not go, said he, How! not go, cry'd Mr. *P*—— would you have me posted for a Coward? Not so, replyed the other, but if you will give me leave to take this Letter with me, I will go along with the Porter to him, and engage shall order matters to the Satisfaction of you both; which I am sure is much better, than losing your Blood in a Cause so unworthy of it.

It was with great Difficulty Mr. *P*—— was persuaded; but knowing his Friend to be a Man who hated a mean thing, as much as himself, he at last consented he should act in it as he thought proper; only bid him be carefull of his Honour, and his Friend assuring him he would be so, went with the Porter to the Place where the Letter had been given to him, and where *Vardine* still waited his Return in Expectation of an Answer.

It was a Coffee-House, but few People being there, the Gentleman had opportunity enough to say what he intended, without Interruption. He told him that not having quitted Mr. P—— since the Skirmish, and happening to rise first, he took the Letter instead of him to whom it was directed; and suspecting the Purport open'd it, and was come to reason with him on the Affair, before Mr. P—— knew anything of it; and also, if he could to prevent the fatal Consequences which else might possibly ensue. *Vardine* did not seem displeased in the least at his Proceeding; and when they came to argue on the Provocation Mr. P—— had received, and the almost unparalled Deceit and Ingratitude of *Syrena*, *Vardine* acknowledged that he could not be expected to act otherwise than he had done; and concluded with saying, that he thought now, that they ought to exchange Pardons with each other, for added he, I was prevailed on by the Entreaties of that Woman to joyn in the Deception put upon Mr. P——, in order to draw him in to marry her; and have as much Occasion for his Forgiveness on that Score, as he has of mine for forcing into my Room. The Friend of Mr. P—— then proposed a Meeting between them three, the same Evening to conclude all Animosities over a Bottle, the other agreed to it, and Mr. P—— at hearing what had past was perfectly satisfyed with the Gentleman's Conduct, and went with him to the Appointment, at the time prefix'd, with as much Chearfullness as his Circumstances would admit of—all the Love he had bore *Syrena*, while he believed her sincere, was now turn'd into as great a Contempt, and *Vardine* expressing the same, and protesting never to see her more, added to his Satisfaction.

Thus ended an Affair, which tho' much to the Prejudice of Mr. P——, had it not been for the prudent Management of his Friend, might have been much worse, and afforded Business for the Old Bailey; and ought to be a Warning to all Gentlemen how they suffer themselves to be beguiled in the Manner he was, or expect Sincerity from Persons whom they commence an Acquaintance with in the Street.

Syrena was now once more at Home with her Mother, who knowing how little was to be got either by Mr. P—— or *Vardine* who resolved to see her no more as well as the other, was not much troubled at what had happened; but her Daughter was of a different Way of thinking; she had for a long time been accustomed to be admired and caress'd; and to live without the Conversation of a Man was wretchedly irksome, and what her gay and amorous Constitution could not endure with any tollerable degree of Patience—she made some Efforts to retain *Vardine*, but that young Gentleman finding what a consummate Jilt she was grown, and fearful of being brought into more Broils on her Account, declined any farther Acceptance of her Favours; this, together with the Poverty to which she was reduced, made her almost distracted; the Notion she had been bred up in, that a Woman who had Beauty to attract the Men, and Cunning to manage them afterwards, was secure of making her Fortune, appeared now altogether fallacious; since she had not been able to do it in four Years incessant Application, and such a Variety of Adventures, as in that time she had been engaged in. This naturally led her to reproach her Mother for having given her ill Advice; and the Mother retorted that the Misfortunes and Disappointments she had met with, had not been owing to her Advice, but to her own ill Conduct—what, said she, hindred you from being married to Mr. *W*—— but your Amour with his Son? or what from being still the Darling of Mr. *P*—— but your renewing your Acquaintance with *Vardine*? by which you have lost both, and will always do so while you are silly enough to love any Man.—And pray, interrupted *Syrena*, whom may I thank for losing Mr. *D*—— but you, first for counselling me to be Captain *H*——'s Mistress, and then by your unlucky Letter betraying it to the other—Thus with mutual Upbraidings did they add to their ill Fate, and as there can be neither true Duty or Affection where Interest presides, that prevailing Guide being at present suspended, whoever had seen them together, and heard the bitter things they said, without knowing who they were would little have imagined, how near they were by Blood.

The manner in which *Syrena* had lived, entitled her not to keep any reputable Company of her own Sex, and as for Women of the Town, she always avoided any Acquaintance with them, as being too much addicted to tattling, and also malicious to a Face prefer'd before their own; so that whenever she went to the Play or Opera, or walk'd in the Park, she had been always obliged to dress up some Tirewoman, Sempstress, or such like Person to accompany her; but she had now a very poor Stock of Cloaths, most of those as well as her Watch and Jewels being gone to satisfy Demands of a more pressing Nature; so that she had no Opportunity to shew herself to advantage; for a Woman can give herself a thousand enticing Airs, when she has somebody to talk to, which cannot be practis'd when alone. To stay at home, however, she knew could be of no Service to her, so she went out everyday, sometimes to Church, and sometimes to Shops, cheapening Goods, and to all the Auctions she could hear of.

It was at one of these last Places, she had the Good-Luck, as she then thought it, to be taken particular notice of by Mr. *E*——, a Gentleman of a vast Estate, and most agreeable Person: He had seen her in the Park some Months before, and then languished for an Opportunity to entertain her; but a Relation of his Wife, for he was married, being with him, he was obliged to put a Constraint upon his Inclinations, at that time, and Fortune had never since thrown her in his way. To meet with her, therefore, in a Place where the most reserved of either Sex, make no Scruple of speaking to each other, was an infinite Satisfaction to him: He went round the Room with her, as if examining the Value of the Goods; but in reality telling her how handsome she was, and how much he admired her: To give her some Proof, that what he said were not Words of course, a fine India Cabinet being put up to sale, which she seem'd to praise, he out-bid all the Company, and made her a Present of it.—This he did in hope of knowing by that means, where he might wait upon her; and she, no less desirous that he should do so, took care to give very exact Directions to the Auctioneer where it should be sent. Tho' she affected to receive a Favour of this kind, from a Gentleman who was a perfect Stranger to her, with a great deal of Reluctance; yet she omitted not to let fall Hints, as if she accepted the Donation merely for the sake of the Donor; having found by Experience, that Men, as well as Women have Vanity enough to be delighted, with the Belief they have anything in them capable of charming at first Sight, she call'd so much Tenderness into her Voice and Eyes, whenever she look'd upon him, or spoke to him; yet at the same time blended with it such an Innocence, as made him, while he flatter'd himself with having inspired her with the softest Passion, imagine also, that she was asham'd of her own Thoughts, and was endeavouring all she could to suppress the rising Inclination: He fancy'd he saw in every Glance, Desire struggling with Modesty, and the sweet Contest, which he fancy'd he found there, so heighten'd the Idea of her Charms, that he look'd upon himself as the happiest Man alive.

As she was about leaving the Room, I would attend you to your Chair, Madam, said he; but, as I know how to direct, will give you the Trouble of a Line, if I may be permitted to hope you will allow it the Favour of a Perusal. I am too fond of improving the little Genius I owe to Nature, answer'd she, with the most seemingly artless Blush, not to read with Pleasure whatever falls from the Pen of a Gentleman like you. She waited not to hear how he would reply; but believing he would think she had said enough, turn'd hastily away, in an admirably well dissembled Confusion, and went home to acquaint her Mother with what had happen'd.

Early the next Morning a Porter brought a Letter directed to Miss *Tricksy*; her Orders to the Auctioneer being to carry the Cabinet to Mrs. *Tricksy* at Mr. *N*——'s in H——street; and her Youth and seeming Innocence making Mr. *E*—— suppose her unmarried, occasion'd him to write the Superscription in that manner. She open'd it with Impatience enough, and found in it these Words:

Charming Miss,

As it is impossible to see you without feeling a Mixture of Love and Admiration, I fear you are to much accustom'd to Declarations of this Nature, to have that Compassion which is necessary to save the Life of your Votaries;—permit me, however, to tell you, that I have a Claim beyond what yet you have been sensible of, which is having adored you for a great length of time—Yes, most angelic Creature! I have languish'd in a hopeless Flame for many Months—One Sight of you at a Distance, made me your everlasting Slave; and tho' I have taken all imaginable Pains, I never since that fatal Moment could gain a second interview; till Yesterday, Chance, more favourable than my Industry, restor'd you to my longing Eyes.—What Agonies I have sustain'd till then, you cannot be able to comprehend, nor am I to describe—But as I have already past those Sufferings, which are a kind of Probation that Love exacts from all those who profess themselves his Votaries; if you are equally just as fair, you will allow some little Recompence is due from one who is an old Lover, tho' a new Acquaintance—that of being permitted to visit you sometimes, and to sigh my Wishes at your Feet, is all I yet presume to implore, who am,

> *Divinest of your Sex,*
> *Your most humble, most passionate, and most faithful*
> *Adorer*

P.S. If I have your leave to visit you, I will inform you, not only who I am, but everything you shall ask; and also endeavour to give you greater Proofs than Words of the Sincerity of my Flame. In the mean time, favour me with an Answer directed to A. Z.

ELIZA HAYWOOD

There was something so particular in the Stile of this Letter, that neither *Syrena* nor her Mother knew how to form a Judgment of it; by some Expressions they would have imagin'd, he took her for a Girl of Virtue, and intended to address her on the most honourable Score, had not others again contradicted that Belief—As they yet were ignorant of the Circumstances of him who wrote it, there was, indeed, no Possibility of fathoming his Design; but as there was a Necessity of giving an Answer, and the Porter waited, they contrived one between both, which should encourage him to be more open, and at the same time leave him as much in the dark concerning their Affairs, as they were at present on the Account of his.

To Mr. A. Z.

SIR,

Tho' without ever having been what they call, in Love myself, I have suffered so much from that Passion, that I have Reason to tremble at the very Name; yet as I cannot be vain enough to imagine what is meant by it in yours, anymore than mere Gallantry, I shall make no Difficulty of receiving the Visits of a Person who has so much the Appearance of a Man of Honour, and whose Civilities to me demand somewhat as an Acknowledgement from a grateful Mind; which is all the Merit to be boasted of by,

Sir,
Your most oblig'd, and Humble Servant,
SYRENA TRICKSY

Mr. *E*— was too impatient to defer any longer than the Evening of the same Day waiting on the admired Object, but was a little startled when he found there was a Mother in the way; and who, in the midst of the Civilities she received him with, mingled a certain Severity, which render'd him very much at a loss how to behave: *Syrena*, however, said a thousand obliging things to him, and whenever she had an Opportunity, gave him Looks sufficient to have encouraged a Man who had a less Opinion of himself. Tea was not over when a pretended Messenger came to inform Mrs. *Tricksy* her Company was desired on a Business of great Importance—She made an Apology for being oblig'd to leave him, which he very readily excused, rejoiced to be rid of the Company of one, who seem'd not likely to favour the purpose he came there upon.

She was no sooner gone, than he declared himself in the most passionate manner to *Syrena*, who reply'd to all he said with a well-affected Modesty; but with a Kindness also, which confirmed the Hopes her Glances had before inspired him with. She told him the same Story of her Marriage and Widowhood, as she had done others, and gave him to understand her Circumstances were none of the best.—He, in return for her suppos'd Sincerity, acquainted her that he was married, obliged by his Friends to enter into that State when he was very young; but that he never loved his Lady, nor, indeed, any other Woman, till he saw the Object before him.—*Syrena* seem'd shock'd at hearing he had a Wife, and gave him an Opportunity of discovering, as he imagin'd, that she lik'd him infinitely.—She told him, her Mother would never permit her to receive his Visits when she should know it; and as it was impossible it could be long kept a Secret from her, she could not but look on herself as very unhappy in being deprived of the Company of a Man, who by an irresistable Impulse, she could not help wishing to be eternally with. All this she spoke as in the first Emotions of her Surprize, and as tho' it scaped her without Design—then afterwards appeared confounded at having so far betrayed herself.

Mr. *E*——, who by this Behaviour had Reason to believe she loved him to a very great Excess, was transported, and used many more Arguments than he need to have done, to persuade her to leave her Mother, and retire to Lodgings of his preparing for her.

Syrena thought it not proper to yield to these Proposals immediately, but did not seem altogether averse to them; and in this first Visit he had Cause to expect everything he could wish, so departed highly satisfied; not that he imagined he had to deal with a Woman of that strict Virtue she pretended; but his Opinion of her was, that if she had fallen, it was merely for the Sake of Interest, and that if he gain'd any Favours, they would be the Effect of Love: In effect, he languish'd not long; the Circumstances *Syrena* and her Mother were in at this Juncture, would not permit them time for the Artifices they might otherwise have practised on this Gentleman, so thought it best to accept of his Offer, and trust to his future Generosity and their own Management, for a Settlement.

In fine, the Agreement in a few Days was concluded between the amorous Pair, and *Syrena* went to an Apartment he had provided, the Elegance of which shew'd both his Love and Liberality; he made her a Present of 500*l.* the Moment she set her Foot in it; and assured her, that whatever he was Master of she should command; Mrs. *Tricksy* was to seem ignorant of all this, to the End, that finding it out afterwards, the Reproaches of a Mother might oblige him to do something farther to appease her.

Many Stratagems they had in Embrio, in order to impose upon him, but they were all rendred abortive, by a Misfortune which fell upon them when they least expected it, and from a Quarter they little dream'd of.

Syrena had now provoked a Woman no less cunning, tho' more virtuous than herself, the Wife of Mr. *E*——, who being informed by some Spies, she ever kept upon his Actions, of his Fondness of this new Favourite, resolved to break off the Intimacy between them, and affected it by this Means.

She had among her Acquaintance a Lady extremely jealous of her Husband, and of a Temper too violent and outrageous to forgive the least Infringement on her Rights; this Person she contrived to make her Instrument of Revenge on *Syrena*, without being seen in it herself, or giving Mr. *E*—— any Reason to imagine she even knew of the Injury he did her.

Mr. *C*——was a Man of a very amorous Constitution, tho' secret in his Amours, on Account of his Wife's excessive tenaciousness that way; to him did Mrs. *E*—— contrive a Letter should be sent, containing these Lines.

To Mr. C——

SIR,

Love being a Passion that admits of no Controul, the Custom that obliges Women to conceal it, is cruel and unjust; and what I hope you'll excuse the breach of, when made in Favour of yourself.—In fine, Sir, there is a Lady in the World, who for a long time has looked on you with the Eyes of Tenderness—the Circumstances both of you are in, will not permit her to take any other Steps, than she now does to let you know it; but if you will venture to meet her at the King's Arms in— Street, Tomorrow at Six in the Evening, I believe you will not think your Time ill bestowed—she is a Woman of Reputation, young, and accounted handsome—as to the rest, a few Hours of her Conversation will enable you to judge better, than any Description can be given by

Sir,
Your unknown humble Servant

P.S. Enquire for Number I.

Mrs. *E*—— took care to make the Appointment, contained in this Letter, at a time when she knew her Husband was too deeply engaged with other Company, to be able to see his Mistress; and early in the Morning sent a Porter to *Syrena*, as from Mr. *E*——, to tell her, that an extraordinary Accident had made it improper for him to come to her Lodgings anymore; and that he desired to see her to inform her of it, at the King's-Arms Tavern in—Street. Everything happened as Mrs. *E*—— wish'd—*Syrena* told the Porter she would come; and the subtle Wife having a Letter ready prepar'd, sent it directly to Mrs. *C*—, the Contents of it were as follows.

To Mrs. C——

Madam, I am sorry to acquaint you that you are injured in the most tender Part—Mr. *C*—— has long kept Company with one of the most leud, expensive, insinuating Women about Town, who if not timely prevented, will be the ruin of his Estate, as she has already been of his Honour and Fidelity, to so excellent a Wife—to accuse him will be of little Consequence; he is too firmly attached to the Creature, to break off with her by any moderate Measures; but if you think proper to assert the Prerogative the Law allows a Wife wrong'd in this Manner, and take a Warrant and proper Officers with you; you will find her with your Husband at Six this Evening, at the King's-Arms in—Street:— Slight not this Intelligence, because it comes from one you know not, but convince yourself of the Truth, and at the same time punish the Wretch who dares to invade your Right—her Name is *Syrena Tricksy*, she passes for a Widow, and at this time lodges in Maiden-Lane; but as Mr. *C*—— seldom sees her at home, you can never have an Opportunity like the present of doing yourself Justice, and reclaiming the Man, whom both divine and human Laws ought to bind entirely to you. I am,

Madam,
Your sincere Well-wisher

P.S. If you enquire for Number I, you will be shewn directly to the Scene of Guilt and Shame.

The Rage this Lady was in at the Receipt of this, was not at all inferior to what Mrs. *E*—— imagined—she went immediately to a Justice of Peace, obtained a Warrant, and had a Constable ready to attend her when the Hour should arrive.

ELIZA HAYWOOD

Mrs. *E*—— in the mean time was not idle, she knew her Husband was engaged the whole Day with his Lawyers on some Business relating to an Estate in Debate between him, and a near Relation. So she disguised herself, and went to the Tavern, resolving to be a Witness how her Plot succeeded. Having placed herself in a convenient Room, she saw Mr. *C*—— come in, and soon after him the deceiving, but now deceived *Syrena*, what would she have given for the gratification of her Curiosity in hearing what passed between them, but that was impossible, and she was obliged to content herself with that of her Revenge which she soon saw compleated to her Wish.

The Reader however, must not be left in Ignorance; when *Syrena* first came into the Room, and found a strange Gentleman instead of him she expected; she guess'd the Drawer who shew'd her up, had made some Mistake, and was turning to go out of again, but Mr. *C*—— taking it as Modesty or Affectation prevented her, by saying, Sure Madam you do not already repent of your Goodness, and would leave me before I tell you how happy I think myself in meeting you here. Sir, answered she, I ask'd for Number I, being to see a Friend here by that Token, but perhaps it may so have happened, that there may be two who left that Direction at the Bar—I know not that, Madam, replyed he, but I was made to hope, I should here meet with a Lady young, beautiful, but one altogether a Stranger to me; so whether you are the Person who design'd me that Favour or not, I am certain you have all the Marks, and must at least detain you till another more agreeable than yourself (which is altogether impossible) shall come and relieve you.—*Syrena* was at a Loss what to make of this Adventure, she could have liked well enough to stay with him, but she feared some Trick in the Case: She was apprehensive that Mr. *E*—— had form'd this Contrivance to make tryal of her Constancy, and might be in the next Room a Witness of her Behaviour; so with all the Appearance of a virtuous Indignation, she told Mr. *C*—— who had fast hold of her Hand, that she was surprized at the Accident which had brought two Persons together, in such a Place, who were entire Strangers to each other—that she came there to meet a near Relation and Friend on Business, which since she was disappointed in, begged he would not pretend to enforce her Stay, nor imagine she was a Woman who would submit to anything, that the most strict Modesty would not allow of.

She spoke this with so serious and resolute an Air, that Mr. *C*—— began indeed to fear this was not the Person from whose Kindness he had so much to expect—to convince himself he took the Letter had been sent him out of his Pocket, and shew'd it to her, which made her more than before imagine that there was something in Agitation against her—she assured him, as indeed she well might, that she knew nothing of the sending it—had never seen him before to her Knowledge; or if I had, continued she, blushing, have a Heart already too much taken up to entertain the Thoughts of any other, tho' ever so deserving. As she still was possess'd of the Opinion, that this Gentleman was a Friend of Mr. E——, and would report to him everything she said, she spoke this the more to ingratiate herself with him, when he should be told it; but the Amazement Mr. C—— was in, and the Vexation he express'd to find he had been impos'd upon, a little stagger'd her former Conjecture—I wish, Sir, said she, there is not some Treachery put in Practice against us both; but for what End, or from what Quarter, I cannot guess.—But, added she, the surest way to disappoint it, is immediately to separate—therefore, I beg Sir, you'll not offer to detain me longer. With these Words she endeavoured to draw back her Hand; but he, whose Desires had been raised by the Expectation of a different Entertainment, and were now quite enflamed by so pleasing an Object, could not tell how to let her go so easily; and instead of quitting his hold, threw his other Arm about her Neck, and in that defenceless Posture almost smother'd her with Kisses.—She was no less susceptible than himself of the strenuous Embrace; and beginning now to believe, that if there was a Plot, he at least had no Hand in it, made but faint Efforts to oblige him to desist what was equally pleasing to her as to himself, till quite overcome with the dangerous Temptation, he found her Lips not only yield, but return Kiss for Kiss—the amorous Pair thus equally dissolved, had not stopp'd here, but were proceeding to much greater Liberties, when Mrs. C— rush'd into the Room more like a Fury than a Woman—she flew upon *Syrena*, call'd her all the Names that jealous Rage could suggest; then turning to her Husband, ungrateful Monster, cry'd she! Is this the Reward of all my Love and Virtue?—was it for this I slighted so many noble Matches, and brought you such a Fortune? he was beginning to protest his Innocence, but the very mention made her more outrageous.—O! horrid Impudence, said she, have I not caught you almost in the odious Act! dare you deny it.—But I forbear saying farther to you at present—your Strumpet here shall curse the Hour she ever tempted you to wrong my Bed—as she spoke these Words she stamp'd with her Foot, and immediately came up the Constable, and other Persons she had placed in a Room under that where they were—do your Office, Man, cry'd she, and carry that filthy Creature, where your Warrant directs. Mr. C—— begg'd she would not expose herself and him; and *Syrena* frighted almost to Death, fell on her Knees, and entreated her Mercy and Forgiveness—but all Attempts to quell her Fury, were like fencing the Sea with a Battledor, when it was Mountains high—the more they humbled themselves, the more insolent and impetuous she became; and Mrs. E——, who in her Disguise was now mingled with the croud of Servants, Porters, and others, whom the Noise drew together, had the Satisfaction to see her hated Rival in Mr. E——'s Affections, dragg'd away like the lowest and most common Prostitute, that plies the Streets for the poor Pittance of a Half-Crown Fare; a Fate, indeed, she long since had deserv'd, tho' fallen on her when she gave the least Occasion.

How Mr. C—— and his Spouse made up this Quarrel between themselves, is not to our present Purpose; but Mrs. E—— who knew not but *Syrena* might have the Confidence to send to her Husband, even from the Place she now was in, in hopes of being set at Liberty; did not here give over. She had by Bribes and incessant Application, made herself thoroughly acquainted with every Circumstance of *Syrena's* Family and Circumstances; she knew she had pretty near Kindred in the City, who were Men of Worth and Character, and very rich: To one of these she went, and having made an Apology for coming on a Business, which she knew could not but be shocking, told him that *Syrena*, was at that time a Prisoner in the House of Correction: The Lady whose Resentment confines her there, said she, is my particular Friend; but having suffer'd a great deal from her Husband's Intimacy with loose Women, all I can say in Favour of your unhappy Cousin, will not prevail on her to give her a Release; unless she could be certain of her being removed too far from London, for her Husband to continue any Correspondence with her.—Now, Sir, added she, tho' she alone is guilty, her Brothers, unfortunate in being so, will share in her Disgrace—they are young, and might be eminent Men in time; but what sober Person will match his Daughter, where so near a Relative as a Sister is, everyday, nay every Hour, guilty of Actions, which render her a Shame, not only to her Family, but her whole Sex?—besides, Sir, if she continues in the wretched Place she now is, the horrid Society she in time will there become acquainted with, may excite her to Crimes worthy of her second Removal to Newgate,—in fine, there is no knowing to what Lengths, Crimes will extend in a Person of abandon'd Morals; so that for the sake of her Family, I could wish she were dispos'd of, so as not to bring herself to farther Infamy, nor her Friends to trouble by the hearing it.

The Person to whom this Speech was address'd, seem'd infinitely shock'd, tho' by somethings he had heard of his Kinswoman's Behaviour, he had dreaded to receive some such Intelligence for a long time. He thank'd Mrs. E—— however, with the utmost Civility, and told her he would consult with someothers of the Family; and she might depend upon it, order the Affair, so that the Lady her Friend, should receive no farther Injury from his abandoned Relative.

This worthy Citizen, in effect, summon'd all who were unhappy enough to be nearly ally'd to the wicked *Syrena*, and having made them a brief Recital of what Crimes had come to his Knowledge, committed by her, and the shameful Situation she now was in, they all agreed, that to avoid hearing anything farther of her Viciousness, it was best to send her to some remote Place, where she should be strictly confined, till time, and a just Sensibility of her Infamy, should bring her to an Abhorrence of her past Life. One of them having a handsome Estate in the farther part of Wales, proposed sending her to a Tenant he had there; to which the others readily comply'd and each promis'd to contribute somewhat towards her keeping there.

This being agreed upon, the Person to whom Mrs. E—— had spoke, having her Directions, waited on her, and begg'd she would now perform her Promise in exerting her whole Interest with Mrs. C——, for the Discharge of *Syrena*; and he would engage in return, that the unhappy Girl should never wrong her more. Mrs. E—— assured him, she would undertake the Office.—She did so, and Mrs. C—— was easily enough prevail'd upon, on the Conditions her Friend mentioned.

All that remain'd now was to let *Syrena* know what had been done for her, who, glad to submit to anything that would deliver her from the Place she was in, made a thousand Vows never to return to London anymore.

Thus was *Syrena* taken from the first Captivity she had ever been in; but when she consider'd, she was going to a second, which, tho' less shameful, would in all Probability deprive her entirely from all Conversation with Mankind, she was almost inconsolable—Fatal

ELIZA HAYWOOD

Necessity, however, must be obey'd, and she was sent under the Conduct of an old Servant of one of her Kinsmen to Wales, where what befel her, must be the Subject of future Entertainment.

FINIS

A Note About the Author

Eliza Haywood (1693–1756) was an English novelist, poet, playwright, actress, and publisher. Notoriously private, Haywood is a major figure in English literature about whom little is known for certain. Scholars believe she was born Eliza Fowler in Shropshire or London, but are unclear on the socioeconomic status of her family. She first appears in the public record in 1715, when she performed in an adaptation of Shakespeare's *Timon of Athens* in Dublin. Famously portrayed as a woman of ill-repute in Alexander Pope's *Dunciad* (1743), it is believed that Haywood had been deserted by her husband to raise their children alone. Pope's account is likely to have come from poet Richard Savage, with whom Haywood was friends for several years beginning in 1719 before their falling out. This period coincided with the publication of *Love in Excess* (1719-1720), Haywood's first and best-known novel. Alongside Delarivier Manley and Aphra Behn, Haywood was considered one of the leading romance writers of her time. Haywood's novels, such as *Idalia; or The Unfortunate Mistress* (1723) and *The Distress'd Orphan; or Love in a Madhouse* (1726), often explore the domination and oppression of women by men. *The History of Miss Betsy Thoughtless* (1751), one of Haywood's final novels, is a powerful story of a woman who leaves her abusive husband, experiences independence, and is pressured to marry once more. Highly regarded by feminist scholars today, Haywood was a prolific writer who revolutionized the English novel while raising a family, running a pamphlet shop in Covent Gardens, and pursuing a career as an actress and writer for some of London's most prominent theaters.

A Note from the Publisher

Spanning many genres, from non-fiction essays to literature classics to children's books and lyric poetry, Mint Edition books showcase the master works of our time in a modern new package. The text is freshly typeset, is clean and easy to read, and features a new note about the author in each volume. Many books also include exclusive new introductory material. Every book boasts a striking new cover, which makes it as appropriate for collecting as it is for gift giving. Mint Edition books are only printed when a reader orders them, so natural resources are not wasted. We're proud that our books are never manufactured in excess and exist only in the exact quantity they need to be read and enjoyed.

Discover more of your favorite classics with Bookfinity™.

- Track your reading with custom book lists.
- Get great book recommendations for your personalized Reader Type.
- Add reviews for your favorite books.
- AND MUCH MORE!

Visit **bookfinity.com** and take the fun Reader Type quiz to get started.

Enjoy our classic and modern companion pairings!